**Books by Jude Deveraux**

Published by POCKET BOOKS

# Jude Deveraux

## The Maiden

**POCKET BOOKS**

New York   London   Toronto   Sydney   Singapore

This book is a work of historical fiction. Names, characters, places, and incidents relating to nonhistorical figures are either the product of the author's imagination or are used fictitiously. Any resemblance of such nonhistorical incidents, places or figures to actual events or locales or persons, living or dead, is entirely coincidental.

An *Original* Publication of POCKET BOOKS

POCKET BOOKS, a division of Simon & Schuster, Inc.
1230 Avenue of the Americas, New York, NY 10020

ISBN: 0-671-74379-1

First Pocket Books printing October 1988

32  31  30  29  28  27  26  25  24  23

POCKET and colophon are registered trademarks of
Simon & Schuster, Inc.

For information regarding special discounts for bulk purchases,
please contact Simon & Schuster Special Sales at 1-800-456-6798
or business@simonandschuster.com

Front cover illustration by Melody Cassen;
Photo credit: Corbis

Printed in the U.S.A.

# The
# Maiden

# Chapter One

*1299 England*

WILLIAM DE BOHUN stood hidden in the shadows of the castle's stone walls and looked at his nephew, who sat in the window enclosure, Rowan's golden hair bathed in sunlight, his handsome face frowning in concentration as he studied the manuscript before him. William didn't like to think how much this young man had come to mean to him over the years. Rowan was the son he wished he had been able to breed.

As William looked at the tall, broad-shouldered, slim-hipped, handsome young man, he once again wondered how that dark, ugly Thal could have bred someone like Rowan. Thal called himself King of Lanconia but he wore animal skins, his long dirty hair hung past his shoulders, and he ate and spoke like the barbarian he was. William was disgusted by him and only allowed him to remain in his house at the request of King Edward. William had given the man the hospitality of his estate and had instructed his steward to plan entertainments for the loud, crude vulgarian, but William himself had stayed as far as possible from the hideous young man.

Now, looking at Rowan, William's stomach tightened in remembered anguish. While William was busying himself far away from the barbarian king, his beautiful, kind, dear sister, Anne, had been falling in love with the odious man. By the time William realized what was happening, Anne was so deeply bewitched by the man that she was vowing to kill herself if she could not have him. The stupid barbarian king didn't even seem to realize that Anne was endangering her immortal soul by the mere mention of suicide.

Nothing William said could dissuade Anne. William pointed out the repulsiveness of Thal's person and Anne looked at him as if he were stupid. "He's not repulsive to a woman," she had said, laughing in a way that made William slightly queasy as he thought of that dark greasy man's hands on Anne's slim, blonde person.

In the end, King Edward had made William's decision for him. He said there weren't many Lanconians but they were a fierce lot, and if their king wanted a rich English bride, he should have her.

So King Thal married William's beautiful sister Anne. William stayed drunk for ten days, hoping that when he sobered it would all turn out to be his imagination. But when he woke from his drunken stupor he saw Thal, a head taller than his tall sister, swooping down on her, enveloping her fair loveliness with his darkness.

Nine months later Rowan had been born. From the first William had been inordinately fond of the pretty blond child. His own childless marriage made him hungry for a son. Thal showed no interest in the babe. "Bah! It screams at one end and stinks at the other.

2

Children belong to women. I'll wait until he's a man," Thal had grunted in that strangely accented English of his. He was much more interested in when Anne would be well enough to return to his bed.

William had adopted Rowan as his own, spending endless hours making toys for the boy, playing with the child, holding his chubby fingers as he took his first steps. Rowan was fast becoming William's reason for living.

When Rowan was just over a year old, his sister Lora was born. Like her brother, she was a pretty blonde child, and looked as if she had inherited nothing from her swarthy father.

When Lora was five days old, Anne had died.

In his grief, William saw nothing but his own misery. He did not see the brooding emptiness of Thal. All William knew was that Thal was the cause of his beloved sister's death. He ordered Thal from his house.

Heavily, Thal had said he would pack his men and children and leave in the morning to return to Lanconia.

William had not comprehended Thal's words, but when he heard noise in the courtyard below, he realized that Thal meant to take Rowan and the new baby from him. William went berserk. A normally sane man, he acted out of rage, grief, and fear. He gathered his own knights from the barracks and attacked Thal and his personal guard while they slept.

William had never seen men fight as these Lanconians did. They were outnumbered four to one but still, three of them, including Thal, managed to escape.

Dripping blood from several deep slashes in his

arms and legs and one across his right cheek, Thal stood on the castle wall in the pink light of dawn and cursed William and his issue. Thal said he knew William wanted Prince Rowan but he would never get him. Rowan was Lanconian, not English, and someday Rowan would come home to him.

Then Thal and his men had escaped over the wall and disappeared into the forest.

William's bad luck began with that night. Where once his life had been touched with gold, it soon turned to lead. His wife had died of the pox a month later, then the pox had killed over half his peasants, leaving the grain unharvested in the fields. An early snow left the fields rotting.

William married again, this time to a fat healthy fifteen-year-old who proved to be fertile as a rabbit. She gave him four sons in four years then conveniently died with the last one. William did not grieve since he had found that when his infatuation with her beautiful young body had worn off, she was a stupid, frivolous girl who was no companion.

William had the care of his own four sons and Anne's two children. The contrast was stark. Rowan and Lora were tall and beautiful, golden-haired and handsome. They were intelligent, eager to learn, polite, while his own sons were stupid and clumsy, sullen and resentful. They hated Rowan and teased Lora viciously. William knew this was his punishment for what he had done to Thal. He even began to believe it was Anne's ghost repaying him for his crime against her husband.

When Rowan was ten, a man came to William's castle, an old man with a beard hanging to the middle of his chest, a circle of gold set with four rubies on his head. He said his name was Feilan and that he was Lanconian and that he had come to teach Rowan Lanconian ways.

William had been ready to run the old man through with a sword until Rowan had stepped forward. It was almost as if the boy had known the man was going to come and had been waiting for him. "I am Prince Rowan," he had said solemnly.

In that moment William knew he was losing the most precious thing on earth to him—and there was nothing he could do to prevent the loss.

The old Lanconian remained, sleeping somewhere deep within the castle—William didn't ask where—and spent every waking moment with Rowan. Rowan had always been a serious child, had always taken whatever duties William gave him seriously, but now it seemed that Rowan's capacity for study was limitless. The old Lanconian taught Rowan both in the classroom and on the training field. At first William objected because some of the Lanconian methods of fighting were, to a knight like William, entirely without honor. Neither Rowan nor Feilan paid him any attention and Rowan learned to fight on his feet with sword and lance, with a stick, with clubs, and, to William's horror, with his fists. No knight fought except from the back of a horse.

Rowan did not foster as other aristocratic young men did but remained at his uncle's castle and studied with the Lanconian. William's own sons left, one by one, to live with other knights and train as their squires. They returned with their spurs and their knighthood, their resentment for Rowan even stronger. One by one, William's sons reached manhood and challenged Rowan to a tilt, hoping to lay him low and so gain their father's esteem.

There was no contest as Rowan easily knocked each young man from his horse then returned to his studies without so much as raising a sweat.

William's sons loudly protested their cousin's presence in their home and William watched as his ignorant sons put burrs under Rowan's saddle, stole his precious books, laughed at him in front of guests. But Rowan never got angry, a fact that infuriated his loutish cousins. The only time William saw Rowan get angry was when his sister, Lora, asked permission to marry a lessor land baron who was visiting William. Rowan had raged at Lora that she was Lanconian and when she was called she must return to her home. William was stunned, partly by Rowan's show of temper, but more so by Rowan's referring to Lanconia as "home." He felt betrayed, as if all the love he had given the boy was not returned. William helped Lora in her marriage plans. But her husband had died after only two years of marriage and Lora returned to her uncle's home with her baby son, Phillip. Rowan had smiled and welcomed her. "Now we will be ready," he had said, putting his arm around Lora and holding his new nephew.

Today William was looking at Rowan. It was twenty-five years since a golden child had been born to William's lovely sister and in that time William had come to love the boy more than he loved his own soul. But it was over now, for outside stood a hundred of the tall, dark, scarred Lanconian warriors, sitting atop their short-legged, barrel-chested horses, each man wearing a grim expression and a hundred pounds of weapons. They were obviously prepared for a fight. Their leader rode forward and announced to William that they had come for the children of Thal, that Thal lay on his deathbed and Rowan was to be made king.

William's inclination was to refuse, to fight to keep Rowan until he had no more breath, but William's oldest son had pushed his hesitant father aside and welcomed the Lanconians with open arms. William knew defeat when he saw it. One could not fight to keep something that did not want to be kept.

With a heavy heart he went up the stairs to Lora's solar, where Rowan sat in the window enclosure studying. His tutor, old to begin with, was now ancient, but when he saw William's face, he eased his arthritic body from the chair and went to stand before Rowan, then slowly dropped to one knee. As Rowan looked at his old tutor's face, understanding came to him.

"Long live King Rowan," the old man said, his head bowed.

Rowan nodded solemnly and looked at Lora, who had dropped her sewing. "It is time," he said softly. "Now we go home."

William slipped away so the tears in his eyes would not be seen.

## Lanconia

Jura stood very still in the knee-deep water, her light spear held aloft, poised above the lazily swimming fish, waiting for the moment to skewer the fish. The sun wasn't quite up yet, just enough to silhouette the Tarnovian Mountains behind her and the shadowy fish at her feet. She had discarded the loose trousers to her warrior's uniform on the bank and now wore only the soft, embroidered tunic that was the badge of her profession, her legs bare from the middle of her thigh down. The water was icy cold but she was used to discomfort and had been trained from an early age to ignore pain.

To her left she heard a footstep and knew someone was coming, a woman by the lightness of the step. She didn't show any outward sign of movement but her muscles tensed, ready to spring. She continued holding the spear above her right shoulder but now she was ready to turn and cast the spear at the intruder.

She smiled without moving her face. It was Cilean. Cilean, her teacher and her friend, was soundlessly— almost anyway—moving through the forest.

Jura speared a fat fish. "Will you join me for breakfast, Cilean?" she called as she pulled the flopping fish from the spear and walked toward the bank. Jura was six feet tall with a body made magnificent by years of hard, demanding exercise.

Cilean stepped from the trees and smiled at her friend. "Your hearing is excellent, as always." She also wore the white tunic and trousers of the Irial warrior, soft leather boots reaching to her knees, wrapped with cross garters from ankle to knee. She was as tall as Jura, with long, lean legs, high, firm breasts, a supple spine, and she held herself as erect as a birch, but her face did not have that startling quality of beauty that Jura's did. Her face was also beginning to show her age of twenty-four when she was next to Jura's fresh eighteen.

"He has come," Cilean said softly.

The only indication Jura gave that she had heard

was the slightest hesitation as she arranged the twigs to build a fire to roast her fish.

"Jura," Cilean said, her voice pleading, "you have to face this someday." She spoke in the Irial dialect of Lanconian, a language of soft sounds and rolled *l*'s. "He will be our king."

Jura straightened and whirled to face her friend, her black, braided hair moving and her beautiful face showing her rage. "He is not *my* king! He will never be my king. He is English, not Lanconian. His mother was a soft weak Englishwoman who sits by the fire all day and sews. She did not even have the strength to bear Thal many children. Geralt is the rightful king. He had a Lanconian mother."

Cilean had heard this a hundred times. "Yes, Astrie was a wonderful woman and Geralt is a great warrior but he was not the firstborn son nor was Astrie the legal wife of Thal."

Jura turned away, trying to get her anger under control. In training she could be so cool, could keep her thoughts clear even when Cilean devised some trick, such as ordering five women to attack Jura at once, but there was one area where Jura's fury at the injustice of it could not be controlled, and that was when she thought of Geralt. Years before Jura was born, King Thal had traveled to England to talk to the English king, to try to make an alliance with England. Instead of attending to the purpose of his journey, he had neglected Lanconian business and fallen under the spell of some vapid, weak, useless Englishwoman. He had married her and remained in England for two years, producing two puny, mewling brats who were too weak to return to Lanconia with him after his frail wife had died.

People said Thal was never the same after he returned from England. He refused to marry a proper Lanconian woman, although he spent some time in bed with the beautiful, nobly born Astrie. She bore him Geralt, a son who was everything a man could want, but Thal still kept brooding. In despair, hoping to force him into marrying her, Astrie asked permission to marry Johst, Thal's most trusted guard. Thal barely shrugged his shoulders as he agreed. Three years after Geralt's birth, Astrie gave birth to Jura.

"Geralt has the right to be king," Jura repeated, her voice calmer.

"Thal has made his choice. If he wants his English son to be king, then we must honor that choice."

Jura was angrily scaling the fish with her knife. "I hear he has white skin and white hair. I hear he is as thin and frail as a stalk of wheat. He has a sister too. No doubt she will cry and whine for her English comforts. How can we respect an English king when he knows nothing of us?"

"Thal sent Feilan to him years ago. I have heard legends of the man's wisdom."

"Bah! He is Poilen," Jura said with contempt, referring to another tribe of the Lanconians. The Poilens believed they could fight wars with words. The young men trained with books and learning rather than with swords. "How can a Poilen teach a man to be *king?* No doubt Feilan taught him to read and tell stories. What does a Poilen know of battle? When the Zernas attack our city, will our new king try to tell them fairy tales until they fall off their horses in sleep?"

"Jura, you aren't being fair. We haven't met the man. He is Thal's son and—"

"So is Geralt!" Jura spat. "Can this Englishman know half what Geralt does about Lanconia?" She gestured to the mountains to the north, those beloved mountains that had protected Lanconia from centuries of invaders. "He has never even seen our mountains," she said as if this were the final disgrace.

"Nor has he seen me," Cilean said softly.

Jura's eyes widened. Thal, long ago, had said he wanted his son Rowan to marry Cilean. "Surely Thal has forgotten that. He said that years ago. You were only a child at the time."

"No, he has not forgotten. This morning when he heard his English son was near the Ciar River, he revived enough to send for me. He wants Daire and me to meet him."

"Daire?" Jura gasped then smiled as she thought of the tall, handsome, dark-eyed Daire, the man she was to marry, the man she had loved since she was a child.

Cilean gave her friend a look of disgust. "Your concern is only for the man you love? You care nothing that I am being ordered to marry a man who you have described as weak, puny—"

"I am sorry," Jura said, and felt guilty for thinking only of herself. It would truly be awful to have to marry someone one did not know. To think of living day in and day out with a man whose every movement, every thought was strange and abhorrent to her. "I apologize. Did Thal really say he planned for you to *marry* this . . . this . . . ?" She could think of no description for this foreigner.

"He said it is what he has always planned." Cilean sat down on the ground by the little fire Jura now had going and her face showed her anguish. "I think Thal fears what you fear, that this son of his that he has not seen in over twenty years will be all that you think he is. But Thal is determined to have his way. The more people who try to dissuade him, the more adamant he becomes."

"I see," Jura said thoughtfully, and looked at Cilean for a long moment. Perhaps Thal wasn't such a doting fool after all. Cilean was a logical, intelligent woman who had proved herself on several battlefields in the past. Cilean was able to control her emotions, and, most important, her temper, under the most stressing of conditions. If this English prince was as weak as people said, Cilean's intelligence and wisdom could perhaps keep Lanconia from falling under his rule. "Lanconia may get a sulking English brat for a king but we will have a wise Lanconian woman for queen."

"Thank you," Cilean said. "Yes, that is what I think Thal has in mind and I am honored by his trust in me but I . . ."

"You want a *man* for a husband," Jura said with feeling. "You want someone like Daire: tall and strong and lusty and intelligent and—"

Cilean laughed. "Yes, I can admit to you, my closest friend, that on one hand I am greatly honored, but on the other, I am thinking with the softness of a woman. Does this Englishman *really* have white hair? Who told you that?"

"Thal," Jura answered. "When he was in his cups, he talked about the English woman he so stupidly married. He did it once in front of my mother, and my father took her from the room." Jura's mouth tightened into a grimace, although the expression did not take away from her beauty. Both of her parents had died when she was five and Thal had taken her in and raised her—raised her in that big stone fortress-house of his without the companionship of women. When a washerwoman had stopped Jura from playing with a sharp, long-handled ax for fear she would cut her toes off, Thal had dismissed the woman.

"Thal told us more than we wanted to know about his time in England," Jura continued. Cilean knew the "we" referred to Geralt, Jura's half-brother, and Daire, who had been raised with them.

"Jura," Cilean said sharply, "are you going to eat that fish or not? If so, hurry up so you can help me decide what to take on the journey. Do you think Thal's son's sister will be wearing silks? Will she be utterly divinely beautiful? Will she look down her nose at us Lanconian women as those Frankish women did two years ago?"

Jura's eyes gleamed. "Then we shall do to her what we did to those women," she said, mouth full of fish.

"You are wicked," Cilean said, laughing. "We cannot do *that* to a woman who will be my sister-in-law."

"I have no such compunction. We ought to make plans for what to do to protect ourselves from their English snobbery. Of course all we have to do is lead this Rowan into a single battle and that will be the end of him. Or do you think he sits on velvet-cushioned chairs and drinks ale while watching the battle from afar?" Jura stood and kicked dirt over the fire then pulled on her trousers and laced her boots. "And Daire is to go with you?"

"Yes," Cilean said, smiling. "You can bear to be without him for a few days. We ride out to meet this Englishman and escort him back. I think Thal may be afraid of the Zernas." The Zernas were the fiercest tribe of Lanconia. The Zernas were as devoted to battle as the Poilens were to books. The Zernas attacked anyone at any time and what they did to captives was what gave grown warriors nightmares.

"No Irial is afraid of a Zerna," Jura said angrily, coming to her feet.

"Yes, but this prince is English and the English king believes himself to be king of *all* Lanconia."

Jura smiled in a nasty way. "Someone should let him walk up to Brocain, the king of the Zernas, and announce his kingship. That would be the end of our worries. At least Thal's English son would be *buried* on Lanconian soil, and, I swear, we would bury every piece Brocain hacked from him."

Cilean laughed. "Come on, help me choose what to take. We will leave in another hour and you must say goodbye to Daire."

"That will take much longer than an hour," Jura said seductively, making Cilean laugh again.

"Perhaps I can borrow Daire's virility some lonely night after I am married to this limp Englishman."

"That will be the night you die," Jura said calmly, then smiled. "Let us pray Thal lives long enough to see this English softling of his and sees the error of his ways and corrects it. Geralt will be our king, as he should be. Come on, I'll race you to the walls."

# Chapter Two

*R*OWAN WAS STRETCHED out on the western bank of the Ciar River, his arm behind his head and sleepily looking up into the trees. His chest was bare, sunlight and shadow playing on the muscles in his stomach and chest, glinting on the thick mat of dark gold hair. He wore only his short, baggy breeches and hose that stretched over heavy, muscular legs.

Outwardly, he looked to be calm but then he had had years of training in keeping his emotions hidden. His old Lanconian tutor had never missed an opportunity to tell Rowan he was only half Lanconian and that the weak, crying English half had to be cut out, burned out, or removed in some other fashion. According to Feilan, Lanconians were stronger than steel, more immovable than mountains, and Rowan was only half a Lanconian.

Absently, he felt the scar on the back of his thigh twitch, as it always did when he thought of Feilan, but he did not scratch it. Lanconians did not show fear; Lanconians thought of their country first; Lanconians allowed no emotion to govern their thoughts and Lanconians did not cry. His tutor had pounded that into his head well enough. When, as a child, Rowan's favorite dog, an animal that had comforted him many a lonely night, had died, Rowan had cried, and the old tutor had been enraged. He had laid a red-hot poker across the back of Rowan's thigh and warned the child that if he cried or so much as flinched, he'd receive a second branding.

Rowan had not cried again.

Behind him he heard someone hurrying toward him. Instantly, he was alert and grabbed his sword, which lay by his hand.

"It's me," he heard Lora say, and there was anger in her voice.

He reached for his tunic. In the distance he could hear the Lanconian warriors moving about, no doubt looking for him, afraid he might see a gnat and be frightened of it. He wiped the grimace from his face and looked up at his sister.

"No," Lora said, "don't bother to dress. I've seen unclothed men before." She sat on the ground not far from him and was silent for a moment, her knees bent, her arms wrapped around them, her slim young body rigid with what could only be anger. She was heedless of the dampness of the earth seeping into her brocade gown. When she spoke, it was more of an eruption. "They are *awful* men!" she said furiously, her eyes fixed straight ahead. Her jaw set in rage. "They treat me as if I am stupid, as if I am some spoiled, lazy child who must be patronized at all times. They will not let me walk two steps without aid. As if I were an invalid! And that Xante is the worst. One more of his looks of contempt directed toward me and I'll set him on his ear." She stopped when she heard Rowan's soft chuckle and turned blazing blue eyes on him. She was quite pretty, with delicate features and a tall, slender body, and her anger gave added color to her face.

"How *dare* you laugh," she said through clenched teeth. "The way they treat us is your fault. Every time one of them offers you a pillow, you sigh and smile. And yesterday, holding my yarn! You have *never* done that before, you were always too busy sharpening a sword or knife, but now you delight in pretending to be weak and soft. Why don't you cuff a few of them, especially that Xante?"

Rowan's smile softened his square jaw. He was classically handsome with his dark blond hair and deep blue eyes, and next to the Lanconians he looked to be of another species of human. Where their eyes blazed, his twinkled. Where their jaws were gaunt and weathered, Rowan's cheeks were pale and smooth. Lora was accustomed to seeing men smile at Rowan, thinking they were about to joust with a beardless boy whose tall, big body was no doubt all fat. Lora often laughed with glee when Rowan unseated the smirking knight so easily. The men found out that Rowan's face changed from softness to blond English oak within seconds—and that big body of his was about two hundred pounds of solid muscle.

"And why don't you speak their language to them?" Lora continued, her anger in no way abated by Rowan's seeming unconcern. "Why do you have them translate for you? And who are these Zernas they fear so much? I thought Zernas were Lanconians. Rowan! Stop laughing. They are insolent, arrogant men."

"Especially Xante?" he asked in his deep voice, smiling at her.

She looked away from him, her jaw working in

anger. "You may laugh about them, but your men and your squire do not. Young Montgomery was sporting some nasty bruises this morning and I think he got them defending your name. You ought to—"

"I should what?" Rowan asked softly, looking up at the trees overhead. He would not let Lora see what he felt at the Lanconians' treatment of him. These Lanconians were his own people, but they treated him with great contempt and made it clear that he was not wanted. He could not let Lora see that he was just as angry as she because Lora needed her fire dampened, not inflamed. "I should fight one of them?" he said teasingly. "Kill or maim one of my own men? Xante is the captain of the King's Guard. What good would it do me to harm him?"

"You seem awfully sure you are capable of winning a fight with that strutting monster."

Rowan wasn't sure he could win a fight at all. These Lanconians were all like Feilan, so sure he was weak and useless that at times he almost believed they were right.

"Would you *want* me to win over your Xante?" Rowan asked seriously.

*"My?"* she gasped, then grabbed a handful of grass and tossed it at him. "All right, maybe you shouldn't fight your own man but you must stop the way they are treating you. It is not respectful."

"I'm beginning to like a soft pillow offered whenever I sit down." Rowan smiled toward the trees then turned serious. He knew he could confide in her. "I am listening to them," he said after a moment. "I sit quietly on the edge of a circle of men and listen to them."

Lora was beginning to calm down. She should have

known Rowan had a reason for playing the fool. But oh, how she had hated it since they had left England. She and Rowan, her son, three of Rowan's knights, and his squire, Montgomery de Warbrooke, had ridden away with the silent, black-eyed Lanconians. That first day she had felt marvelous, as if her destiny had come at last. But the Lanconians had made it clear that she and Rowan were English, not Lanconian, and they believed that the English were soft, useless people. They missed no opportunity to show their contempt for their English burdens. The first night Neile, one of Rowan's three knights, had been about to draw his sword on a Lanconian warrior when Rowan stopped him.

Xante, the tall, fierce-looking captain of the guard, asked Rowan if he had ever held a sword before. Young Montgomery had nearly attacked the man, and considering that Montgomery, at sixteen, was nearly as tall as Xante, Lora was sorry when Rowan stopped the fight. Montgomery walked away in disgust when Rowan asked Xante to please show him his sword, as Rowan had always wanted to see one at close view.

Until now, Lora had hated Rowan's act so much that she had not considered he had a reason for what he was doing—except that there were a hundred of the dark, watching Lanconians and only six Englishmen and a child. She should not have doubted her brother.

"What have you heard?" she asked softly.

"Feilan told me of the tribes of Lanconia, but he did not tell me or perhaps I assumed that they were more or less united." Rowan was quiet for a moment. "It seems that I am to be king of the Irials only."

"Our father, Thal, is Irial, isn't he?"

"Yes."

"And the Irials are the ruling class, so, therefore, you are king of all Lanconians, whatever they call themselves."

Rowan chuckled and wished life could be as simple as Lora sometimes saw it. If she decided she loved a man, she married him. She did not worry about what would happen in the future if she were called to Lanconia and she was bound to an English husband. But for Rowan, destiny and duty were everything. "That is the way the Irials see it, but I fear the other tribes do not agree. Right now we are only miles from land the Zernas claim as their own and the Irials are concerned and watchful. The Zernas are reputed to be very fierce."

"You mean these Lanconians are *afraid* of them?" Lora asked breathlessly.

"Zernas are also Lanconians, and these men with us, these Irials, are more cautious than afraid."

"But if the *Irials* fear them . . ."

Rowan understood her meaning and smiled. These tall, scowling, scarred, humorless Irials did not seem to fear anything on this earth. No doubt the devil did not risk tempting a Lanconian. "I have yet to see these Lanconians do anything but swagger and talk of war. I've not seen one in battle."

"Yes, but Uncle William said they fought like demons, like no Englishman ever had."

"William is a soft, lazy man. No! Don't protest, I love him too, but love doesn't keep me from seeing him clearly. His men are fat and spend their time fighting among themselves."

"Not to mention his sons," Lora said under her breath.

"Would you rather be with William's four buffoons or here in this beautiful land of ours?"

She looked at the wide, deep, rapidly flowing river. "I like the country but without these men. This morning a Lanconian told me to turn away while he skinned a rabbit because he said he feared for my health at the sight. Grrrh! Remember the boar I shot last year? Who does he think I am?"

"A soft English lady. What do you suppose their women are like?" Rowan asked.

"These men are the sort who lock their women away in a cellar and bring them out twice a year, once to impregnate them, once to take the child."

"Doesn't sound like a bad idea to me."

"What?" Lora gasped.

"If the women look like the men, they *should be* locked away."

"But the men aren't bad looking," Lora protested, "merely bad tempered."

"Oh?" Rowan looked at her, one eyebrow arched.

Lora blushed. "I do want to be fair. They are all rather wonderfully tall and not at all fat and their eyes are—" She stopped talking when Rowan's smile grew into a knowing smirk.

"That is why we are here. I assume our mother felt the same way about the Lanconians as you do."

Lora despised his smirk and while she was cursing all men everywhere, she suddenly stopped and smiled. "I'll wager I heard something you didn't. Our father has chosen a bride for you. Her name is Cilean and she is the captain of something called the Women's Guard. She is a female knight." Lora was pleased to see Rowan's smile vanish; she had his attention now. "From what I can find out, she is as tall as you are and spends her days learning to use a sword. I believe she even has her own armor." She smiled at Rowan and batted her lashes. "Do you think her bridal veil will be chain mail?"

Rowan's face had changed from soft, smiling boyishness to one of cold steel. "No," was the one word he uttered.

"No, what?" Lora asked innocently. "No chain mail?"

"I did not choose to be king, it was given to me before birth, but I have dedicated my life to it. I will marry a Lanconian woman—I had planned that—but I will marry no bull of a woman. There are some sacrifices a man cannot make for his country. I will marry a woman I can love."

"I imagine the Lanconians would consider that a soft attitude. They marry but I cannot imagine one of them in love. Can you see Xante with his scarred forehead offering a bouquet of flowers to a woman?"

Rowan didn't answer. He was thinking of all the lovely women in England he could have married but didn't. No one, not even Lora, knew of the pain, both physical and mental, that Rowan had suffered through Feilan as that old man tried to beat the English half of Rowan out of him. The old man seemed able to read Rowan's mind. If the boy had a doubt about himself, Feilan sensed it and worked to drive it away. Outwardly, Rowan had learned never to allow anyone to see his fear or see that he sometimes believed he was not the right one to rule Lanconia. But after years of Feilan's training, Rowan honestly believed he could now laugh in the face of death. What he felt inside would *never* show to anyone.

But, through all the years with Feilan, he had kept a

dream of someday being able to share himself with a woman, someone soft and gentle, someone loving, someone whom he could *trust*.

Every year Feilan had sent a letter to Rowan's father Thal, listing Rowan's every fault and telling Thal he had doubts that the boy would ever be fully Lanconian. Feilan had complained of Rowan being like his English mother, and that he wanted to spend too much time in his sister's gentle company.

Silently, Rowan had fought old Feilan on this. He trained all day, endured whatever the man could devise in the way of torture, but he also learned to play the lute and sing a few songs. And he found he needed Lora's softness. Perhaps he never would be wholly Lanconian, for he imagined his home life being like what he shared with Lora. As they were growing up, they had grown close as they clung to each other against Uncle William's stupid, cruel sons. Rowan used to hold Lora as she cried after the boys had taunted her with sticks for an hour, scratching her face and tearing her clothes. He calmed her by telling her stories of Lanconia.

As they grew older they learned to stay close to one another for the physical protection of Lora, and Rowan had grown to love Lora's soft ways. After a day on the training field when Feilan had once again tried to kill him, Rowan would ease his tired, sore body to the floor at Lora's feet and she would sing to him or tell him a story or just caress his hair. The only time he had allowed his emotions to show since he was a child was when Lora said she planned to marry and leave him. He had been miserably lonely the two years she was away when she was married, but she had returned with Phillip. Sometimes Rowan thought they were a family, and when he imagined a wife, he knew he wanted her to be soft and sweet like Lora, with a woman's anger over minor jealousies and squabbles. He did *not* want some female Lanconian warrior.

"There are some privileges a king has, and one is to marry whomever he wants," he said with finality.

Lora frowned. "Rowan, that's not at all true. Kings marry to form alliances with other countries."

He started to rise, quickly pulling on his clothes in a way that let Lora know that was the end of the matter. "I will make an alliance with England if I must. I'll ask Warbrooke for one of his daughters, but I will not marry some witch who wears armor. Come on, let's go. I'm hungry."

Lora wished she had never brought the subject up. As much as she felt she knew her brother, there were times when she felt she knew nothing about him. There was a part of him that remained secret. She took his extended arm. "Will you teach me Lanconian?" She hoped to get his mind to a different subject and so bring back his good mood.

"There are three Lanconian languages. Which one do you want to learn?"

"Xantian," she said quickly then gasped. "I . . . I mean the Irials' language."

Rowan was smirking knowingly again but at least he wasn't angry anymore.

They had not reached camp yet before Xante met them. He was six feet four inches tall, broad-shouldered, with a body as strong and lean as a rawhide whip. His black hair hung in heavy rivulets to his shoulders, framing a dark-skinned face with heavy black brows, deep-set black eyes, a thick black mustache, and a chin that was square and rigid. A deep scar on his forehead was emphasized by the scowl he now wore.

"We have visitors. We have been searching for you," Xante said in his harsh voice. He wore a belted bearskin over a short-skirted tunic that left his muscular legs bare.

Lora started to reply to Xante's insolence to his king but Rowan squeezed her fingers painfully.

Rowan did not explain his absence from camp even though Xante had told him he was not to leave the sight of the Lanconians who were to protect him. "Who has come?" Rowan asked. He was a couple of inches shorter than Xante but younger and thicker. Xante had had too many lean winters to have the thick muscle of Rowan.

"Thal has sent Cilean and Daire with another hundred men."

"Cilean?" Lora asked. "Is this the woman Rowan is to marry?"

Xante gave her a sharp look, as if to tell her to mind her own business.

Lora glared at him in defiance.

"Shall we ride to meet them?" Rowan asked, a slight frown on his handsome face.

His horse was saddled and waiting for him and, as always, he was surrounded by fifty Lanconians, rather like a child who needs constant protection. They rode northwest, toward the mountains, where, in the setting sun, he could see the outline of many troops. As they drew closer together, he braced himself to meet this woman who had been given the equivalent of knighthood.

He saw her from a long way off. There was no mistaking her form for that of a man: tall, slim, erect, high firm breasts, a three-inch-wide belt around her narrow waist, curving hips below.

He kicked his horse forward, ignoring the protests of the men around him, and went forward to meet her. When he saw her face, he smiled. She was quite lovely with her dark eyes and deep red lips.

"My lady, I welcome you," he said, and smiled at her. "I am Rowan, humble prince of your magnificent country."

Around him the Lanconians were silent. This was no way for a man to act, especially not a man destined to be king. They looked at the setting sun glinting off his blond hair and they knew that everything they had feared about this man was true: he was a stupid English softling.

At the first guffaw behind Cilean, she urged her horse forward and held out her hand to touch Rowan's in greeting. She, too, was disappointed. He was good-looking enough but the silly grin he wore made her agree with her men's opinion of him.

Rowan held Cilean's hand for a moment and saw her thoughts in her dark eyes. Around him he could feel the superior attitude of the Lanconians and his anger almost came to the surface. Whether it was anger at himself or the Lanconians he did not know. The scar on his leg twitched and his smile faded.

Rowan dropped Cilean's hand with his smile. It was one thing to look the buffoon before men, but before this magnificent creature who was to be his wife . . .

Rowan reined his horse around. "We return to camp," he ordered, not looking at anyone. He knew his own three English knights were the first to obey him.

Suddenly a shout went up and the Lanconians circled Rowan and his three men protectively.

"You are too close to Zernas," Rowan heard a man say in the Irial language. He was a young serious-looking man, riding next to Cilean, and now he was berating Xante. This must be Daire, Rowan thought.

Even though the Lanconians tried to halt him, Rowan urged his horse to the front of the group to see what had caused the alarm.

On a hill, silhouetted by the dying sun, were three men.

"Zerna," Xante said to Rowan as if that explained everything. "We will take you back to camp. Daire! Choose fifty men and prepare to fight."

Rowan's temper that he had suppressed for days could no longer be contained. "Like hell you will!" he said to Xante in perfect Irial Lanconian. "You will not harm my men and, make no mistake, the Zernas are mine as much as the Irials are. I will greet these men. Neile! Watelin! Belsur!" he called to his three knights.

Never had any men so readily obeyed an order, for they were sick of the Lanconians' treatment of them. They arrogantly shoved their way through the Lanconians to stand behind Rowan.

"Stop the fool," Daire said to Xante. "Thal will never forgive us if he's killed."

Rowan turned deadly eyes to Daire. "You follow *my* orders," he said, and Daire stopped speaking.

Xante was looking at Rowan with some interest, but he was older than Daire and less easily intimidated. When he spoke, his voice held great patience. "They are Zerna and do not recognize an Irial king. They believe Brocain is their king and they would delight in killing you."

"I do not please people so easily. We ride," he said over his shoulder to his own men.

Behind him Xante stopped the Irials from following Rowan. "It is better that the fool is killed now before Thal makes him king," he said. The Lanconians watched with impassive faces as the prince they disliked so much rode toward certain death.

The three Zernas on the hill stood still as Rowan and his knights approached. He could see, as he drew closer, that they were young men out hunting and no doubt startled at the sight of so many Irials where they shouldn't be.

Rowan's anger was still pounding in his ears. Always, he had been taught that he was to be king of all the Lanconians, and here the Irials were trying to kill the Zernas.

Rowan motioned for his knights to remain behind as he rode forward to greet the three young men alone. He halted about a hundred yards from the young hunters. "I am Prince Rowan, son of Thal," he called in the Irial language that the Zernas spoke also, "and I offer you greetings and peace."

The three young men still sat motionless on their horses, obviously fascinated by this lone blond man, such an oddity in this country, riding toward them on his tall, beautiful roan horse. The middle Zerna, little more than a boy, was the first to recover his senses. With a movement like lightning, he drew his bow and an arrow and shot at Rowan.

Rowan swerved to the right only just before the arrow reached him and he felt it graze his left arm. He cursed under his breath and spurred his horse to a swift gallop. He had had more than he could bear from these Lanconians. Contempt and laughter were one thing, but being shot at by a boy after he'd offered peace was the last insult he could tolerate. He reached the boy in seconds and, while still galloping, pulled him from his horse and flung him to the ground. Rowan was off his horse instantly, holding the fighting boy to the ground with the weight of his big body. Behind him he could hear the thunder of the hooves of two hundred approaching Lanconian horses.

"Get out of here!" he bellowed to the two boys still on their horses.

"We cannot," one said, looking in horror at the boy Rowan was pinning to the ground, his voice little more than a whisper. "He is our king's son."

"*I* am your king," Rowan bellowed, all of his anger behind his voice. He looked up to see his own knights approaching. "Get them out of here," he ordered, motioning toward the two Zerna boys. "Xante will tear them apart."

Rowan's knights charged the two young men and sent them racing.

Rowan looked down at the boy he held. He was a handsome youth, about seventeen and as mad as a cat in water.

"You are not my king," the boy screeched. "My father, the great Brocain, is king." He spat a mouthful of saliva in Rowan's face.

Rowan wiped his face then slapped the boy in an insulting way, like a man might slap a woman whose quick tongue was more than he could bear. He jerked him upright. "You'll come with me."

"I'll die before—"

Rowan turned the boy to face the approaching Irial troops, who were now very close. They were a formidable sight of muscled men, muscled horses, and weapons gleaming in the sunlight. "They will kill you if you try to run."

"No Zerna fears an Irial," he said, but his face had lost all color.

"There are times when a man uses his brain instead of his right arm. Act like a man now. Make your father proud." He released his hold on the boy, and after a moment's hesitation, the boy stood where he was. Rowan could only hope the boy had sense enough not to do something stupid. No doubt the Irials would take great pleasure in killing this Zerna boy.

The Lanconians surrounded Rowan and the boy, their horses sweaty, nostrils open, the men with their black brows drawn together, weapons at the ready. They were enough to make Rowan want to turn tail and run.

"Good," Xante said, "you have a captive. We will execute him now for trying to kill an Irial."

Rowan was proud that the boy did not waver or show any signs of cowardice at Xante's autocratic words. Rowan's anger, momentarily exorcised by his tussle with the boy, came to the surface again. Now was the time to establish his right to rule. He pushed his anger down and looked up at Xante. "I have a *guest,*" he said pointedly. "This is Brocain's son and he has agreed to travel with us and to direct us through his father's land."

Xante snorted as loudly as his horse. "It was this *guest* who shot you?"

Rowan was aware of the blood streaming down his

arm but he would not back down now. "I cut myself on a rock," he said, his eyes challenging Xante's.

Cilean urged her horse forward, placing herself between the two men. "We welcome a guest, even though he be Zerna," she said as if she were welcoming a poisonous snake into her bed. Her eyes were on Rowan, watching him as he glared up at the formidable Xante. Not many men dared challenge Xante and she never would have believed this soft blond Englishman would do so. But she had watched him ride against the Zerna, rather amazingly dodge an arrow, leap from his horse onto the boy, and now the Zerna boy stood close to the Englishman as if this blond man could stay the hands of the Irials. And now this Rowan was daring Xante in a way she had never seen before. Perhaps this man was a fool but perhaps there was more to him than they thought.

Rowan's knight Belsur held the reins to Rowan's horse. Rowan mounted then offered his hand to the Zerna boy to mount behind him. As Rowan turned his horse to start back to the camp, he asked, "What is your name?"

"Keon," the boy said proudly, but there was a catch in his throat, betraying his fear at his narrow brush with death. "Son of the Zerna king."

"I think we'd better give your father another title. *I* am the only king of this country."

The boy laughed in a derogatory way. "My father will destroy you. No Irial will ever rule a Zerna."

"We shall see, but for tonight, maybe you'd better consider me Zerna and stay near me. I'm not sure my other Lanconians are as forgiving as I am."

Behind them rode Rowan's knights and then the

cluster of Lanconians, Daire, Cilean, and Xante in front.

"Is he always such a fool?" Daire asked Xante, looking at the back of this man who was supposed to be an Irial but who treated the Zerna boy as a friend. "How have you kept him alive?" he asked in wonder.

Xante was looking at Rowan and the Zerna boy thoughtfully. "Until tonight he has been as tame as a pet dog. His sister has shown more fire than he has. And, until tonight, he has spoken only English."

"If he continues riding alone against the Zernas, he will not live long," Daire said. "We should not try to prevent him from whatever foolishness he wishes to try. Judging by what he did today, he will open the gates of Escalon to any invader. Lanconia could fall under a ruler as stupid as he is. No, we will not try to prevent his riding alone against the enemy. We will be well rid of him. Geralt will be our king."

"*Is* he stupid?" Cilean asked. "If we had attacked those boys and killed Brocain's son, we wouldn't know peace until Brocain had killed hundreds of our people. And now we have an important hostage. Brocain cannot attack us for fear of killing his son. And you say this Rowan has not, in weeks of travel, let you know he speaks our language? Come, Xante, I am surprised at you. What else does the man know about us that you do not know about him?" She urged her horse forward to ride beside Rowan.

All evening Cilean watched Rowan and his sister and his nephew and his men, encircled by darkness around a fire in front of Rowan's beautiful silk tent. The Zerna boy, Keon, sat near them, quiet, sullen, watchful. Cilean imagined that Rowan's ways were as strange to him as they were to the Irials. Rowan held his young nephew on his lap and whispered things that made the boy laugh and squeal. No Lanconian child of that age would be held by his father. By four the boys were already being taught to use weapons and so were the girls who had been chosen for the Women's Guard.

Cilean watched the way Rowan smiled at his sister, heard him ask after her comfort, and she began to wonder what it would be like to live with this man of contradictions, who rode alone against three Zernas and two hours later cuddled a child and teased a woman. How could such a man be a fighter? How could he be a king?

Early the next morning, before the sun was up, the alarm horns were blown by the guardsmen standing watch. Instantly, the Lanconians were out of their light sleeping blankets and on their feet.

Rowan came out of his tent wearing only his loincloth, giving the Lanconians their first sight of the body of the man they had thought soft. Muscle like Rowan's had been created by hard, heavy work.

"What is it?" he yelled in Lanconian at Xante.

"Zerna," was Xante's terse answer. "Brocain comes to fight for his son. We will meet him." He was already mounting his horse.

Rowan grabbed Xante's shoulder and pulled him about. "We do not attack because of what you believe to be true. Keon!" he yelled past Xante. "Prepare to ride to meet your father."

Xante gave Rowan a cold look. "It is your life you lose."

Rowan choked back words of anger and gave a look

of warning to Neile, who took a step toward Xante. He had expected them to doubt him, but they did not merely doubt, they were *sure* he was useless.

Within minutes he was dressed. He did not dress in chain mail as for battle but in embroidered velvet as if for a social event. Rowan grimaced when the Lanconians smiled at the stupidity of this foreigner and Keon shook his head in wonder. At the moment Keon wished he had been killed yesterday, as death was preferable to facing his father.

Cilean, watching from a distance, saw the anger quickly cross Rowan's face then disappear. If she were to marry this man, it might be good to ally herself with him now. And, besides, she was very interested in how he planned to deal with an old, treacherous man like Brocain.

"May I ride with you?" Cilean asked Rowan.

"No!" Daire and Xante yelled in unison.

Rowan looked at them, his eyes as cold as steel. "They can spare the life of an English prince but not one of their own," he said, the bitterness he felt showing in his voice.

Cilean held a tall spear, a bow, and a quiver of arrows flung to her back. "I am a guard; I make my own decisions."

Rowan grinned at her and Cilean found herself blinking as if against too bright a sun. By the gods above, the man was handsome! "Get your horse then," he said, and Cilean hurried to her horse like a novice anxious to please her teachers.

Rowan looked after her. Feilan had not told him of the intelligence and generosity of the Lanconian women.

The other Lanconians were not affected by Rowan's

personal appearance and sat on their horses in a long line, watching silently as Rowan, Cilean, the three English knights, and Keon rode to meet two hundred Zerna warriors and certain death.

"Straighten your spine, boy," Rowan said to Keon. "It is not as if you were facing the wrath of your king."

"My father *is* king," Keon shot back, his dark face almost as pale as Rowan's.

A hundred yards from the Zernas, who sat still and waited for the approach of the small band, Rowan rode forth alone. Sun hit the gold embroidery of his tunic, flashed off his golden hair, winked in the diamond in his sword hilt, played along the trappings of his horse. The Lanconians, neither Irial nor Zerna, had never seen anything like this richly dressed man. He was as different looking from them as possible, a rose amid a field of sand burrs. They gaped at him in wonder.

After a moment's hesitation, a big man rode toward Rowan. His face was scarred, one deep gouge running from his left eye down to his neck, and half of one ear was gone. There were more scars on his legs and arms. He looked as if he had never smiled in his life.

"Are you the Englishman who took my son?" he asked in a voice that made Rowan's horse dance about. The animal recognized danger.

Rowan smiled at the man, successfully covering the fact that his heart was pounding in his ears. He doubted if any amount of combat training could prepare one to fight with such a man as this. "I am Lanconian, King Thal's successor. I am to be king of all the Lanconians," he said with an amazing amount of firmness in his voice.

For a moment, the older man's mouth dropped

open, then he closed it again. "I will kill a hundred men for each hair that is harmed on my son's head."

Rowan yelled over his shoulder. "Keon! Come forward."

Brocain looked his son up and down, grunted satisfaction that he was unharmed, then told him to join the Zernas on the hill.

"No!" Rowan said sharply. His hand dropped to his knee, so that it was inches from his sword hilt. Whatever fear he felt, he could not let it show and he could not let this man have Keon. Fate had delivered the boy into his hands and Rowan meant to keep him. He was not going to let this small chance at peace escape him. "I'm afraid I cannot allow that. Keon stays with me."

Once again, Brocain's mouth dropped open but he recovered himself quickly. This man's words and attitude did not match his handsome, unscarred, pale-skinned face. "We will fight for him," he said, reaching for his sword.

"I'd as soon not," Rowan said pleasantly, and hoped no one saw the greenish tinge his skin was taking, "but I will if necessary. I want to keep Keon with me because I believe he is your successor."

Brocain gave a quick look to Keon. "He is if one so stupid can be allowed to rule."

"He's not stupid, merely young and hot-blooded and a very poor shot. I'd like to keep him with me, to show him that we Irials are not demons, and perhaps someday there can be peace between our people." Rowan's eyes twinkled. "And I would like to teach him to shoot straight."

Brocain looked at Rowan for a long time and Rowan knew the hideous old man was deciding on life or death for his son and this Englishman. Rowan did not believe a man such as Brocain would be moved by such a weak emotion as love for his son. "Old Thal did not raise you," he said at last. "He would have killed my son by now. What guarantee do I have for his safety?"

"My word," Rowan said solemnly. "I will give you my life if he is harmed by an Irial." Rowan was holding his breath.

"You are asking for a great deal of trust," Brocain said. "If he is harmed, I will kill you so slowly you will pray for death."

Rowan nodded.

Brocain did not speak for a while as he studied Rowan. There was something different about this man—different from any Lanconian. And even though he was dressed more gaudily than any woman, Brocain sensed that there was more to him than first appeared. Suddenly, Brocain felt old and tired. He had seen son after son killed; he had lost three wives in battle. All he had left was this young boy.

Brocain turned to look at his son. "Go with this man. Learn from him." He turned back to Rowan. "Three years. Send him home three years from today or I will burn your city to the ground." He reined his horse away and went back to his men on the hill.

Keon turned to Rowan with eyes wide in wonder, but he didn't say anything.

"Come on, boy, let's go home," Rowan said at last, releasing his breath and feeling as if he'd just escaped death of a most vile nature. "Stay close to me until people get used to seeing you. I don't like the idea of being tortured."

As Rowan and the boy rode past Cilean, Rowan

nodded at her and she followed them. She was beyond speech. This Englishman who dressed in clothes as pretty as a courting bird's feathers had just won a verbal battle with old Brocain. "I'd as soon not," he'd said when challenged to fight, yet Cilean had seen the way he kept his hand near his sword. And the way he'd told Brocain that the Irials would keep the Zerna boy! He had not flinched a muscle, had not registered any fear.

She rode back to the others and still could not speak. This Rowan not only looked different, he was different. Either he was the biggest fool ever made or the bravest man on earth. She hoped for Lanconia's sake and—she smiled—for her future life as his wife that it was the latter.

# Chapter Three

JURA STAYED MOTIONLESS, her bow drawn back, ready to fire as she waited for the buck to turn toward her. The dark green of her tunic and trousers concealed her from the animal. The instant the animal turned, she shot and it fell down gracefully and soundlessly.

Out of the trees seven young women came running from their hiding places. They were all tall, slim, and each wore her dark hair in a thick braid down her strong back. They wore the green hunting tunic and trousers of the Women's Guard.

"Good shot, Jura," one woman said.

"Yes," Jura said distractedly, looking about the forest while the women began to skin and gut the buck. She was restless this evening, feeling as if something were about to happen. It had been four days since Cilean and Daire had left and Jura missed her friend very much. She missed Cilean's quiet humor, her intelligence, and she missed having someone to confide in. She also missed Daire. She and Daire had grown up together and she was used to his being around.

She rubbed her bare arms beneath the short sleeves of her tunic. "I'm going swimming," she murmured to the women behind her.

One woman paused in her cutting of a haunch of meat. "Do you want someone to go with you? We are far from the city walls."

Jura didn't turn around. These were trainee guards, none of them over sixteen years old and, by comparison, she felt old and lonely. "No, I'll go alone," she said, and moved through the forest toward the stream.

She walked farther than she meant to, wanting to rid herself of the feeling she had of impending . . . what? Not danger, but somewhat like the air felt before a storm broke.

There had been only one communication from the army that was bringing the English Rowan to the Irial capital city, Escalon, and his dying father. Old Thal was keeping himself alive by sheer willpower as he waited to see what kind of man his son had grown to be. So far, judging from what had been reported, Rowan was proving to be a fool. He involved himself in village disputes, he single-handedly challenged the Zernas while Xante and Daire had to protect him. Rowan was said to be a soft weakling who knew more about velvet than he did about a sword.

The word had spread rapidly throughout Escalon and already there were murmurings of uprisings and revolts in protest against this stupid Englishman who was not fit to rule. Geralt and Daire and Cilean would have to use all their powers to keep this oaf from destroying the tentative peace of the Lanconian nation.

In a secluded glade, Jura removed her clothing and

slipped into the water. Perhaps a long swim would ease her troubled mind.

Rowan rode as hard and fast as his horse would go. He needed to get away, to be alone, to escape the censoring eyes of the Lanconians. Two days ago they had ridden past a peasant's hut that was blazing. When Rowan halted the army of Lanconians and ordered them to put the fire out, they had merely stared at him in contempt. They had sat on their horses and watched while Rowan and his English men had directed the peasants in dousing the flames.

When the fire was out, the peasants had told a garbled story of a feud between two families. Rowan had told them to come to Escalon and he would hear their case and he the king would personally judge it. The peasants had laughed at the idea of a king. The king ruled the soldiers who trampled their fields; he did not rule the workingman.

Rowan rode back to the Lanconians, who looked at him with contempt for having involved himself with the petty disputes of the farmers.

But Rowan knew that if he was to be king and there was to be peace between the tribes, he must be king of all the Lanconians, the Zernas, the Ultens, the Vatells, all the tribes and all their people, from the lowest peasant to Brocain, who ruled hundreds of men.

Today, Rowan had had enough of the silent hostility and sometimes not so silent hostility of the Lanconians and he had broken away, telling his own knights to keep the Lanconians away. Their eyes reflected every fear he had stowed within himself. Their obvious doubts of him made his own doubts come closer to the surface. He needed to be alone, to have some time to think, and to pray.

He knew he was only miles from the walls of Escalon when he came to a river tributary, a peaceful, lovely stream, so unlike everything else he had experienced in Lanconia.

He dismounted and tied his horse, then fell to his knees, his hands folded in prayer.

"Oh Lord," he prayed in a choked whisper that betrayed the depth of his pain, "I have tried to ready myself for the duty that You and my earthly father have placed upon my head, but I am only one man. If I am to accomplish what I know to be right, I need Your help. The people are against me and I do not know how to win their loyalty. I beg You, dear God, please show me the way. Guide me. Direct me. I place myself in Your hands. If I am wrong, let me know. Give me a sign. If I am right, then I plead for Your help."

He hung his head for a moment, feeling spent and exhausted. He had come to Lanconia knowing what he was to do, but with each passing day his confidence had been draining. Every hour of every day he had to prove himself as a man to these Lanconians. They had made up their minds about him and nothing he did changed their opinions. If he was brave, they murmured that fools are often brave. If he cared about his people, they said his ways were foreign. What did he have to do to prove himself? Torture and kill some innocent Zerna boy who they seemed to think was the devil incarnate?

He stood, his legs shaky from the emotion he had exerted, then cared for his horse. He removed his sweaty clothes then stepped into the cool, clear water. He dove, he swam, he let the water take some of the anger and feelings of helplessness out of his body, and an hour later when he returned to the bank he felt better. He put on his loincloth, then all at once, his senses came alive. He had heard a noise to his right. It sounded like a person moving about. He pulled his sword from the saddle scabbard and silently crept along the edge of the water toward the noise.

He was not prepared for the blow that hit him. Someone swung from a tree branch above his head, feet slammed into Rowan's shoulders, and caught off balance, he fell to the ground. Instantly, he felt a steel point at his throat.

"Don't," said a woman's voice.

Rowan had been reaching for his fallen sword, but as he looked up, he forgot about his sword. Straddling him, her legs bare to midthigh, was the most beautiful female Rowan had ever seen in his life. His uncle William's men had always teased Rowan that he lived like a monk. They laughed because he had no desire to tumble a peasant girl in a haystack. He had had a few sexual encounters, but no woman had ever inflamed his senses so that he desired her above all else in life. If sex was offered and the girl was clean, he took it if he had nothing else to do.

Until now.

As Rowan looked up at this woman, up past high breasts, up to her face with black eyes that burned as hot as coals, he felt as if his body were on fire. Every pore in his skin was alive, awake as it had never been before. He could feel her, smell her. It was as if the warmth from her body were merging with his and becoming one.

His hands moved to touch her ankles, clasped them, and his eyes followed his hands as he drank of the beauty of her long, lean, muscular legs. The sword point at his throat fell away but he wasn't aware of it. He saw and felt only his touch of those magnificent legs, his hands traveling higher, caressing, kneading her tanned, beautiful, smooth flesh.

He thought he heard her groan but he wasn't sure it wasn't the sound of his own heart melting in ecstasy.

As his hands traveled upward as far as they could reach, her knees began to bend in a slow way, like a wax candle melting when placed too near a blazing fire. His hands moved up and up, lifting the damp tunic she wore. She had on nothing beneath and he saw the precious jewel of her as his hands moved up to clasp the high firm cheeks of her buttocks.

She sank to his chest, and when her bare flesh touched his, Rowan quivered with desire. Her skin was as hot as his, like red-hot iron in the farrier's forge. His hands moved up her back and pulled her forward.

Her face was near his, her eyes half closed with desire, her lips red and full and open to receive him, her skin pale and perfect. He pulled her face to his.

At the first touch of their lips, she sprang away from him and looked at him. But she seemed to feel the same surprise that he did. But the next moment his surprise was gone as she flung her arms around his neck and kissed him with all the passion he felt. His arms tightened about her so hard, it was a wonder her ribs didn't break. He pushed her to her back, never breaking contact with her lips as he kissed her violently, deeply, with years of desire that had been waiting for this one woman and this one moment.

Her legs went about his waist as he rolled over with her and his loincloth came off of its own accord.

"Jura," someone called.

He ate at her lips, gnawing them, trying to get more and more of her. He nestled his hard body into the woman's saddle of her.

"Jura, are you all right?"

The woman beneath Rowan was beating on his bare back with her fists, but he was too stupid with desire to feel pain.

"They will see us," she whispered urgently with a shaky voice that went up and down in pitch. "Release me."

If a horse had run over him, he wouldn't have felt it. His hand searched for and found her breast.

"Jura!" The voice was closer.

Jura grabbed a rock and brought it down on the man's head. She didn't mean to hit him so hard, only to get his attention, but he collapsed senseless on her body.

She could hear the guardswomen coming closer now. With urgency and a great deal of regret, she pushed the man off of her. For a moment she looked down at his magnificent body. Never had she seen a more perfect man, muscular yet lean, thick but not heavy, with a face like one of God's angels.

She ran her hand over his body, down his thick thighs and back up to his face. She kissed his lips.

"Jura! Where are you?"

She cursed the stupid trainees who had interrupted her, then stood so they could see her. The tall grasses hid the man at her feet. "I am here," she called. "No, don't come any closer, the mud is deep here. Wait for me at the path."

"It's growing dark, Jura," one who was little more than a girl said.

"Yes, I can see that," Jura snapped. "Go on. I won't be but a moment." Impatiently, she watched the women go out of sight then knelt to the unconscious man.

Perhaps she should feel guilty about what she had almost done with this stranger, but she didn't. She touched his chest again. Who was he? He wasn't Zerna, nor was he Vatell like Daire. Perhaps he was of the Fearens, the horsepeople who lived in the mountains and kept to themselves. But he was too large to be a Fearen.

He was beginning to stir and Jura knew she had to get away from him before he looked at her again with those hooded eyes that threatened her sanity.

She ran toward the bank, grabbed her clothing, and dressed as she ran toward the trainees. She could still feel his hands and lips on her body.

"Jura, you look flushed," one of the girls said.

"Probably because Daire is returning soon," another one said slyly.

"Daire?" Jura said as if she'd never heard the word before. "Oh, yes, Daire," she said quickly. Daire had never made her heart leap to her throat or made the muscles in her legs turn to fluid. "Yes, Daire," she said firmly.

The girls looked at one another knowingly. Jura was getting old and losing her mind.

"Rowan! Where have you been?" Lora questioned sharply.

"I . . . I went swimming." He was dazed, befuddled. His head swam with images of the woman. He could feel her skin against his palms and he was sure his chest was still red where she had sat on him.

He had been able to dress and saddle his horse only because he had done it so often before.

"Rowan," Lora said softly. "Are you all right?"

"Never better," he murmured. So this was lust, he thought. So this was the feeling that drove men to do things they wouldn't ordinarily do. If this woman had asked him to kill for her, to desert his country, to betray his men, he doubted if he would have hesitated.

Rowan became aware that people were looking at him. He was leaning on the high, wide pommel of his saddle, his body relaxed, a half smile on his lips, and below him Lanconian and English alike were gaping at him.

He straightened, cleared his throat, then dismounted. "The ride refreshed me," he said in a dreamy-sounding voice. "Here, Montgomery, take my horse and give it extra feed." The dear animal led me to her, he thought as he caressed the horse's neck.

Montgomery moved close to his master. "They thought you couldn't take care of yourself for even a few hours," he whispered bitterly.

Rowan patted Montgomery's shoulder. "I could take care of the world tonight, my boy." He turned away toward his tent and stopped near Daire. Daire was a tall, silent man whose face did not show what he was thinking as Xante's did. Somehow, Rowan did not feel as much contempt coming from Daire as from the others.

"Have you heard of a woman named Jura?"

Daire hesitated before answering. "She is Thal's daughter."

Rowan's horror showed in his face. "My sister?" he choked out.

"Not by blood. The king adopted her as a child."

Rowan nearly wept with relief. "But we are not blood related?"

Daire was watching him. "Geralt is your brother by blood. Jura and he share a mother while you and Geralt share a father."

"I see." All Rowan cared about was that she was not a blood relative. "She is a guardswoman? Like Cilean?"

Again, Daire hesitated. "Yes, although Jura is younger."

Rowan smiled. "She is the perfect age, whatever that is. Good night."

Rowan didn't sleep much that night but lay awake in his tent, his hands behind his head, staring into the darkness and savoring every moment of his time with Jura.

He would marry her, of course. He would make her his queen and together they would rule Lanconia . . . or at least the Irials. Jura would be the softness in his life to make up for the Lanconians' lack of belief in him. Jura would be the one he could share himself with. As God said, a helpmate for man. He had asked God for a sign and moments later Jura was there.

Before dawn he heard the first stirrings of camp and rose and dressed and went outside. The mountains were hazy in the distance and the air was crisp and cool. Lanconia had never looked so beautiful to him.

Cilean stopped near him. "Good morning. I am going fishing. Perhaps you would join me?"

Rowan looked at Cilean for a long moment, and for the first time realized there might be a bit of a problem in his plans to marry Jura. "Yes," he said. "I will go."

They walked together into the forest toward a wide stream.

"We'll reach Escalon today," Cilean said.

Rowan didn't answer. What if King Thal insisted he marry Cilean? What if, in order to be made king, he would have to marry Cilean? Every punishment Feilan had devised for him rose to his throat. "May I kiss you?" he asked abruptly.

Cilean turned startled eyes toward him and color rose to her cheeks.

"I mean, if we are to be married, I thought—"

He broke off because Cilean put her hand to the back of his head and pressed her lips to his. It was a pleasant kiss but it didn't make Rowan forget who he was or where he was, nor did it tempt him to sign a pact with the devil.

Gently, he broke away and smiled at her. He was sure now. Jura was the one God had chosen for him. Companionably, they walked together to the stream, Rowan with his thoughts on Jura and unaware of Cilean's happiness. She thought she had been kissed by the man she was to marry, and she was more than satisfied with the coming marriage.

It was a five-hour ride northwest to Escalon. The roads were practically nonexistent and Rowan vowed to set up a road maintenance system right away. The Lanconians cursed the fourteen baggage wagons that Rowan and Lora had brought with them from England that carried their furniture and household goods. The Irials' one concession to comfort was their walled city, and when they traveled, they took only what could be carried on their horses. Rowan had an idea they stole their food from the peasants as they traveled.

Escalon lay on the banks of the Ciar River, naturally protected by a curve of the river on two sides and a steep hillside on another. A twelve-foot-high wall surrounded the two square miles of the city. Inside, Rowan could see another wall, another rise of land, and on that the sprawling stone castle that must be his father's house.

"We are almost home," Lora said from her horse beside Rowan. Young Phillip sat in front of her, his little face showing his weariness from weeks of travel. Lora sighed. "Hot food, a hot bath, a soft bed, and someone to talk to besides these warmongers. Do you think the court musicians will know any English songs? What dances do these Lanconians perform?"

Rowan didn't have an answer for his sister as Feilan had not thought it important to talk of the pleasures of Lanconians. Besides, there was only one pleasure in Lanconia that interested Rowan and that was the beautiful, delicious Jura, the most perfect of women, the most . . . He daydreamed all the way into the city.

Their procession into the city of Escalon caused very little interest. It was a dirty place, filled with animals and men, and the sounds were deafening as iron hammers banged on steel, as horses were shod, as men yelled at each other. Lora held a pomander to her nose against the smell.

"Where are the women?" she shouted to Xante over the noise.

"Not in the city. The city is for men."

"Do you have the women locked away somewhere?" she shot back at him. "Do you not allow them out into the fresh air and sunshine?"

Daire turned to look at her with interest and mild surprise on his face.

"We dig pits in the side of the mountains and keep

them there," Xante said. "Once a week we throw them a wolf. If they can kill it, they can eat it."

Lora glared at him, not knowing how much of the truth he was telling.

At the northwest corner of the walled city, in the most protected spot, rose the sprawling stone fortress of Thal's house. It was not a castle as Rowan knew a castle, but lower, longer, and more impenetrable. The stones were as dark as the Lanconians.

Before the fortress was another stone wall, eight feet thick and twenty feet high. There was a rusty iron double gate, covered with vines, in the center of the wall, and to the left was a smaller gate, wide enough only to allow the passage of one horse at a time.

Xante shouted an order and the Lanconian troops began to form themselves into a single line and move toward this narrow gate.

"Wait," Rowan called, "we'll have to use the wide gate to get the wagons through."

Xante reined his horse to stand in front of Rowan. His face showed that his patience was at an end. He looked like a man who had been forced to care for a spoiled, stupid, annoying child. "The wagons cannot go through. They will have to be unloaded and what furniture that will not fit through the gate will have to be taken apart."

Rowan ground his back teeth together. He was reaching his breaking point. Had these people no respect for a man who was to be their king? "You will order your men to open the double gate."

"This gate does not open," Xante said contemptuously. "It has not been opened in a hundred years."

"Then it is time it *was* opened," Rowan bellowed at

the insolent man. He turned in his saddle and saw four men carrying a twelve-foot-long log toward a carpenter's shop. "Montgomery!"

"Yes sir!" Montgomery answered happily. He loved disobeying the Lanconians.

"Get that log and open the gate."

Rowan's three knights were off their horses at once. They were eager to do anything the Lanconians said shouldn't be done. They grabbed, by the scruff of their dirty necks, six of the brawniest workers and set them to using the log as a battering ram.

Rowan sat stiff and straight on his horse and watched as the men rammed the rusty old gate again and again. It didn't budge. He didn't dare look at the smirking faces of the Lanconians.

"The gate was welded shut and it does not open," Xante said, and Rowan could hear the smile of superiority in the man's voice.

Rowan knew there was some superstition attached to the gate but he thought he would die before he asked what it was. Right now necessity outweighed any primitive superstition of these arrogant people. *"I* will open the gate," he said as he dismounted, not looking into the face of a single Lanconian.

He had with him his war horse and those of his three knights. They were huge, heavy animals, capable of pulling tons of weight. Since the battering ram did not work, perhaps he could throw chains about the gate and the horses could pull it down.

Crowds were gathering now as workers ceased their tasks and came to watch this English prince make a fool of himself. On the walls above them were more guardsmen looking down on the scene with great amusement. So this was Thal's weakling brat who thought he could open St. Helen's Gate.

"Xante," someone bellowed down, "is this our new king?"

The laughter was uproarious and it rang in Rowan's ears as he walked toward the gate. Lora was right. He should have challenged a couple of men to a fight the first day and established who was in charge.

He stood before the gate and looked at it. It looked to be ancient, covered with rust and thorny vines. He pulled away a vine, thorns tearing his hands and making his palms bleed, and studied the old lock. It was a solid piece of iron with no sign of a weak joint. As far as he could tell, the battering ram hadn't moved the lock.

"This blond Englishman thinks *he* can open the gate?" a man taunted.

"Didn't someone tell him that only a Lanconian could open it?"

The crowd laughed derisively.

"I *am* Lanconian," Rowan whispered, his eyes on the gate. "I am more Lanconian than they will ever know. God, help me. I beg You. Help me."

He put his hands on the gate, both bloody palms touching the rusty surface, and leaned forward to get a closer look at the thick piece of iron holding the gate shut.

Beneath his palms, he felt the gates tremble.

"Open!" he whispered. "Open for your Lanconian king."

Rust trickled down from the top, sprinkling his face and hair. "Yes!" he said, his eyes closed as he directed all of his energy into his palms. "I am your king. I command you to open."

"Look!" screamed someone behind him. "The gate moves!"

The crowd and the guards on the wall quietened as the ancient gate began to creak. It seemed to shudder like something alive.

There was complete silence, even the animals were still, as the old iron lock fell at Rowan's feet. He pushed the left gate back a couple of feet and the ancient hinges cried out in protest.

Rowan turned to his own men. "Now bring the baggage wagons through," he said, and suddenly felt very, very tired.

But no one moved. The English were looking at the Lanconians and the Lanconians, hundreds of them, both peasants and guardsmen, were staring at Rowan with eyes filled with wonder.

"What's wrong now?" Rowan bellowed up at Xante. "I opened the gate for you, now *use* it."

Still no one moved. Montgomery whispered, "What's wrong with them?"

Xante, as if he were walking in his sleep, very slowly dismounted his horse. His movements amid the absolute stillness seemed dramatic and of great significance. Rowan watched him, wondering what this man planned now to make his contempt known.

To Rowan's utter astonishment, Xante moved to stand in front of him, dropped to his knees, bowed his head, and said, "Long live Prince Rowan."

Rowan looked over his head to Lora, who still sat on her horse. Lora looked as bewildered as Rowan felt.

"Long live Prince Rowan," someone else said, then another, and soon the chant became a shout.

Watelin, Rowan's knight, a most sensible man,

came forward. "Shall we get the wagons through, sire, before the fools decide you're a demon instead of a god?"

Rowan laughed, but before he could answer, Xante was on his feet, glaring at Watelin.

"He is *our* prince," Xante said, "our *Lanconian* prince. *We* will take his wagons through." Xante turned and started bellowing orders to the guardsmen and peasants alike.

Rowan shrugged and mounted his horse as he smiled at Lora. "It seems that opening a rusty old gate was the right thing to do. Shall we enter our kingdom, dear sister?"

"*Princess* sister, if you don't mind," Lora said, laughing.

Inside the walls, men and women of the guard stood quietly with their heads bowed as Rowan and Lora passed them. Rowan searched each face, hoping for a sight of Jura, but she was nowhere to be seen.

At the front of the old stone fortress, Rowan helped Lora dismount. "Shall we go to meet our father?" he asked, and Lora nodded.

# Chapter Four

J URA WAS THE only person on the long training field. There were targets for lance and bow practice at either end, bare patches for wrestling practice, a foot-race course, obstacles for jumping. Now, with one lone woman on the field, it looked enormous. The other guardswomen had rushed back to the city when a runner had come to say the new prince was approaching.

"Prince, ha!" Jura muttered, and heaved her javelin at the target and hit it square in the middle. He was *English* and he wanted to take her brother's rightful place on the throne. At least she was comforted by the knowledge that all Lanconia agreed with her. For once, all the tribes were united in something: this Englishman was no more their king than the English Edward was.

At a sound behind her, she whirled, her javelin aloft. The point stood ready at Daire's throat.

"Too late," he said, smiling. "I could have used a bow from the edge of the field. You should not be here alone with no one standing guard."

"Daire, oh Daire," she cried, and flung her arms

about his neck. "I have missed you very, very, very much." She wanted to touch him, hold him, kiss him—and rid herself of the memory of the man by the river. Last night she had awakened with her body drenched in sweat and all she could think of was that stranger, a man she had never seen before, a peasant for all she knew, some muscular woodcutter on his way home to his wife and brats. "Kiss me," she pleaded.

Daire kissed her, but it wasn't the same as the kiss of the man in the forest. She felt no burning desire, no uncontrollable lust. She opened her mouth under his and put her tongue in his mouth.

Daire drew back, a frown on his face. He was a handsome man with his dark eyes and high cheekbones, but he wasn't as handsome as the man in the woods, Jura thought involuntarily.

"What is wrong?" Daire asked huskily.

Jura dropped her arms and turned away to hide her red face, afraid he might read her thoughts. "I have missed you, that is all. Can't a woman greet her intended with enthusiasm?" Daire was silent for so long that she turned to look at him. They had been reared together. Daire was of the Vatell tribe, and on a raid led by Thal, Daire's father had killed Jura's father. Thal had killed Daire's father, then the twelve-year-old boy had attacked Thal with a rock and a broken lance. Thal had slung the boy over his saddle and taken him back to Escalon. Since Jura's mother had died two weeks before, Thal took in Jura and Thal's son Geralt and supervised the education and training of all three children. Jura, only five at the time, and feeling lost and lonely at the loss of both her parents in so short a time, had clung to the tall, silent

Daire. As they grew up she never stopped clinging to
him. But just because she had spent most of her life
near him didn't mean she could tell what he was
thinking.

"Has he come?" she asked, wanting to make him
stop looking at her as he had when she was six and had
eaten some dried fruit of his then lied when he asked
her if she knew who had stolen it.

"He has come," Daire said softly, still watching her.

"And did the people hiss at him? Did they let this
English usurper know what they thought of him? Did
they—"

"He opened St. Helen's Gate."

Jura let out a guffaw. "With how many horses? Thal
will not be pleased when he hears how his cowardly
son—"

"He opened it with his palms."

Jura stared at Daire.

"He wanted the gate open so he could get his
wagons through, so he ordered his men to use a
battering ram. It had no effect, so Prince Rowan put
his palms against the gate and prayed for God to help
him. The gate swung open."

Jura could do nothing but gape. The legend was that
when the true king of Lanconia arrived the gate would
open for him.

She recovered herself. "No one has tried to open
that gate in years; it must be rusted through. No doubt
the battering ram knocked it loose, then when this
Englishman pushed on it, it opened. Surely everyone
knew that."

"Xante went on his knees before the prince."

"Xante?" Jura asked, eyes wide. "Xante? The one
who laughs whenever the Englishman is mentioned?

The same Xante who sent back messages saying what a fool the man was?"

"He bowed his head and called him Prince. *All* the guard and all the people who were there bowed before him."

Jura looked away. "This will make it harder. The peasants are a superstitious lot, although I had hoped better of the guard. We will have to make them see that they were just a pair of rusty gates. Has Thal been told?"

"Yes," Daire answered. "They are with him now."

"They?"

"Prince Rowan, his sister, and her son."

Jura toyed with her javelin and began to feel overwhelmed. It felt as if she were the only sane person left. Was all Lanconia willing to throw away what it knew to be true merely because some rusty gate opened *after* being hit with a battering ram? Surely at least Daire did not believe in this usurper. "We must convince Thal that Geralt should be king. Tell me, are they *very* English? Do they look and act foreign?"

Suddenly, as quick as a snake, Daire's arm shot out and grabbed the thick braid of Jura's hair and wrapped it about his wrist and forced her face close to his.

"Daire!" she gasped. She had not been prepared for his movement. When she was with him, her guard was down; he had her complete trust.

"You are mine," he said throatily. "You have been mine since you were five years old. I'll share you with no one."

The light in his eyes frightened her. "What has happened?" she whispered. "What has this Rowan done?"

"Perhaps you can answer that better than I."

She recovered from her fear. She still held her javelin in her left hand and now she pushed the point against his ribs. "Release me or I'll put a hole in you."

As abruptly as he had grabbed her, he released her hair then smiled.

Jura did not return his smile. "You will explain yourself."

Daire shrugged. "Cannot a lover be jealous?"

"Jealous of whom?" Jura asked angrily.

He didn't answer her and she didn't like the way his lips were smiling but his eyes were not. They had been together too many years, for he was able to read her thoughts. Somehow he had been able to see through that first kiss of hers, and her talk of the Englishman had not led him from the scent. She had betrayed herself in that kiss and let him know that something was wrong.

She smiled at him. "You have no reason to be jealous. Perhaps it is my anger that makes me—" she hesitated—"seek you out." She looked at him and silently pleaded with him to not press her further.

At last he, too, smiled. "Come," he said, "don't you want to meet your new prince?"

She breathed a sigh of relief that the tense moment was over and lifted her javelin again. "I'd as soon walk into the Ultens' camp alone." That odd look returned to Daire's face, but this time she was not going to ask its cause. "Go on, go back to him," she said. "Thal will want you. Everyone will be needed to bring this soft white Englishman his sweetmeats."

Daire stayed where he was. "I'm sure there will be feasting later."

Jura threw her javelin hard and hit the target in the

red center. "I don't think I'll be in the least hungry tonight. Go on, get out of here. I need to train."

Daire was frowning at her as if something puzzled him, and without another word he turned back toward the walled city.

Angrily, Jura jerked her javelin from the straw-filled target. So much for a lover's return, she thought. She threw her arms about him and he pushed her away, yet a moment later he pulled her hair and told her he was jealous. Why didn't he *show* his jealousy with a few kisses? Why hadn't he done something to erase the memory of the man by the river?

She threw her javelin again and again. She planned to spend the day in hard exercise so that tonight she would be too tired to remember that man's hands on her legs, or his lips on hers or— She uttered a curse and heaved the javelin and missed the target completely. "Men!" she said in anger. Daire stared at her, pulled her hair, and another man caressed her thighs, while an Englishman threatened all of Lanconia. She threw her javelin again and this time hit the center perfectly.

Rowan stood outside the door to his father's chamber and tried to brush some of the travel dust from his clothes. He had not been given time to change and make himself presentable. He had been told that Thal insisted upon seeing him immediately, that he would wait for nothing.

Upon reflection, Rowan doubted if his dusty clothes would matter much to Thal after having seen the squalor of his house. Rowan kicked a gnawed bone from under his feet, straightened his shoulders, and pushed the heavy oak door open. The room was very

dim and it took his eyes a moment to adjust. His
father seemed content not to speak as he studied his
son and thus allowed Rowan time to look at his father.

Thal lay on a pile of furs, long-haired, rough-
looking furs that perfectly suited him, for he was a
rough-looking man. He was extraordinarily tall, at
least four inches taller than Rowan, but unlike Rowan,
he was lean, without Rowan's thickness. Perhaps his
face had once been handsome, but now it was covered
with too many scars from too many battles. Rowan
could easily imagine this man atop a charging stallion,
brandishing a sword above his head and leading a
thousand men into a battle that he would win.

"Come to me, son," Thal whispered in a deep voice
that told of the pain he was in. "Come sit by me."

Rowan went to sit on the edge of the bed by his
father and used every bit of training he had to conceal
the anxiety he felt. He had worked for years to make
his tutor's reports to Thal as good as possible. He had
always wanted to please this man he had never met
and to live up to what was expected of him. Now,
looking at Thal's dark harshness, he felt the man
would be disappointed in his blond, pale son. But
Rowan let none of these feelings show.

Thal put up a scarred hand, still strong, and
touched his son's cheek. His old, dark eyes softened
with unshed tears. "You look like her. You look like
my beautiful Anne." He ran his hand down Rowan's
arm. "And you have the size of the men in her
family." His eyes and lips smiled. "But you have the
height of a Lanconian. At least you got something
from me, for I see no other resemblance. And that
hair! That's Anne's hair."

Thal nearly laughed but it turned into a cough.

Rowan sensed that his father would not want comfort, so Rowan sat still until the spasm was over.

"There is something eating my insides away. I've known it for a long time but I put death off until I had seen you. Did William treat you well?"

"Very well," Rowan said softly. "I couldn't have asked for better."

Thal smiled and closed his eyes a moment. "I knew he would. He always did love you. From the day you were born he loved you. After Anne died . . ." He paused and swallowed. "Death brings back memories. I am praying to see your mother again soon. After my dear Anne's death I would have given you to William to raise if he had asked, but he attacked my men and me; he tried to *take* you."

Thal coughed again but soon controlled the spasm.

"You could have sent for me," Rowan said gently. "I would have come."

Thal smiled and seemed to be comforted by this. "Yes, but I *wanted* you to grow up with the English. Anne showed me peace." He took Rowan's hand. "No one has conquered Lanconians, boy. We have survived the Huns, the Slavs, the Avars, the Romans, and Charlemagne." He paused and smiled. "We didn't survive the priests, though. They made Christians of us. But we fought off the invaders. We Lanconians can outfight anyone—except ourselves," he added sadly.

"The tribes fight each other," Rowan said. "I have seen it myself."

Thal squeezed Rowan's hand. "I heard you walked against the Zernas alone, that you faced Brocain himself."

"The Zernas are Lanconian."

"Yes," Thal said forcefully, and Rowan waited

while he controlled another coughing fit. "When I went to England, when I met Anne, I saw then how a country could have one king. I am called the King of Lanconia but I am actually the king of the Irials only. No Zerna or Vatell will call me king. We will always be a divided nation of tribes. But if we are not united, Lanconia will die."

Rowan was beginning to understand what his father was asking of him. "You want me to unite the Lanconians?" He did not fully keep the horror from his voice. He had not realized how separate the tribes were until he came to Lanconia. Because he had stood up to three young boys and an old man did not mean he could conquer a whole country.

"I left you to be raised outside of my country," Thal continued. "You are not Irial, and perhaps because you are half English the other tribes will accept you."

"I see," Rowan said, and for a moment his eyes closed. He had known for days that there must be peace in Lanconia and, as king, he'd hoped he could stave off war between the tribes. But *unite* them? He was being asked to make old Brocain and the arrogant Xante *friends!* Could one man do this in one lifetime? Now they believed, because he'd opened some old rusty gate, that he was meant to be king, but Rowan didn't think their belief in him would last. All he had to do was one English-seeming thing and again he'd be the outsider, the foreigner. "I was chosen over Geralt because I am English," he said softly. "The Lanconians believe my half-brother should be king."

Thal's expression changed to anger. "Geralt is Irial. He hates anyone not Irial. I hear you have Brocain's son with you. Protect him. Geralt will kill him if he can. Geralt dreams of a Lanconia peopled only by Irials."

"And the other tribes dream of owning Lanconia also?" Rowan said tiredly.

"Yes," Thal said. "In my father's father's time we had outsiders to fight and we were happy. War is in our blood, but now we have no invaders, so we attack each other." He held up his scarred hands. "I have killed too many of my own people with these hands. I could not stop, for I am Irial."

He clutched Rowan's hand and his eyes were pleading. "I am leaving Lanconia to you and you must save it. You can. You opened Saint Helen's Gate."

Rowan smiled at his dying father but inside he was remembering an heiress who had been offered to him and he had refused her. If he had accepted her, he could now be sitting by a fire, a hound at his feet, a child or two in his lap. "It's a wonder the wind didn't knock those gates down twenty years ago." Because of a boy, and an old man, and some rusty gates, he was believed to be capable of *anything*. Part of him wanted to jump on a horse and ride out of Lanconia as fast as possible. But the scar on his leg began to twitch.

Thal smiled and lay back against the pillows. "You have Anne's modesty and, I hear, her sweet temper also. Were my Lanconians hard on you on the journey here?"

"Fearful," Rowan said, smiling genuinely. "They don't have a high opinion of Englishmen."

"Lanconians believe only in Lanconians." He looked at Rowan as if trying to memorize Rowan's blond hair and blue eyes. "But you will change that. You will do what I could not. Perhaps if Anne had lived, I could have done something to bring about peace, but I lost my spirit when she died. Lanconians will kill each other off if the tribes are not united. We will be so busy fighting each other we won't see the next invading horde that comes over the mountains. I'm putting my faith in you, boy."

Thal closed his eyes, as if trying to gather his strength, while Rowan considered the enormity of what his father was asking of him. Because Thal had fallen in love with a beautiful woman, he believed the son of that union capable of great feats. Rowan wished he had half as much faith in himself as his father did. The thought of what was ahead of him, dealing with the hardheaded Lanconians, trying to change the way they had thought for centuries, seemed like more than he could bear. Again, he wanted to run away. Home to England, home to safety. But then he remembered Jura. Jura was the one Lanconian he could understand. Perhaps, with Jura beside him, he could indeed conquer a country.

"Father," Rowan said softly, "is it true that you mean for me to marry Cilean?"

Thal opened his tired eyes. "I chose her when she was just a child. She reminds me of Anne, so calm and kind, yet strong inside. She is the captain of the Women's Guard. She is as strong as she is wise and beautiful. She will make you an excellent wife."

"Yes, I'm sure she would but—" Rowan broke off at Thal's glare. The old man's body might be dying but his mind was perfectly healthy.

"You have not married an Englishwoman, have you? Your children would be more English than Lanconian."

"There is no other *English* woman," Rowan said

pointedly, and his father waited, his eyes piercing into Rowan's, making Rowan shift on the seat. He had felt less fear of Brocain than he did of this old man when he looked like that. No wonder he had ruled for so long. "There is another woman. I believe she is also of the guard and eligible for my wife. Her name is Jura."

Thal dropped his head back on the furs as if in agony. "How strong are your feelings for her?"

Rowan felt somewhat embarrassed but he tried to control the blood rushing to his face. He wanted Jura enough to risk disappointing this father whom he had always lived for. "Strong," he managed to say, and in that one word he told of his lust and desire and need for her. He hoped his father would understand that he was willing to fight for Jura.

Thal lifted his head again and looked hard into his son's eyes. There was strength there, the strength of generations of Lanconian kings. "When I wanted Anne, I wanted her. I would have stolen her in the night if the English king had denied me her. Does Jura feel the same as you?"

Rowan could remember the passion with which she returned his kisses. "Yes," he said. "It is the same."

"I don't want to hear how you met her. She was, no doubt, where she should not have been, which is like Jura. Oh, my son, why couldn't you have loved Cilean? Jura is a problem. She is as hotheaded as her brother, and as angry as her mother. The girl's mother tried to threaten me into marrying her after she gave birth to Geralt. To punish me she married my most loyal man, Johst, and made his life hell."

Thal paused, resting his voice and his mind. "If I give Jura to you, it will cause many problems. Cilean will become your enemy, and the Irials love Cilean and they would hate you for dishonoring this beloved woman. And Jura is promised in marriage to—"

"Promised?" Rowan gasped.

"Yes," Thal answered. "She is to marry the son of Brita who is the leader of the Vatells. It would not do to anger Brita."

Rowan's mouth dropped open. "A *woman* is the leader of a tribe?" He was to conquer a *woman?* Did these Lanconians expect him to meet her in hand-to-hand combat?

Thal smiled at his son. "She uses her brain where we men use our backs. She has been the leader since her husband was killed. Brita already hates the Irials, me and my issue in particular, and it would not do to further enrage her. You are going to have a difficult enough time with the people who support Geralt. Cannot you reconsider and marry Cilean? Or someone else perhaps? Jura is—"

"The one I want," Rowan said flatly, his jaw set rigid.

Thal gave a deep sigh. "There is a way."

"I will take it."

"She might lose. You might lose both Jura and Cilean."

"If it is a fight, I will meet the challenge."

"It will not be your fight but Jura's," Thal said, then began to explain. "Lanconian women have always been strong. They protect their men's backs in battle. They protect themselves when the men are away. It has always been good to have a strong wife, and at one time a man could choose a wife through an Honorium."

"Which is?" Rowan asked.

"It's rather like your English tournament, only the women are the participants."

"The *women* joust?" Rowan asked, incredulous.

"No, they have contests of skill, shooting, javelin tossing, running, leaping a bar, wrestling, there are many contests. The winner wins the man who has called the Honorium."

Before Rowan could speak, Thal took his son's hand. "An invitation must go out to all the tribes when the king is involved. Jura is young and has never been in a battle. You do not know how she will react in a contest. She could very well lose." He paused. "As could Cilean."

"It is a chance I will have to take."

"You do not understand. Most of our guardswomen are beautiful, but the other tribes, to show their contempt for the Irial king, will send women who are beasts." Thal's lip curled. "You have never seen an Ulten woman. They are filthy creatures who are sly and dishonest. They will steal your hair while you sleep if they can find a buyer. And Brocain will send someone hideous, no doubt. I have oxen smaller and better looking than Zerna women. Think what you are doing, boy, and take Cilean. She is beautiful and—"

"Would you have dared an Honorium to win my mother?"

"Yes," Thal said softly. "I would have dared anything when I was young and my blood was boiling at the sight of her."

"My blood boils for Jura," Rowan answered firmly. "Call the Honorium."

Thal nodded. "It will be done, but stay away from her. Let no one know of your intention to win her. You do not know what anger you will stir up if you slight Brita's son. I will say the Honorium is to show your intention of being fair to all the tribes. All the tribes will have a chance to put a queen on the throne. Now, you must go. Send Siomun to me so that I may announce the Honorium."

"I thought perhaps you would like to see your daughter and your grandson."

Thal's eyes widened. "Lora? The infant girl I left behind? She is with you?"

"Yes, and she brought her son Phillip. He's a clever child."

"Not as clever as you were as a child, I'll wager," Thal said, smiling. "Yes, do send them in. I just pray Lora wants no unsuitable man."

Rowan smiled. "I don't think so, although she seems somewhat taken with Xante."

Thal laughed until he began to cough. "That ol' war horse? Ah, that would be a good match. He has never been married and it would take a woman of great fire to melt his old heart."

"Lora can do it if anyone can." Rowan rose, then on impulse lifted his father's hand and kissed it. "I regret . . . I regret that—"

"No!" Thal said sharply. "No regrets. You are what I prayed every night you would be: you are of no tribe. You are a Lanconian king who has loyalty to no particular tribe. You can unite the country. I just hope the wife by your side— No, no regrets. Send my daughter to me, and the boy."

"Yes, my father," Rowan said, and started to leave the room.

"Son," Thal called, "get Siomun to give you some proper clothes so you won't look like an Englishman."

Rowan nodded and left the room.

Outside Thal's room, Rowan leaned against the dark stone wall and closed his eyes, feeling the enormity of the burden of faith his father was placing on him. He had always thought he was to be king of a single country, but now he found he was to unite six tribes who hated each other, six tribes who stole from each other, killed each other without guilt. He took a moment to pray for guidance from God. He would do the best he could and rely on God for help. And Jura, he thought, opening his eyes. Jura would be there to help him too. He made his way through the dark corridor and stopped when he heard Lora's voice raised in anger, followed by Xante's deep chuckle.

"If I may interrupt," Rowan said, "our father would like to see you and Phillip and, Xante, could you find someone named Siomun for me?"

"Yes, my lord," Xante said reverently, and walked away.

"First Siomun," Rowan whispered, "then Jura." He followed Xante, whistling.


Jura left the training field with regret but the young man who had come to her said she was needed urgently. It seemed odd that she was needed in the stables, but lately everything had been odd. Ever since Thal had sent for his English son, her world had turned upside down. She would go now and find out who wanted her, then she would find Geralt and offer him what comfort she could.

The stables were dark and empty of people. She thought with disgust that now the Zerna could attack and win because of the disorganization of the Irial.

"Hello?" she called but no one answered. She drew

her knife as her suspicions rose and began to creep slowly along the hall, her back to the horses' stalls.

As cautious as she was, she was not prepared for the hand that shot out and clamped about her mouth. Another strong arm knocked the knife from her hand and she was pulled back into the darkness of a horse stall.

She began to struggle but, as if her strength were nothing, the man turned her about in his arms and clutched her body to his. Even though she couldn't see his face in the darkness, her body told her it was *him*.

When his mouth swooped down on hers, she responded with all the passion she felt. Since yesterday she had told herself that her reaction to this handsome stranger was a fluke, something that could not happen again. It had been the time and the place. She had been lonely for Daire, and, too, when she saw the man, both of them had been half naked. It was no wonder she had reacted as she did. She had also minimized the passion she had felt. It was natural to feel so good at the kiss of such a good-looking man.

But Jura had forgotten her feelings by half. She had not remembered the way she felt in this man's arms, the way her body weakened and quivered at his touch.

When he lifted his head, her arms were about his neck, her fingers entangled in his hair—and she wanted more of him.

"Jura," he whispered, and his voice seemed to penetrate her. "We will be together now," he murmured against her lips.

She opened her mouth against his, like a flower opening to a bee, wanting her pollen to be taken. Together meant making love, and she was ready for him. She did not think of the consequences or where they were. For all she cared, they could be in the midst of a banquet hall.

She opened her legs a bit, pressed her hips against his, and let him hold her upright as he supported her weight.

"My love," he whispered, kissing hungrily at her neck as if he were trying to eat her skin. "We will be together. I have arranged it."

"Yes," she murmured, her eyes closed, her head back. "Together. Now."

He pulled away from her to look at her face. "You tempt me very much, more than I would have thought possible. Jura, my love, I didn't know I could feel this way. Tell me that you love me. Let me hear the words."

She had no thought of words; she only felt. She felt his body next to hers, felt his big, hard thighs pressed against hers. She wanted to put her skin next to his, to entangle her toes with his, to feel her breasts against the hair on his chest. She wanted to run her hands, her fingertips, her nails over his skin.

"Jura!" he gasped, and plunged his mouth against hers so hard that she lost balance and fell backward, her back slamming against the stone wall of the stable. He didn't release her but kept kissing her, his body crushing into hers until Jura thought she might die from the weight of him, yet, instead of struggling for release, she pulled him closer.

Suddenly, he released her and moved away from her into the deep shadows of the corner of the stall.

"Go," he said raggedly. "Go or you are a maiden no more. Leave me, Jura."

She held herself upright by clutching at the stones behind her, the roughness cutting into her palms. Her heart was pounding in her throat and her body seemed to be pulsating in undulating waves.

"Get out of here before someone sees you," he said.

Jura's mind was beginning to function again. Yes, no one must see her. She struggled to stand upright on her weak knees and she fumbled a few steps forward, clutching at the stall wall for support.

"Jura," he called.

She did not turn around. Her muscles were too weak, too fluid to make any unnecessary movements.

"Remember that you are mine," he said. "Do not let Brita's son touch you."

She nodded, too dazed to understand what he was saying, and made her way out of the stables. She was glad her feet remembered the way to the women's barracks because her mind was full of nothing but him. She kept rubbing her fingertips, remembering the feel of him.

"Jura," someone called, but she didn't respond.

"Jura!" Cilean said sharply. "What is wrong with you? Where is your knife? Why is your hair loose? What are those marks on your neck? Have you been attacked?"

Jura gave her friend a crooked smile. "I am fine," she whispered.

Frowning, Cilean took Jura's arm and forcibly led her to her chamber. It was a Spartan room with only the necessities of a bed, a table, a chair, a washstand, and a large chest for clothing. Weapons hung on the walls, and over the bed was a carved wooden Christian cross.

"Sit down," Cilean ordered Jura, pushing her toward the bed. Cilean dampened a cloth and pressed it to Jura's forehead. "Now tell me what has happened to you."

Jura was beginning to recover herself. "I . . . I am all right. Nothing has happened to me." She pulled the cloth away. Her hands were still shaky but she was recovering. She *must* stay away from that man. He was like a disease that only she could catch—a disease that was going to kill her.

"Tell me your news," Jura said. "You have met this English pretender?" Perhaps her hatred of the Englishman could make her forget her passion. "Is he as stupid as we thought?"

Cilean was still puzzled by her friend's looks. "He is not stupid at all. In fact he seems extraordinarily brave. He rode against Brocain alone."

Jura snorted. "That is stupider than I thought. His ignorance no doubt protected him this time, but it won't again. You should go to Thal while he still lives and beg him to release you from marriage to this repulsive man."

Cilean smiled knowingly. "He is not repulsive. He kissed me and it was very, very pleasant."

Jura gave Cilean a hard look. "He presumes too much. Does he think we Lanconian women are lax in our morals? How dare he kiss a guardswoman as if she were a peasant?" Even as she said this, Jura could feel her face growing hot. A man had more than dared to kiss her, and instead of thinking of morals she had nearly mated with him on the stable floor amid the straw and horse manure.

"He has my permission to presume whenever he

wants," Cilean said, then turned away. "But it is not to be. Thal has called an Honorium to fight for the new king."

"An Honorium?" Jura said in disbelief, at last giving her full attention to her friend. "But there has not been such a thing in my lifetime, nor, I doubt, in Thal's." She jumped to her feet. "How dare this upstart declare such a thing? It is an insult to you. It's as if he were saying the woman chosen for him weren't good enough. He is a bastard! He is a cowardly, sniveling—"

"Jura!" Cilean said, turning. "You are wrong about him and it's Thal who has called the Honorium. He says his son is to be king of *all* Lanconians and therefore his wife should be chosen from all tribes. It is a noble thing Rowan has done when he agreed to this. What if a Zerna woman wins? Or an Ulten?" she said, this last question delivered with horror in her voice. "Not many men would be so noble as to allow such a contest. An Honorium has not been held since King Lorcan won Queen Metta. I hear she was a brute of a woman with half her nose gone from battles and she was older than the king by ten years. There were no children from the match. Yet Prince Rowan has agreed to marry the winner of the Honorium."

Jura turned away and offered a silent prayer for help. Why did everyone endow this foreigner with noble characteristics? "He is no doubt ignorant of the possible outcome. He has seen you and thinks all Lanconian warriors are like you. Or else he is such an obedient dog he does what he is told without question." Cilean's laugh made Jura turn back.

"Prince Rowan is anything but obedient. Jura, you must meet him. There is feasting tonight. Come and I will introduce you and you will see for yourself what he is like."

Jura let her anger show. "I will not betray my brother. Geralt should be king and, so far, what I have heard of this Englishman makes me more sure of that. You go to the feast and sit with him, I will not. Someone should stay here and see to the camp, and I have weapons to sharpen."

"Such as your knife?" Cilean asked pointedly, nodding toward Jura's empty scabbard.

"I . . . I fell in the dark," Jura said haltingly, the blood rushing to her cheeks as she again remembered the man in the stable. "I will go back and find my knife. You go to this feast and I will see you in the morning." Jura left Cilean's room quickly, before Cilean began asking more questions about Jura's knife and the marks on her neck the man had made.

Just the thought of the man made Jura's body begin to warm and she was glad for the cool darkness that hid her red face.

The knife was not in the stables and she knew without a doubt that *he* had it. She leaned against the stall a moment and closed her eyes and cursed herself for being such a fool. Twice she had met this crude oaf and had fallen into his arms like a woman of the streets, yet she didn't know his name or even his station in life. For all she knew he was one of the slaves who worked in the city. Except that he was clean and the Irial language he spoke in that deep, smooth voice of his was perfectly pronounced, not like the foreign slaves' guttural attempts at the language.

He could cause her trouble, she thought. He could use the knife as blackmail. The knife was marked with her sign of two lions rampant and people would know it was hers. He had merely to show it to Daire—what had he said?—Brita's son. If Daire saw her knife in another man's possession, there could be trouble between the Vatells and the Irials.

"Fool!" she cursed herself aloud. "You are a stupid, loose-skirted fool who does not deserve to be a guard." She left the stables still cursing herself.

# Chapter Five

J URA DIDN'T SLEEP much that night, and before dawn
Geralt's pounding on the door made her pull on her
tunic and trousers and shove the bolt back. Geralt
strode in angrily.

"Have you seen him?" Geralt demanded. "He has
bewitched my father. Because he opened a rusty gate,
my father thinks he is capable of *anything. I* should
have pushed that gate open years ago."

Jura, still groggy with sleep, blinked at her brother.
Geralt was a dark man in a tribe of dark men, his
black hair about his shoulders, his heavy black brows
nearly meeting now as he frowned, the dark skin of his
lips twisted in anger.

Geralt slammed his fist into his palm. "Already he
talks of roads and of—" He broke off, sounding as if
he were choking on the words. "He talks of trade fairs.
How does he think we Lanconians survived against
those who have tried to invade us? We allow *no* one
in—not Vikings, not Huns, and most of all not those
wily merchants. Who knows whether they carry an
army in their wagons? Yet this . . . this usurper wants

to open our borders to them. He will wipe us out within ten years."

Geralt paused to draw breath but did not allow Jura to speak. "He has Brocain's son, yet he protects the boy as if he were his own child. I say we hang the pup, and when Brocain attacks, we kill him. Zerna are our enemy. We must protect ourselves."

"Open our borders?" Jura murmured. "I had not heard this. We will cease to exist. We will be swallowed by invaders." It was but one more in a growing list of reasons why the Englishman should not be king. Thal's mind was as sick as his body. She looked at Geralt. But here at last was someone who agreed with her, someone who did not think this Englishman was a second cousin to God.

"Yes, but Thal does not see it. I tried to talk to him this morning but he ordered me from his room." Geralt's head came up. "You have heard of the Honorium? Do you realize that we could have a foreign queen in our midst? I hear Brocain has daughters. What if one of them won?"

Jura could only stare at her brother in horror. She had not thought of this.

Geralt came to sit by her on the bed and put his arm about her shoulders. "Winning is in your hands."

"Me?" she asked, confused.

"You must see that Cilean wins the man. You must enter the Honorium and fight as you have never fought before. You must defeat all comers until it is you against Cilean."

"Yes," Jura said, nodding. "Cilean will fight for him."

Geralt gave a look of disgust. "She looks at the man

with dreamy eyes. She cannot see him clearly, cannot hear what he says."

Immediately, Jura defended her friend. "Cilean is a guard. She must see that he is a fool."

"Cilean is also a woman and she sees him as if she were a girl just coming of age." He raised one eyebrow. "Have you seen him yet?"

"No, but what can I see that will change what I know about him?"

"He is pale-skinned with pale hair and some of the women seem to be taken with him. They think with their bodies instead of their minds." He was watching her closely.

She glared at him. "And you think I might be one of these women?" she said with all the contempt she felt. "I don't care if he is as handsome as the god Naos, he will not change my mind. He has no right to be King of Lanconia."

"Good!" Geralt said, slapping her on the back as if she were one of his guard and making her fall forward. "My father asks that you come to the castle and be presented to this imposter prince. The king was distressed that you did not attend the feast last night."

"Did Thal go?" She was surprised.

"He cannot bear to let his English son out of his sight." Geralt turned away for a moment and Jura knew he was trying to conceal his anguish at the way Thal was displaying his love for this son whom he had not seen since Rowan was a child. Geralt had always worshiped his father but Thal had not thought enough of his son to make him king.

Geralt turned back to his sister and he was calmer. "We have to protect Lanconia. Whatever this man does to thwart us, we have to protect the country the best way we can by working around him. First we must put an Irial queen beside him. We cannot allow a queen of another tribe to infiltrate Escalon. She would bring foreign retainers and they would open gates at night and bribe guards. No, we must stop it before it begins. We *must* put Cilean on the throne. Do you believe you can win against the challengers?"

"Yes, of course I can," she said—at that moment she was sure she could.

"Good." He stood. "Come with me. You are to meet my father's son."

Jura grimaced. "Now? Before breakfast?"

"Now. My father demands it."

Feeling as if she were being led to her own execution, she hurriedly finished dressing and followed Geralt. She didn't bother putting on her long gown but, instead, wore her guard uniform of trousers and tunic with her big blue wool cloak flung over one shoulder. She hesitated over her empty knife scabbard, then decided to wear it pushed toward her back, hidden by her cloak.

Geralt was complaining that she was taking too long to dress, so she flung open the door and left behind him. Her brother did not pay her the courtesy of walking beside her but strode ahead, Jura trailing behind him as if she were his annoying little sister—which she was.

He led her to the men's training ground, to the edge of the field where the archery targets were set up. Jura paused a moment to look at the scene before her. In the shade of a tree to her left lay old Thal, gaunt and gray from his illness, on a bed covered with a pile of pillows. She had never seen the hard old man accept any softness in his life, but here he was surrounded by embroidered feather pillows atop what looked to be a tapestry. In a chair beside him sat a beautiful young woman with golden hair and wearing a long dress of some fabric that glowed and shimmered in the daylight. A little boy, golden-haired like his mother, stood near her chair. The three of them were looking toward the archery range at the back of two men.

One of the men they were watching Jura knew was the young captive Zerna, for he wore the distinctive purple-and-red-striped tunic of that tribe. Jura dismissed him, because, even with his back to her, it was the other figure who commanded attention.

He was nearly as tall as a Lanconian, perhaps, Jura grudgingly thought, as tall as some of them, but he was heavier. Fat, she thought, he was covered with fat from his lazy life. His hair was trimmed to just above his collar and the sun flashed off it. It was not white as she had been told but the color of old gold, and looked to be as soft as a girl's.

If Jura had not been angry before she saw him, she would have been, for he wore a tunic that her mother had embroidered for Thal years ago. It had been loose on Thal but it hugged this man's plump shoulders, and the sumptuous blue and green embroidery emphasized the broadness of his back. Below the tunic showed his heavily muscled thighs and the cross-gartered boots clung to his big calves.

Jura sniffed. Perhaps he fooled other women, but he wouldn't fool her. She was used to handsome men. Wasn't Daire beautiful enough to make the moon jealous?

She straightened her shoulders and went forward to greet her king while Geralt moved away to the center of the training field and his men.

She hated to see Thal as he was now: weak and helpless, just waiting to die, but she would never tell him so. There had always been animosity toward him on her side and grudging respect on his. She had always felt that it was his fault for the early deaths of both her parents. She had been five when she had been orphaned and Thal had taken her into his court, and she had wanted comfort and consoling, but Thal had told her to stop sniveling and had given her a sword to play with. Daire had started teaching her to shoot a bow and arrow when she was six.

"You sent for me?" Jura asked, looking down at Thal. Her expression showed what she felt about the softness of his bed and she refused to look at the Englishwoman.

"Ah, Jura," Thal said with a smile. He looked like a fatuous old man, not the great Lanconian warrior who had repelled thousands of invaders. "Such a beautiful day. Have you met my daughter?"

Jura did not change her expression. "You have one true child, a Lanconian son." She heard the English-woman's gasp of breath and Jura smiled to herself. It was good that someone let these intruders know they were not wanted.

Thal sighed and lay back against his pillows. "Ah, Jura, why are you so hard? These are my children as much as Geralt is." He looked past Jura and smiled, and she knew that his son, the Englishman who wanted the throne, was approaching. "Here is someone who will no doubt make you smile."

Jura stiffened her spine, hardened her jaw, and turned to meet this man she already hated.

The first jolt that ran through her when she saw him made her knees buckle. He put out his hand and caught her forearm and even that slight touch sent chills through her body.

*Him!* How could he be the one she had had her secret trysts with? How had she not seen his golden hair? Then she remembered that at their first meeting his hair had been wet and dark, and their encounter in the stables had been in the darkness.

She jerked her arm from his grasp and somehow managed to turn her back on him.

"You have met before?" Thal asked knowingly.

"No," Jura managed to say.

"Yes," Rowan said at the same time.

Jura stood rigid, her back to him, refusing to look at him. He was standing too close to her to allow her to think, but already she realized how she had been used. He thought that if he could get her on his side, then perhaps Geralt and the men who followed Geralt as the true prince would come to this English usurper.

"I have had the honor of seeing the lady," Rowan said from behind Jura. "But only from afar."

To Jura's horror, he slipped his hand to her back and clutched the tail of her braid.

"And I had heard of you, also," Lora said politely, but Jura did not look at the woman. "I heard only of your skills of war but not of your beauty."

Jura stood rigid, looking at the tree in front of her.

"Jura!" Thal bellowed, then collapsed into coughing. The woman Lora clucked over him and, to Jura's disgust, Thal not only allowed it but seemed to want such soft attention. Jura wanted to move away from Rowan but he held her braid fast.

"You will treat my children with respect," Thal said raggedly, his throat raw from coughing. "You will thank my daughter for her pretty compliment."

Jura stared straight ahead and said nothing. It was difficult to concentrate on the world around her with this man standing so close.

When Thal started to rise again, Lora soothed him. "Please, Father, do not vex yourself. I'm sure Jura is used to such compliments. Rowan, your squire and your captive look as if they might kill each other. Perhaps you should attend to them."

Jura didn't look at him but she felt his hesitation. He moved only when the clash of steel on steel rang out. In spite of herself, Jura turned to watch him move toward the two tall boys who were attempting to kill one another. Jura recognized one as the young man who had told her she was wanted in the stables. He was as dark as a Lanconian and she had not realized he was English. Since he had delivered his message in Lanconian, she wondered if he had memorized the message and repeated it by rote.

She watched Rowan stalk across the field toward the boys. He showed no fear or hesitation as he moved into the middle of the fighting young men with their swords flashing in rage. Rowan merely slammed his open palm into the chest of each boy and sent him flying. The boys landed on their seats in a cloud of dust.

"My men do not fight each other," Rowan said in a low voice that carried more threat than a shout.

"I am not *your* man," Keon yelled up at Rowan. "My father is Brocain and—"

"*I* am your master," Rowan said, cutting him off. "You are not Zerna, you are Lanconian and *I* am your king. Now, both of you go and polish my mail."

Montgomery, lifting himself from the dust, groaned. To be cleaned, chain mail had to be put in a big leather bag with oil and then tossed from one person to another. It was like tossing a rock back and forth.

Thal chuckled with pleasure at his son's settling of the dispute.

Jura whirled to face him. "Whatever he does pleases you," she spat at the old man. "He claims kingship that is not his to claim. He brags that he is king of *all* Lanconians, but to be that, he would have to declare war on the other tribes. Is he to kill Brocain and Brita? What of Marek and Yaine? We have peace now but will we if this man kills merely to feed his vanity so that he can say he is king of more than the Irial? I beg of you, do not leave us with this braggart for king. We need no more war between the tribes. Each tribe patrols its own borders. If a tribe is destroyed we will be attacked and we will exist no more. Please, I beg you, we all beg you, give us a king who understands what must be."

Thal glared at her, his face turning purple with a suppressed rage that was making his need to cough so strong that he could not contain it.

"Go!" Lora yelled, coming to her feet and hovering over Thal like a protective she-bear. "You have upset him enough."

Jura turned on her heel, looking neither left nor right, and left the training field.

Rowan walked back to his father but his eyes were on Jura's back.

"You are a fool," Thal croaked up at his son. "She will make your life miserable."

Rowan smiled. "I do not have a choice in the matter. As I am to be king, she is to be mine."

"Yours?" Lora asked. "What is going on? Rowan, tell me you aren't planning a . . . a union with that woman. She is rude, thoughtless, uncaring of anyone but herself, and she has no respect for your right to be king. She is altogether unsuitable to even live in our house much less in a position of honor."

"Mmm," was all Rowan said, and turned back toward the archery range.

Jura trained harder than anyone would have thought possible over the next few days. She attended no banquets of welcome for the arriving contestants nor did she leave the fields to greet them. She was up before dawn, running for miles on the long, winding trails outside the city walls. She jumped across wide streams, walked across four-inch-wide logs, practiced throwing her spear and shooting her arrows. She stopped only long enough to wolf down vast meals and at night fall into bed into a deep, dreamless sleep.

"Jura," Cilean said on the fourth day, "slow down. You will be too tired to compete."

"I must be ready. I must win."

"You want to win?" Cilean asked softly.

"Winning to me is making sure that you win. He must have someone of wisdom on the throne beside him. His vanity and stupidity are overwhelming. Without you beside him, I fear he will destroy Lanconia."

Cilean frowned. "Jura, I'm not so sure you're right. He doesn't seem vain at all. He trains almost as much as you do and he oversees the men all day. He is very fair and impartial in settling disputes and he is very kind to the women who are arriving for the Honorium." She stopped and laughed. "Do you remember three years ago when we came upon that hunting party of Zerna? You and I were alone and they stopped to water their horses."

"Yes, we hid in the bushes and waited for them to leave."

"Remember the leader? That big woman with the scarred face?"

"We heard her speak and thought she was a man."

"Yes," Cilean said, "that's the one. Her name is Mealla and she has come to try for Rowan's hand in marriage."

Jura smiled wickedly. "He deserves such as her." Her face changed. "But we Irial do not. Cilean, you *must* win."

Cilean looked at her friend sharply. "Why is it that you hate him so much? Since he opened the gate, most of us are willing to give him a chance to prove himself."

"Yes," Jura snapped, "all of you are willing to forget how he does not belong here, how he is taking Geralt's rightful place. You look at his pretty form and do not see the treachery inside his soul."

"I did not know you knew him so well."

"I do not know him at all," Jura answered, and knew she was giving herself away. The man haunted her every waking moment, and in the morning before she fully woke, she reached for him in her bed. "I do not *want* to know him. Are we going to talk all day or train?"

Jura beat everyone at every contest during training.

The Honorium was to be three long, hard days of games, and the contestants were awarded points for how they placed in the contests. At the end of the first day, one third of the entrants with the lowest scores were eliminated, another third at the end of the second day. On the third day, all the games were replayed but only with pairs of contestants. The loser of each match was eliminated. By the end of the day there would only be two women left and the winner of the final match, a hand-to-hand battle with wooden poles, won the prize—which happened to be the queenship of Lanconia. Twice Jura received messages that she was urgently needed in some dark, secluded spot but both times she refused to appear. He thought she was a lightskirt, someone who was easy prey for his lusts, and twice she had fallen under his spell, but she wouldn't be such a fool again. She wondered how many other women he was secretly seducing. Every time she saw one of the trainees return from Escalon, her face flushed, her voice hushed, her eyes alight, she wondered if she had been with Rowan.

"And who has he chosen for his bed?" she blurted once to Cilean. She was drenched in sweat and her muscles ached but she wouldn't stop training.

"He? Who?"

"Thal's son, of course," Jura said tightly. "Who else does everyone speak of? Who else is Lanconia obsessed with?"

"You seem to be also," Cilean said thoughtfully.

"Me? I *hate* him." She threw her javelin with ferocity and hit the target exactly in the red center.

"How can you hate someone you've met only once? You should come with me tonight and speak with him."

Jura retrieved her javelin. "Is that all you do? Speak with him? No doubt he is as celibate as a saint and he does not bed a different woman each night."

"I have not heard a whispered word of what he does in bed at night. If he has a woman, he is very discreet about it. Somehow, I do not believe he does. I think he sleeps alone or everyone in the city would know about it. The chosen women would no doubt brag."

"Brag about what? That some soft English—"

"Soft?" Cilean laughed. "Rowan may be called many things but soft isn't one of them. You should come with me and watch him train. When he removes his tunic and—"

"I have no desire to see his nakedness," Jura said shrilly. "Shouldn't you be practicing your jumping? You are weak on that."

Cilean looked at her friend for a long moment. "Jura, be careful that you do not protest too much or you will make people think the opposite is true."

Jura started to reply, but she closed her mouth and threw her javelin with renewed vigor.


Jura had been training so hard for so many days that she was unaware of the preparations that had been made for the Honorium. Wooden seats had been built outside the city walls, sections of them canopied for Thal's family and for any tribal leaders who might attend the games. Vast quantities of food, whole cows and boars, vats of vegetables, bins of loaves of bread, and barrels of ale had been prepared. Anyone who came to the games would be fed at Thal's expense for three full days.

At dawn on the first day was to be a parade of the contestants, to walk through the watching, cheering, leering crowd and to pause before the stands and Prince Rowan.

The women gathered on the Irial training field before dawn and Jura had her first good look at her competition. There were two women from the Ulten tribe and Jura knew they had come only for the excitement and the chance to steal what they could. They were small women but she knew them to be quick and agile. How they rolled their big, liquid eyes from one person to another and smiled in their secret, infuriating way, she thought. There were a half dozen Vatells, each woman wearing about her upper arm one of the beautiful bracelets the Vatells made. These women could be fierce fighters.

There were eight Fearens, and Jura dismissed these women. On horses the people of this tribe were formidable, but they were like fish on dry land when out of the saddle.

No Poilen women came, nor did anyone expect them to. If the contest had been for the memorization of epic poems, the Poilen would have won, but they were people who did not battle unless forced to—and then they were unbeatable.

The fifty women left were Zernas and Irials. All the Women's Guard of the Irials were participating, even the trainees, in hopes that they would win Rowan's hand in marriage. The Zerna women were a sight to behold: big, muscular, many of them scarred from brawls with each other. Jura knew they would be the only competition, for although the Irials would win the contests of speed and agility, few could overcome the sheer muscle of the Zernas.

Cilean nudged Jura and nodded toward Mealla. She

was the largest, the oldest, the most frightening of the Zernas.

The trumpets sounded and the parade began.

The women stood in a long line before the canopied stands, and Rowan, resplendent in a green silk tunic of Lanconian design, came down the steps to walk before them, murmuring good luck to each woman. He paused for a long time before Mealla, looking her in the eye. The tip of her nose had been cut off in some previous battle. Cilean smiled when he offered Mealla good luck also, but Jura did not.

When Rowan stopped in front of Jura, she did not look at him, but gazed fixedly somewhere to the right of his head.

"May God be with you," he whispered.

Minutes later a shout went up and the games began.

This first day was easy and Jura held herself back, reserving her strength for the days to come. All she needed to do was place high in the winners of each event to be able to compete the next day. She was always in the top four of each race and each contest, but never the winner. Besides, she did not want to show everyone her skill this first day. Mealla won every event she entered, even the foot race, although she elbowed aside an Irial trainee at the last moment.

Jura had no idea how the Zerna woman's place in the events was affecting Rowan. Each time Mealla was declared a winner, he died a little inside, until by the end of the day he looked more tired than the contestants.

Jura left the field pleased with the day's events and went back to the women's barracks to bathe and rest.

By the end of the second day there were only sixteen

women left to compete with each other for the final day's events.

"Jura," Cilean said, "whoever draws Mealla for the wrestling will lose against her."

"Perhaps not," Jura said, but she was lying. Early tomorrow morning lots would be drawn to see who competed with whom in which event. Most anyone could beat Mealla in the contests of speed but the wrestling event would eliminate someone. "Perhaps another woman will draw her, and she will be the one to lose."

"I just worry that one of us will be pitted against her."

"Me," Jura said quickly. "She might beat me but at least you will only have the poles to use against her. And she will be tired after a battle with me. I can assure you of that."

Cilean did not smile. "Come with me, I want to go into the city."

"Why?" Jura asked sharply. "There is nothing in the city for us and we need rest."

"I am meeting Prince Rowan," Cilean said quietly.

In spite of herself, Jura felt angry. "Oh? He asks for a taste of what is to be his? Is he bedding the other contestants as well? Mealla perhaps?"

"Stop this!" Cilean commanded. "You have changed since he came. No, I am not planning to spend the night with him. If you must know, Daire is arranging the meeting."

"Daire?" Jura asked, aghast.

"You have been so busy training you have not had time to see your intended, but I am not so. Rowan is my intended, at least I think of him as such, and I want to see him so he can privately wish me luck. I

thought perhaps you might like to go with me and see
Daire."

"Yes," Jura muttered, "of course." She hadn't
thought of Daire in days. "I would very much like to
see him."

The land immediately outside the city walls and all
the area inside the walls was as light as day, with
hundreds of torches lighting scenes of drunken people
dancing and cavorting in celebration. So many people
slapped Jura and Cilean on the back that Jura went to
draw her knife, but met only with an empty scabbard.

Rowan was waiting for them in a shadow of Thal's
stone castle. He had been waiting for quite some time
and the stones were hurting his back, but he would
wait for days if it meant a moment alone with Jura.
She had been better at pretending they did not know
one another than he had. He was almost glad, at the
start of the games, that she had not looked at him
because he might otherwise have forgotten himself.

As the games had progressed and she came in
second, third, even fourth, he began to doubt if she
would eventually win. He had nervously asked Daire
to reassure him of Jura's skill as a guard. At the end of
the second day, he knew he could no longer be
cautious and that he had to risk a private meeting with
Jura and had asked Daire to arrange it.

Now, he stood waiting for her.

Jura sensed his presence before she saw him.
"There," she said to Cilean, her voice choked. Jura
watched as Cilean stepped toward the shadow and
Rowan's big arm came out and grabbed her. Jura's
hands made fists at her side. So it was true, she was
just one of many. This randy old satyr grabbed and
pawed at all women. Did he tell Cilean of his love for

her? Everyone said he trained so hard, but if he spent so much time hiding in stables and kissing women, how much time did he have for training?

"You're Cilean," she heard Rowan say, and the two of them came into the light while Jura stepped back out of sight.

"Didn't Daire tell you to meet me?" Cilean asked.

"He said I was to meet the one— Yes, yes, of course, he did. Are you alone?"

Jura saw him searching the darkness.

"Jura is with me. We came for private good wishes."

His eyes searched the darkness then stopped at Jura, even though she knew he could not see her. "Jura," he said, and held out his hand toward her.

Jura did not move.

"Rowan," Cilean said as he moved toward Jura.

Rowan walked toward Jura, his hand outstretched. "May I give you a kiss of luck?" he asked softly.

She recovered herself. "You have kissed enough for tonight," she spat at him.

It infuriated her that he chuckled. "I have something of yours," he said, and held out her knife. She snatched it from him, careful not to touch his fingertips. "Do I get no thanks for its return?"

Jura was suddenly aware of Cilean standing a little behind Rowan and listening intently to this exchange. "I must go," she said. "Stay and wish Cilean luck." She turned away and fled from the two of them.

She was blind from her anger and did not see or hear Daire until he caught her. Thinking he was Rowan, she struggled fiercely until she realized Daire was holding her.

"Who has harmed you?" he asked, fury in his voice. "What are you running from?"

She clung to him. No one paid them the least attention as many couples were embracing drunkenly and the noise of their singing and brawling was deafening.

"Come," Daire said, and led her away to a farrier's lean-to. It was quieter with only a horse for company. "What has happened?"

She put her arms around his neck. "Nothing. Nothing at all, just hold me, kiss me." He kissed her but it didn't rid Rowan from her mind. "Tomorrow Cilean will win and be married to the Englishman. Could we be married tomorrow also?"

Daire was frowning at her. "Why this sudden interest in me and my kisses? Why do you want to act like a woman?"

She pushed him away. "But I *am* a woman. Because I do not dress as Thal's English daughter doesn't mean I am less of a woman."

"I know you, Jura. I have known you since you were a child. Your emotions do not rule your head."

"They haven't until *now!*" she yelled at him, then pushed away from him and began running back to the barracks.

Cilean was waiting for her and she was very, very angry. "You plan to win for yourself, don't you?" Cilean said with controlled fury. "He kissed me, but he thought I was you. Behind my back you have wooed him and lied to me. You have *never* been my friend. Our friendship is nothing but lies."

Cilean slammed from the room, leaving Jura alone and trembling. *He* had done this. Since he had come to Lanconia, everything in her life had changed: Thal hated her, Cilean hated her, Daire was suspicious of her.

The only way to prove to them all that she was not deceitful was to make sure that Cilean won tomorrow. Cilean would win and Jura would be free of Rowan. She could marry Daire and he would keep her nights so busy that she would think of no other man. Her attraction to Rowan was only physical, and it was no wonder since she was a virginal eighteen-year-old woman. What she needed was a strong, healthy man in bed beside her and she could forget this soft Englishman.

Soft, she thought. If he were soft, she wouldn't have had the trouble she had now.

As she undressed for bed, she resolved to fight to the death if need be in order to win for Cilean. She and Cilean would be pitted together with the poles and the moment Cilean so much as lifted her pole, Jura would fall down, vanquished, the loser.

This time tomorrow Cilean would again be her friend and Daire would be her husband. This time tomorrow she would no longer be a maiden.

# Chapter Six

❧❧❧

*I*N THE MORNING Cilean looked tired and refused to speak to Jura. Jura tried to reassure her friend but Cilean turned away.

The women marched to the field and Jura could feel her blood pumping with anger. Her arms would be torn from their sockets before she lost an event.

The lots were drawn and to her horror Cilean drew Mealla in the wrestling match. The other contestants were visibly relieved, especially because Mealla didn't seem to realize that the matches were games. She played to win.

Jura tried to whisper encouragement to Cilean, but Cilean glared at her. "This should please you. Now you will be queen. Do you mean to poison Rowan and give the throne to your brother? Or is it Rowan himself that you want?"

Jura straightened her spine. "If you cannot beat a Zerna, you do not deserve to be queen." She moved away from a scowling Cilean.

On this last day she had to win only three times and the last game would be against Cilean—if Cilean won the wrestle. If Cilean lost, then Jura would have to fight Mealla, and Jura knew that, win or lose, she would not like the outcome of that match. She would become Rowan's wife or Mealla would become queen.

Cilean *had* to win.

Jura won the first three games easily. She outran one of the Irial trainees then placed six arrows in the dead center of the target to beat a Fearen girl who had surprisingly made it to the finals. The third game was harder: she had to leap a pole set high above the ground. She made it but just barely. She nearly wept with relief when the heavier Zerna woman knocked the pole down and so lost the match.

Now all that remained was Cilean's match with Mealla and Jura had to fight the winner.

Cilean's match with Mealla had already begun and the crowd recognized this as the most serious contest. From the look of the two women, it was like an eagle fighting a hummingbird. Mealla outweighed Cilean by at least fifty pounds and Cilean's main defenses were intelligence, speed, and agility—none of which meant much when an oak tree was wrapping its limbs around you and crushing.

Jura joined the line of contestants along the palisades wall and watched the match. She did not shout like the others, but quite calmly prayed with all her being.

Mealla wrapped her big arms around Cilean's ribs and squeezed.

"Gouge!" Jura whispered. "Go for her weak points. Don't let her beat you." She willed her words to reach her friend and Cilean seemed to hear them as she pushed her thumbs into Mealla's neck and the pain caused the bigger woman to release.

Jura's breath released as the two contestants circled each other. Involuntarily, she looked up into the stands to see Rowan looking down at her. His expression was one of concern. Behind him Daire was also watching Jura. She looked back at the match.

Mealla threw Cilean to the ground then started to jump, but Cilean was too fast as she rolled away and Mealla fell onto empty, hard ground. Instantly, Cilean was on her, twisting her arm behind her back.

Mealla's lack of agility played against her as she could not reach Cilean to push her off. She was trapped.

Cilean held Mealla down for a long while, until the crowd began to scream, "Forfeit! Forfeit!" After a long time of agony for Cilean, Mealla did forfeit the match.

Cilean stood, but her face was not triumphant. It was gray and ashen with pain and exhaustion and she raised only one arm in victory, keeping her other arm to her side.

Jura knew her friend was hurt and ran to her side to see how much damage was done. "Quiet!" Jura commanded when Cilean started to protest. "Lean on me but do not let the crowd see you leaning. How bad are you hurt?"

"At least three ribs are broken," Cilean said quietly, her voice catching. "Should I forfeit to you?"

"No, we will start our match immediately. I will lose it within moments. If you rest, you will not be able to stand. Now turn and smile and wave at the crowd. It will be over very soon."

Jura's heart was pounding wildly as she took up her pole in preparation for her "fight" with Cilean. She had no intention of trying to make the fight look good.

All she wanted was to get it over with, to have her friend declared the winner, then at last she would be able to escape the Englishman's hold on her.

She and Cilean marched to the center of the field side by side.

"When the match begins, lift your pole and hit my head," Jura whispered. "I will fall and you will be the winner. Do it quickly. Do not risk a rib through your lung. Understand me?"

Cilean nodded. There was almost no color in her face.

The two women faced each other in the center of the field. The crowd was silent now, for this was the deciding match.

Trumpets were raised and blown and the match began.

Jura moved to her left. "Hit me," she whispered.

Cilean just stood there, her eyes glazed with pain. Bruises were turning purple under her skin.

"Hit me!" Jura said, beginning to circle. "Think of your precious Rowan. To get him all you have to do is hit me once. Or do you *want* me to have him? You want me in his bed, touching him, caressing him?"

Cilean raised the right side of her pole to strike, and Jura, out of instinct and years of practice, lifted her pole to defend herself. The reverberations of the clashing poles shook Cilean and her hand dropped as Jura's pole lightly clipped her on the temple. It was too much for Cilean's broken body. She fainted, her body crumpling at Jura's feet.

For a moment all was silence as Jura and the crowd stared stupidly at Cilean's inert body. Then Jura fell to her knees just as the crowd began to chant, "Jura, Jura, Jura."

"Cilean!" Jura screamed over the noise. "Wake up! You must *win.*" She began to slap her friend's cheeks but Cilean was dead to the world. "Cilean!" Jura screamed over and over again in desperation.

The crowd reached them and hands began to pull Jura away from Cilean.

"No, no," Jura yelled. "She has only fainted. There was no match. Cilean did not forfeit. I did not win. Cilean is the winner. Cilean, wake up and tell them."

No one heard her as she was lifted onto men's shoulders. Irial trainees ran to Cilean to protect her from trampling feet and watch Jura being carried away. They were jubilant that an Irial had won.

Jura kept screaming and pleading, trying her best to get away from the men carrying her, but she was treated like a bag of grain and paid as much heed. The noise of rejoicing was too loud for her to be heard.

By the time they reached the city walls she was frantic. She couldn't make anyone understand. *Cilean* had won, not her. Cilean was to be queen.

Sitting on horses just inside the gates were Daire and Thal's daughter Lora. Both of them were scowling at her.

"I didn't win," she shouted toward Daire, but she couldn't hear her own words over the noise. She tried to get down and run to Daire, but the hands on her body held her fast.

By the time they reached the inner wall and Thal's old stone castle, she was stunned into silence. This really wasn't happening to her. This was a nightmare.

Thal stood in the doorway, supported by Xante. He lifted one thin hand and gradually the crowd quieted. "Welcome, daughter," he said. "Your bridegroom waits inside."

"No!" Jura yelled into the quiet. 'Cilean won, I—"

Thal's face showed growing anger but it was Xante who interrupted her. His voice boomed out. "Humility and loyalty are good qualities in a queen."

The crowd cheered at his words and carried Jura inside the castle, where a priest and Prince Rowan awaited her.

The Englishman stood beaming at her as if he were an idiot while Jura tried to protect herself from the hands fumbling at her body while they lowered her. She was given no time to bathe or change but merely dropped to stand beside the English usurper, and the priest began the wedding ceremony. She wanted to say no to him, wanted to tell him that he had no right to be in her country, but then she looked at the crowd around her. Their blood was up. They had been drinking for three days now and they wanted to see a proper end to their festivities.

The priest was looking at Jura and, slowly, every other eye turned toward her and she swallowed. Now was the moment of decision. If she turned and walked out now, the consequences could be great. The different tribes could say the contest was a farce—and if this man Rowan was to lead them, he could never do so if a woman refused him at the altar. They would laugh at him. She had competed and she had taken a chance of winning.

"Jura," Rowan said softly from beside her. "Do you want me or not?"

She turned to look at him, and those eyes of his, deep, fathomless blue, seemed to see inside her.

She turned back to the priest. "I will take the man," she whispered through dry lips.

A deafening cheer went up and Jura heard no more of what the priest said. Rowan turned to her and pulled her into his arms. He whispered something to her but she couldn't hear him, and when he tried to kiss her, she turned her head away.

Her movement seemed to please the crowd.

"You'll have to win her, prince or no," someone called.

Jura used the moment to push away from the man who was now her husband and make her way through the crowd to a side door. The crowd was laughing at her but she didn't care. She had to get away and find Daire and Cilean and talk to them.

"You're a fool, Rowan," Lora shouted at her brother. "There is still time, you can repudiate her. Set her aside now before you go to bed with her."

Rowan was eating, as he had been doing for the last hour. For the past three days he had watched the games too intently to be able to eat. His one concern had been that Jura win, and he had not been able to eat for worrying that she wouldn't. "Jura is what I want," he said, his mouth full.

"Yes, but does she want you? Where is she now? Why did she run away from you? Why aren't you with your new wife?"

Rowan took a deep drink of ale. "She has to do women's things, I don't know what they are. Maybe she wanted to bathe and put on a pretty gown. What do most brides do on their wedding day?"

Lora put her fists to her temples in anguish. Outside they could hear the noise of the revelers. "Rowan," she said as calmly as she could, "you have always been a sensible man. You have studied hard to learn about

Lanconia. You have told me how great your responsibility is toward this country, but now you risk everything and I don't understand *why*. You have always been most sensible about women. When that beautiful Lady Jane Whitton visited us last year, every other man could see no farther than her pretty face, but you said she was a viper and you turned out to be right. So why has this Jura bewitched you? She is not as pretty as Lady Jane."

"Jura is more beautiful than a thousand Lady Janes." He was looking over a plate of fruit tarts.

"She is *not!*" Lora shouted. "She is the sister of a man who would like to see you dead. You are taking an enemy into your bed. She could slit your throat at night."

"Lora, please calm yourself. Here, have a cherry tart." He looked up at his sister and saw that she was very serious in her anger. "All right," he said, pushing his chair back. "Perhaps I was a bit hasty, but sometimes a person *knows* when he is right. I knew from the moment I saw her that she was mine."

Lora sat down across from him. "What do you know of her? Besides kisses, besides her beauty, what do you know of her?"

"All that I need to know."

Lora sighed. "Let me tell you of this Jura because I have made it my business to find out about her. She is the loyal, loving sister of a man who wants your throne—and the way to get that is through your death. She had no intention of winning the Honorium today. It was common knowledge among the guardswomen that Jura meant to help Cilean win. If you had looked with open eyes at the match between Jura and Cilean, you would have seen that Cilean was not hit, she fainted. Now she lies in the Women's Barracks with four broken ribs, and a sprained shoulder. It's a wonder she was able to stand on her own feet after the wrestling match."

Rowan was looking at her with a faraway expression and Lora knew she was making no impact on him.

"And then there is her lover," Lora said softly.

Rowan's eyelids lowered a bit. "Brita's son."

"Yes, Brita's son, Daire."

"Daire?" Rowan asked. "But Daire is—"

"Your friend? You *thought* he was your friend. Have you been telling him of your love for Jura? Has he said nothing of the fact that they have been betrothed for years?"

Rowan frowned and Lora hoped he was at last listening to her.

"Jura is your enemy," she said. "She wants you out of Lanconia. She meant for Cilean to marry you, but I think she said yes to the priest because she realized she could get close to you if she were your wife. Oh, Rowan, I beg you to listen to me. I fear for your life. A wife is so close to a man. She could poison you, or stab you and blame someone else. And you are so blinded by her that she could make you do things you ordinarily would not. Look at how you have already called the Honorium in order to get her. Poor, sweet, dear Cilean now lies broken because of your wanting of this woman. Who else will shed blood because of your passion for her? She doesn't like Phillip or me. What will you do if she orders us to leave you?"

"Cease!" Rowan ordered. He stood and began to pace the floor. There was so much truth in what Lora was saying. He knew Jura had power over him, but he had not considered how she might use that power.

"I cannot believe she wants my death," he said softly. "She feels for me as I do for her." Doubt, he thought, doubt seemed to plague his life. But about Jura he had no doubts. Jura's love for him and his for her was the only sure thing he'd encountered since he rode across Lanconia's border.

Lora grimaced. "Rowan, I am a woman and I know how easy men are to trick. Each man believes himself to be the best at all things, believes himself to be the only one a woman loves. But this Jura loves Daire and her brother, and she married you for *them*. She will remove you from their path, and once you are dead she will marry her beloved Daire and Geralt will rule."

"I don't believe you," Rowan said fiercely. "The woman . . . cares for me."

"Then where is she?" Lora shouted. "Why is she not here with you? She is with her lover, I tell you, making plans for what to do with you."

Rowan stared at his sister for a moment, and some of the fog began to clear from his brain. If what Lora said were true . . . "Where is she?" he asked softly.

"I don't know," Lora answered. "I sent Montgomery out to look for her, but he didn't see her. Daire rode out of the city walls after Jura was carried inside. Perhaps she went after him."

Rowan remembered the cool, quiet glade where he had first seen Jura. Perhaps she had gone there. He turned toward the door.

"Where do you go?" Lora asked, anxious.

Rowan's eyes were cool when they looked at her. "I am going to find my wife."

"And if she is with Daire?" Lora whispered.

"She will not be," he said coolly, and left the room.

Lora stood where she was for a moment, then she thought of what could happen if Rowan found the woman he loved in the arms of another man. She ran from the room to search for Xante. Xante would know what to do.

"Meddling fool," Xante said when Lora told him some of what she had said to Rowan. He was saddling his horse. "Jura is no murderer and she is a maiden. She does not lie with Daire. You should not have told Rowan these things and made him doubt."

"He is my brother and I must protect him."

"As Geralt is Jura's brother, but she would no more poison Rowan than you would poison Geralt."

"You don't know women as I do," Lora said stiffly.

"No, but I know Jura." He stopped and looked at Lora, standing there biting her lip with worry. He adjusted his saddle. "Did you love the man you married as much as you love Rowan?"

She was startled. "Yes," she answered.

Xante didn't reply as he mounted his horse. "I have an idea where Jura went. The women hunt there sometimes." He looked down at her. "Go inside. I will protect your brother from himself."


Rowan's head swam with the images Lora had planted there. Since that first meeting with Jura he had known he loved her. No other woman had affected him as she had, so of course it was love. But had she felt the same way? He had assumed she had, but had she *said* so? As he tried to recall their three quick, tempestuous meetings, he couldn't remember her saying much of anything—at least not in words.

He dismounted some distance from the place where he first met Jura and walked silently through the darkness. Already he could hear voices raised in anger. He walked closer until he could hear them.

"You lied to me, Jura," Daire was saying. "How many times did you meet with him in secret? He told me of how you ran to him."

"I did not," Jura said, and her voice was strained as if she were repressing tears. "I met him twice by accident and once he tricked me into meeting him. I never wanted to see him. You know how I've always hated him. He does not belong in Lanconia. Geralt should be king. He has no right—"

"It seems he has *every* right now," Daire spat at her. "He has the right to touch you, to hold you. Is that why you trained so hard, competed so hard? So you could win him and share his bed? Does your lust rule your head as well as your body? Will you pant after him day and night and forget about your people? Will you betray us because of your lust?"

"No!" Jura screamed. "I am no traitor. I do not lust after him." She was lying and she knew it, but she couldn't bear to lose this man who had been her friend for so many years. He used to hide her and lie to Thal about her whereabouts when Thal was angry with her. "He attacks me. I have never invited his touch."

"Ha! Will you say that tonight when he beds you?"

"I wish to God I did not have to bed him," Jura said.

"You shall have your wish," Rowan said, his voice full of controlled fury as he stepped from the shadows and into the moonlight. He drew his sword. "And you," he said to Daire, "shall die for touching my wife."

Daire drew his own sword.

"No!" Jura screamed, and threw herself on Rowan. "Do not hurt him. I will do whatever you want."

Rowan snarled at her. "I want nothing from you." He pushed her aside as if she were an annoying insect, and Jura landed a couple of feet away in the damp grass.

She watched the men circle one another and wished for a way to stop them. She drew her knife, planning to step between them when a big hand clamped onto her shoulder and made her remain seated. She looked up to see Xante.

Quite calmly, Xante stepped between the men, facing Rowan. "You have the right to take this man's life, my lord," Xante said, "but I beg that you do not. Today he lost his betrothed and he has lost her abruptly and publicly."

"There is more to it than that," Rowan snapped. "Out of my way."

"No, sire, there is not," Xante said, not moving. "There is no treachery. Merely two hot young bucks fighting over a female."

Quite suddenly Rowan became aware of what he was doing. He was acting like Feilan always feared he would. He was behaving like an emotional Englishman and not a Lanconian. At all costs he must control himself. The scar on the back of his leg twitched and hurt almost as much as it had the day his tutor had branded him. He straightened and sheathed his sword. "You are right, Xante. Daire, the woman is yours. I will not force myself on her. Take her."

The three of them did not move as Rowan turned back toward his horse.

Xante recovered first. "She is your wife, my lord.

You cannot discard her so easily. The people would be so angered they—"

"Damn the people!" Rowan shouted. "The woman hates me. I cannot take a wife like that. Tell the people that the last match was not fair. I will marry Cilean. Tell them anything."

"And I will be the first to escort you to the border," Xante bellowed. "You do not come here with your English ways and spit on us. You wanted the woman; you wanted the Honorium, and now, by God, you will choose England or Lanconia. Either your English ways or our Lanconian ways. You discard the woman and you lose the kingship."

Rowan knew what he was saying was true. But to live with a woman who *hated* him. A woman who found his touch foul and disgusting. A woman who prayed she wouldn't have to bed him.

Rowan clenched his teeth. "I will take her but, before God, I'll not touch her until she begs me to do so."

Before another word could be spoken, the sound of horses interrupted them. It was Geralt, his dark face almost invisible in the dim moonlight.

Geralt glared at Rowan. "Our father is dead," he said, and reined his horse away and rode back to Escalon.

Rowan did not look at any of the people around him but made his way back to his horse. He was king now. King of a people who didn't want him; husband of a woman who didn't want him.

# Chapter Seven

❧❧❧

JURA LEANED AGAINST a tree, her ribs heaving from her run. It had been a week since Thal's death and, except for the burial ceremony, she had not left the women's field. Over Thal's deep grave she had looked up to see the man who was her husband glaring at her, but he had quickly turned away.

Turned away, she thought with anger, that's how everyone was reacting to her. The guardswomen looked at her with hooded eyes and their whispering stopped when she approached. Three days after the Honorium the trainees stopped obeying her. Onora, a high-tempered, vain girl who dreamed of commanding the guard and who had fought very hard to win Rowan, had sneered at Jura with contempt and said that she had been discarded by the king, so why should they give her their respect? Jura had been faced with ten young recruits, each staring at her with defiance.

Her impulse had been to pull a knife on Onora but Jura was not stupid enough to pit herself against ten strong women. With as much dignity as she could muster, she had turned and left the field.

There seemed to be no one on her side. The guardswomen believed she had lied about not wanting to win and had deliberately knocked Cilean down. As for Cilean, she lay in her chamber, her body slowly healing, and refused to see Jura.

Now, as Jura leaned against the tree, she knew she hated this Rowan who called himself king.

Her anger was so great that at first she didn't hear the approaching footsteps. The man was almost upon her before she drew her knife. It was one of the English knights who had accompanied her enemy from England.

"Put that away," he snapped. He was a young man, dressed in the long robes of the English, and he was scowling at her. "My lord bids you come."

"I do not obey him," Jura said, her knife at the ready.

The man took a step toward her. "Go ahead and threaten me. I'd love to remove a little of your hide. I don't have much use for your people and even less for you."

"Neile!" said a deep voice to Jura's left.

She turned, knife ready, toward the voice. Another English knight stood there, an older man, or at least he looked older, since there was a scar across the part in his hair and the hair had grown white there.

This man turned toward Jura. "My lady—" He stopped in anger at the snort from the other knight. "King Rowan wishes you to come to him."

"I have work to do here," Jura said.

"You bitch!" the younger knight, Neile, said, and took a step toward her.

The older man stepped forward. "It is not a request. Please come with me."

Jura saw the warning in his eyes, letting her know that there would be consequences if she did not go with him. She knew the time had come to pay for her crime of winning the Honorium. She sheathed her knife. "I am ready."

She followed the older knight, the younger one behind her, to the edge of the forest. A saddled horse waited for her and a pack animal was loaded with what she recognized as her meager belongings. She did not comment on their presumption but rode with the two men toward Escalon.

She had been isolated since her marriage and had no idea how the Irial people had reacted to the separation of her and Rowan, but the people soon let her know. They laughed as she rode by and called her the Maiden Queen. They loved the idea of this beautiful young woman, who so many had lusted after, being rejected by the king.

Jura held her head high as they rode into the walled city then through the inner walls to Thal's castle. Inside, the castle was much cleaner than when Jura had lived there and she snorted in contempt. Such a waste of time on frivolities.

The English knight opened a door to a room that Jura knew well. Thal had used this room for planning his war strategies. She walked inside and the door closed behind her. It took her eyes a moment to adjust to the dimness.

Rowan sat at one end of the room, the lack of light making his hair appear dark. "You may sit," he said.

"I will stand," she answered.

She could feel his anger, but it was no stronger than her own.

"We must talk," he said through his teeth.

"I have nothing to say that has not been said," she answered.

"Damn you," he raged. "This is *your* fault for enticing me to believe you wanted me."

For all the man looked nothing like Thal, he sounded like him. Thal never believed any wrong had been caused by him but was always others' fault. "One does not confuse lust with wanting marriage," she said calmly. "I may lust after a well-formed blacksmith but I would not wish to marry him."

"I am your king, not a blacksmith."

She stared at him. "You are not *my* king. You are an Englishman who, because of some cruel jest of the gods, has been made my husband. There are ways for our marriage to be dissolved."

Rowan got up and walked to the narrow arrow slit that passed for a window at the far end of the room. "Yes," he said quietly, "I have looked into that, but I'm afraid it will not be possible. At least not yet, not when the Honorium is so fresh in people's minds." He paused and Jura saw him hunch his shoulders together. "I curse the day my father met my mother. I wish she had married a serf rather than a Lanconian. Always, being a prince has been a grief to me, but this is the worst." He spoke so low that she barely heard him.

He turned back toward her. "I am going to unite the tribes of Lanconia, and I fear the Irials will not follow me if I set aside the half-sister of their old king's son."

Jura smiled at him. "Unite the tribes of Lanconia? And will you also move the Tarnovian Mountains? Perhaps you would like them a little farther south. Or maybe you'd like to move the rivers."

His eyes shot blue fire at her. "Why did I allow my

body to rule my head? Why did I not have one minute's conversation with you before calling the Honorium?"

"*You* called it? I thought Thal ordered it to give all the tribes a chance at the English prince."

"Fool that I was, I called it, as it was the only hope I had of obtaining you. I was sure you would win."

One moment Jura was standing still and the next she was leaping at him with her hands made into fists. "You injured my friend Cilean merely for your lust?" she screamed at him. "You broke my engagement to Daire because of your japing lusts?"

He caught her as she flew at him, his back hitting the stone wall. He was so angry at her, insanely angry, viciously angry, but the moment he touched her his anger turned to desire. He enveloped her in his arms and his mouth crushed down on hers, and Jura responded to him, her body seeming to try to make itself dissolve into his. Her arms went about his neck, pulling him closer as her mouth opened under his. Her anger, her despair, her loneliness turned into desire for him. She was his to do with as he would.

Suddenly, he pushed her from him and Jura went sprawling onto the hard stone floor.

"We must talk," he said through his teeth.

He was panting like a hard-run horse as he looked down at her. A beam of sun came through the arrow slit and lighted the back of his head. "I curse you, Jura," he said, his jaw hard. "I made a vow before God that I'd not touch you and I will not."

Jura was trying to recover her senses. "We are married now," she said. Whatever problems she had with his logic, she had none with her wanting of him.

"Then you must beg me," he said.

"I must what?" she said, rising.

"If you want me in your bed, you must beg me."

Jura blinked at him. "Is this one of your English customs? Do you make your soft Englishwomen beg? Is that a way to further humiliate them and to make yourself feel powerful? Lanconian men need not make their women grovel. Lanconian men are *men.*"

His anger was back and he took a step toward her then moved away, rather like one did when one moved too close to a fire. "I made a vow to God and I will not break it. Now, we have things to discuss."

"I have nothing to discuss with you," Jura said, and started for the door.

He caught her arm but released it instantly. "Sit," he ordered.

With a shrug, Jura obeyed.

Rowan turned away from her and began pacing. "However it happened, through what mean turn of fate, you and I are married. I could dissolve the marriage if the circumstances were different, if I were not half English and therefore suspect or if you were not related to Geralt. But I cannot release us from this marriage; therefore, we will have to make concessions. Tomorrow I leave to go to the Vatell tribe to talk with their leader and you must go with me."

Jura stood. "I most certainly will not."

Rowan stood in front of her and leaned down until his nose was nearly touching hers. "I do not trust you to not try to gather an army to put that loud, arrogant brother of yours on the throne. I will have you near me—both of you—so that I can see what you are doing."

"Or is it that you do not want the people to think

you cannot take your wife's virginity," she said softly. She could feel his breath on her lips.

His eyelids lowered. "I can take it all right, make no mistake of that." He glanced down at her lips and back to her eyes. "But I will not."

She moved away from him. Whatever his stupid English reasons were for rejecting her, he was doing just that, rejecting her. It was another reason in her long list for hating him. "I will remain here and—"

"No!" he said loudly. "Whether you want it or not, you are my wife and you will act as such. If you do not share my bed, you will share my room, or tent, as it may be. I will let nothing stand in my way of uniting the tribes. If the people want to see me with my virginal wife, then they will see me—and I will be able to see that you do nothing evil behind my back."

"If I put a sword through you, it will be in your heart not in your back."

"I assume that is meant to ease my mind," he said dryly.

"Take it how you want," she said, glaring at him, then her expression turned to curiosity. "How do you plan to unite the tribes? Conquer them?"

Rowan moved away toward the window. "In a manner of speaking. I want to marry them to each other so that in a couple of generations they will be so interbred they will not know which tribe they are. They will only be Lanconians."

Jura smiled at him. "And how do you plan to do this? *Ask* them to marry people they hate?" Her smile disappeared. "You know *nothing* of us. The tribes would die before giving up their identity. Why don't you go back to your England and leave us in peace before you cause a war—if you live that long?"

"And will you return with me?"

Jura was aghast. "*Live* in England, where the women must beg the men for their favors?"

Rowan opened his mouth to explain but closed it again. "I will not try to explain to you. Your duty is to obey and nothing else. You are to go with me as I travel across Lanconia and nothing else. I want no advice from you nor any comments. You are to be a proper wife."

"An English mouse, you mean," she said. "You will find a Lanconian woman not so easy to subdue as your pale English dolls. I will go with you. What does it matter? I will be a widow by the next full moon." She turned on her heel and left the room.

As she moved along the dim stone-walled corridors toward the main hall, she thought of what a fool the man was. As if he could march into the main city of each tribe and ask them to please stop hating each other. She was right, someone would kill the fool within days.

And as for his not bedding her, that was truly puzzling. Was it that he did not desire her? That seemed a ridiculous thought or maybe all Englishmen were as passionate about women as this one was about her. Or perhaps he could not consummate their marriage. She shrugged. Who could understand the thoughts of a foreign idiot?

"You are Jura," said a small, breathless voice. "You won."

Jura looked down to see the little son of the Englishwoman. She suspected he was younger than his height indicated, and, to her, his pale skin and hair looked like bread that had not been baked long enough. The wall torch made the boy look as if his face were carved out of a pearl.

"What do you want?" she asked, looking down at the child. He was a young enemy now but he was indeed her enemy.

"I saw you," the boy said, his eyes as round as blue meadow flowers. "I saw you win. I saw you beat everybody. Would you teach me to run like you do? And wrestle? And shoot a bow?"

Jura couldn't keep from smiling. "Perhaps."

The boy smiled up at her.

"There you are," said a voice at the end of the corridor. It was the young man called Montgomery and Jura's hand instinctively went to her knife, but the young man was merely gazing at her in a way that Jura knew was complimentary. Her hand relaxed.

"This is Jura," the boy said proudly.

"Yes, I know," Montgomery said, and smiled. Jura saw that he was going to be a splendid-looking man and she smiled back at him.

"What is this?" Rowan shouted from behind the trio. "Montgomery, have you nothing to do but drool over my wife? No armor to clean? No weapons to sharpen? No lessons to study?"

"Yes, my lord," the boy said, but he gave Jura another smile before he left.

Young Phillip, at the sound of his uncle's shout, had moved between Jura and the wall, his arms going around her thigh and holding on to her. Jura looked down at the boy in surprise.

"Phillip!" Rowan said sharply. "What do you think you are doing?"

"This is Jura," he said as if this were an answer.

"I know full well who she is, now come away from her."

Jura smiled at Rowan. "If you cannot control a child, how do you expect to control Brita and Yaine, who rule the other tribes? And greasy old Marek?"

Rowan grabbed for Phillip's arm but the boy slid behind Jura and she put her body between Rowan and the boy.

Suddenly Rowan straightened. "You have power over me," he said softly. "You make me act younger than my squire. I'll not fight you for the boy; no doubt you have bewitched him also. But remember, he is not my heir. There would be no benefit to you to harm him."

"Harm a child?" Jura asked in horror. "Even an English child? You go too far. I have no need to harm any Englishman as you will do yourselves the most harm. We Lanconians will tire of your self-satisfied superiority and someone besides me will remove a few heads." Her eyes narrowed. "And that Neile of yours will go first."

"Neile?" Rowan asked. "Has he tried for your favors?"

"Get your mind out of your breeches. The man hates us and he lets it be known. Now, I am hungry and I smell food. Am I allowed to eat or have you vowed that I may not?"

Rowan's nostrils flared in anger but he said nothing. "Come. Eat. Who am I to have a say in your life?" He turned and started down the hall.

Jura meant to follow him but Phillip tried to take her hand. "Lanconian warriors do not hold hands," she said, "and straighten your shoulders. How can you be a Lanconian if you slump?"

"Yes sir," Phillip answered, and Jura did not correct him as the boy stood straight.

She smiled down at him. "Perhaps we can find you some proper clothes more befitting an Irial warrior."

"And a knife?" he asked, eyes gleaming.

"By all means a knife."

Long trestle tables had been set up in the main hall and servants were bringing in platters of meat and vegetables. Jura started to take her place toward the end of the table but Rowan, frowning, motioned to the place on the bench beside him. Phillip followed her like a shadow.

"Phillip." Lora called her son from the other side of Rowan, motioning for him to come sit by her.

"Jura will let me sit by her," the boy said, his little spine rigid.

Lora started to rise but Rowan stopped her.

A priest blessed the meal and the fifty or so diners fell to as if they were starving. They were loud as they argued about weapons and horses and who was the greatest fighter.

A quarter way into the meal two men made for each other's throats, each trying to strangle the other.

Rowan, for all he had seen of Lanconian tempers, was still unprepared for these outbursts. He was talking to Lora and did not react immediately.

Not so Jura. She jumped onto the table, took two steps across it, and launched herself onto the men, knocking them off balance so that the three of them fell to the floor amid the debris and the barking dogs.

She drew her knife even as she fell. "I'll have the heart of the next man who interrupts my meal," she yelled.

The men calmed themselves and got up off the floor.

The other Lanconians had barely interrupted their eating at the sight of this very ordinary event, but it was not ordinary to the Englishmen. Jura stood, dusting herself off, and met the eyes of Rowan and his three knights. The Englishwoman stood to one side, her eyes frightened as she clutched her little boy to her.

Jura had no idea what she had done to cause such looks on the faces of these men. Rowan's face was as red as a sunset, the veins standing out in his neck, his jaw muscles working, while his three knights merely looked on in horror.

Jura sheathed her knife. "The food grows cold."

Phillip broke away from his mother and ran to fling his arms around Jura's thighs.

She put her hand on the boy's soft hair, smiled, then bent down, took his shoulders, and held him at arm's length so she could look at him. "What's this?" she asked softly. "Fear from a Lanconian?"

"Girls cannot fight men," the boy whispered.

"True, but this was only Raban and Sexan. They always fight. Now straighten your shoulders and stand tall and—" Jura broke off because Lora, recovering from her shock, grabbed her son away.

"How dare you," Lora said. "How dare you touch my son and teach him your violent ways? You aren't a woman. You aren't fit to be near children."

Jura stood and took a step toward Lora, her eyes cool and hard. Rowan put himself between the two women. "Come with me," he said, looking at Jura with an expression she'd never seen before.

By now the Lanconians had stopped eating to watch this drama. A fight and Jura leaping across the tables caused no comment, but they wondered what these odd English were doing. Anger because a guard had stopped a fight? That was their duty.

"Come with me," Rowan repeated, his jaws clamped shut.

"I am hungry," Jura said, looking toward the tables and the rapidly disappearing food.

Rowan's fingers clamped down on her upper arm as he began to pull her out of the room. Jura tried to jerk away from him but he held her fast, and she cursed him for embarrassing her before her people.

He pulled her into the first open doorway, a small chamber for the storage of barrels of ale and mead.

"Never," he said into her face as soon as the door was closed, "never will my wife behave like that again." He could hardly speak for his anger. "As if you were a common doxy, leaping on the tables and . . . and . . . "—he nearly choked—"throwing your body on those men."

Was this man crazy? "That is my duty," she said patiently. "The guardswomen are trained to settle disputes, and as Thal's representative it was my duty. Had Geralt been at dinner, he would have handled the men."

Rowan's face was turning purple. "Thal is dead," he said. "*I* am king. *I* will settle disputes between my own men. My *wife* will not."

Anger began to rise in Jura. "I begin to understand. It is that I am a woman. Do you think that Lanconian women are as cowardly and as useless as that sister of yours?"

He advanced on her. "Leave my sister out of this. I am telling you that you will not act as if you were my

125

sergeant-at-arms. You are a woman and you will act as one."

The man was absurd. "I must sit and sew in order to prove to you that I am a woman? Do I *look* like a man?"

Involuntarily, Rowan looked down at her body with her high firm breasts, long round thighs, and that short tunic of hers clinging to her curving backside. For the thousandth time he cursed his quick temper that had made him swear he would keep his hands off of her.

"You will obey me or you will regret it," he said.

"What will you do? Order me kept prisoner? And who will obey your commands? Do you think my Lanconians will? You will never be allowed to leave the gates of Escalon alive if you harm me. And that will be the end of your childish plans to unite the tribes."

Rowan clenched his fists at his side. Never had anyone been able to get to him the way she did. He had dealt with his uncle William's stupid sons without once losing his temper. And never had a woman made him angry. Women were sweet, kind things who gave comfort to a man and listened to what he had to say with wide, adoring eyes. If a man went hunting, he was to return to tell his wife of the dangers of the hunt and she was to sigh and exclaim at his bravery. But Jura might bring down a stag bigger than his.

"Have you no women's clothes?" he asked. "Must you wear such a garment as that?" He indicated her loose trousers with her high, cross-gartered boots.

"You are no older than the child," she snapped. "What does it matter what I wear? It helps me perform my duties and—" She stopped because Rowan had pulled her into his arms.

"Your duties are to me," he said huskily. "You do not press your body against other men."

"Do you mean when I stopped the fight?" Her voice was slower and lower. She couldn't think clearly when he touched her.

"Jura, you have done something to me. I do not recognize myself."

"Then I will tell you who you are: you are an Englishman in a country where you do not belong. You should return to England and give the kingship to my brother."

He thrust her from him. "Leave me. Go and fill your belly and do not interfere between me and my men again."

"They are Lanconians, they are not *your* men," she said as she left the room quickly and hurried back to the main hall. She would be lucky to get any food. The tables were being cleared but she managed to grab a venison pie that was only half gone from a servant's tray and began to eat it as she left the castle walls to go outside where she could breathe.

She was walking toward the men's barracks when Geralt came toward her. "You were not at dinner," she said.

"Sit with my enemy?" he asked sneeringly. "I hear you are to live with him now."

"And to travel with him. The fool thinks to unite the tribes," she said, taking the last bite of the pie.

Geralt gave a derisive laugh. "He will be killed by the first tribe's territory he enters."

She could feel her brother watching her. "I have

told him so but he does not listen. He will be killed soon and maybe it is better to get it over with. Some of the men like him. Xante stays too close to him."

Geralt moved closer to her and his voice lowered. "You are in a position to hasten his death."

She spat out a piece of gristle between his feet. "I am no murderer. He will kill himself soon enough."

"So it is true that you have gone to his side. Cilean said that you wanted him for yourself and that is why you knocked her down in the Honorium. Tell me, does your blood boil hotter for this pale foreigner than it does for your own people?"

Her nostrils flared at him. "Do you think that your sly insults will goad me into murdering him? Then you do not know me. I tell you that he is a fool, and he will do himself in with no one's help. You will be made king and you won't have the blood of your English brother on your hands."

"Unless he breeds a child with you," Geralt said.

"There is no chance of that," Jura answered.

"He is not a man?" Geralt asked in wonder.

"I do not know. He says he has made a vow to God that—" She broke off. "There will be no children during the short life of the man. Wait and be patient, you will be king." She turned away from him and walked through the inner gates into the city. It was quiet now, with both man and animals settling down to sleep.

Unite the tribes, she thought. Impossible idea, of course. The tribes hated each other too much to ever get along, and that stupid Englishman would never be able to understand that. One had to be Lanconian to understand the Lanconian mind.

Oh well, she thought, shrugging, it didn't really

matter anyway since the fool was going to get himself killed before long. She paused for a moment. It would be a shame for him to die before she spent some time in bed with him. After all, they were married.

With a yawn, she turned back toward Thal's old castle. Tonight she would be secreted in a room with him and perhaps tomorrow she would no longer be a maiden. She smiled and hastened her step.

# Chapter Eight

❦

JURA CORRECTLY ASSUMED that her husband was using Thal's old room as his own, but when she pushed open the door, he looked up from a table with a startled expression.

"Why are you here?" he snapped.

"You ordered me here," she said patiently. "You had your insolent Englishmen take me from the women's quarters, with my belongings, and bring me here. I assumed I was to take on the duties of being queen—for as long as I am such," she added under her breath.

He looked at her for a long moment. "I guess I must keep you," he said with resignation. "Go and sit over there and be quiet." He turned back to the table, which was littered with books and rolled papers.

Jura wondered if he had brought the books with him or if they had been taken from Thal's meager and mostly unused library. She had no intention of obeying him, so she went to look over his shoulder.

He whirled on her. "What are you doing?" he snapped.

"Looking," she answered, then nodded toward the

map he was holding. "That is wrong. The Vatells' border is farther north. Thal seized a good bit of the land when I was a child. My father was killed in the battle." She turned away to sit on the edge of the bed and began unwrapping the garters on her legs.

Rowan turned toward her. "What do you know of the borders?"

"More than you do, it seems."

He stood, picked up the map, and put it on the bed behind her. "Show me how things have changed. This map was made by Feilan over twenty years ago. Who else has my father slaughtered in order to take their land?"

Jura pushed off her boots and wiggled her bare toes. "Thal did what he had to do. Half of the Vatells' land is in the mountains where nothing grows, and they were raiding the Irials to steal our grain."

"So my father put an end to their raiding," Rowan said thoughtfully. "How did the Vatells fare through that winter?"

"Not well," Jura said. "Do you plan to hate everything about us?"

Rowan looked surprised. "How can I hate my own people? Here, show me the new borders."

She leaned closer to him and, with her finger, showed him the smaller Vatell territory. "They are reasonable people, at least fairly so," she said, "not like the Zernas or the Ultens. The Vatells—"

"Yes, I know," he said impatiently. "Now show me where the Irials' grain fields are."

"If you know so much, why don't you know that?"

He pointed to a place on the map. "If they have not moved, the fields are here. Protected by three rivers and guarded at regular intervals by Irial guards. The crops are barley, wheat, and rye. Sheep are raised here on this plain. The horses they have are descendants of those stolen from the Fearens, and still the young Irial men raid the Fearen camps at night. They cross Vatell country here in the dense forest then go along a goat path here until—"

"How do you know this?" Jura asked.

"When other boys were chasing a ball in the courtyard, I was hidden away with old Feilan learning the Ulten language."

"Ulten?" Jura asked. "No one speaks that guttural mess of theirs. It is not a language but merely grunts and moans."

Rowan leaned back on the bed, his hand under his head. "It may sound so but it is actually a form of Lanconian. For instance, your word for woman is *telna* while theirs is *te'na*. It is just a quicker way of saying the same thing."

Jura drew her feet up under her. "A lazier way. They are lazy, slimy people. All the tribes hate the Ultens."

"Then all the better to interbreed the tribes. The Ultens stay up in the mountains and they interbreed with each other until their brains are mush."

"Another reason your plan of uniting the tribes will not work," Jura said. "Who would want to marry an Ulten woman?"

Rowan looked at her with merriment in his eyes. "A Zerna man," he said.

Jura laughed and stretched out on the bed. The map was between them as they both lay on the bed.

"During the Honorium I had nightmares about Mealla winning," Rowan said. "The problem I have with intermarrying the tribes is wondering who will marry the Zerna women. Are they *all* like Mealla and the other women who entered the Honorium?"

Jura lifted her head onto her elbow. "The Fearen men might like the Zerna women. Fearen men are small, short, thin little men, and Thal always said they were angry about their size. Zerna women might appeal to the Fearens. Their children would be larger."

Rowan grinned at her as he also lifted onto his elbow. "And the Poilens? Who shall we marry to them?"

"That's not easy," Jura said thoughtfully. "The Poilens believe thought is more important than food or pleasure."

"Then we should give them some of those feisty little Fearen women. *They* would turn a man's thoughts from books to more earthly delights."

Jura was watching him. He was very good-looking and the candlelit room made that golden hair of his glow. She had an urge to touch it and even lifted her hand.

Rowan abruptly got off the bed. "You may sleep there," he said, pointing to a seat formed in the thick stone walls. It would be barely long enough for her.

Jura started to protest the absurdity of their sleeping apart, but then she thought that this arrangement might be better. When he was killed—as he surely would be—it would be better for her not to have become attached to him. And it would be better for the succession if there was no child of his who might want to be king. And Jura didn't know if she could deny her child a throne that would rightfully be his. No, this was better. She would stay a maiden with this man until she was widowed, then Geralt would become king and she would marry Daire and have many children.

She rose from the bed. "You say that we travel tomorrow?"

He had his back to her. "Yes, we start for the Vatells' land, but first we stop at the Irial villages and get men and women."

"For what?" she asked as she untied her loose trousers and slipped them off.

He turned back to her. "For marriages to—" he began but broke off at the sight of her half-nude body. He turned away again. "Go to bed," he said in a deep voice. "Cover yourself."

Jura smiled at his back and climbed beneath the sheepskins that were thrown across the window seat. She watched him as he undressed, his face turned away from her. He removed the tall boots and exposed his big, blond-haired calves. His embroidered tunic, which reached to just above his knees, came off next, and as he slid it over his head, Jura saw again that big, muscular body that had made her forget her senses, her present and her past, on that day at the river when she had first seen him.

The muscles in her legs began to feel as if she had just exerted them to their limit, and her breathing was deeper and slower.

Without looking at her, he blew out the candle by the bed and plunged the room into darkness.

"Rowan," she whispered into the darkness, using his name for the first time.

"Do not speak to me," he said loudly. "And call me 'Englishman.' Do not use my name."

Jura clamped her jaws shut and cursed the stupid foreigner. With his vile temper and his unreasonableness, she gave him only a week before someone put an end to his life. Good riddance, she thought. Lanconia would be better off without him.

She turned to her stomach and thought of Daire. It would be good to be a virgin on her wedding night to Daire.

"Get up!"

Lazily, Jura turned over in the warm bed. It was still dark. Rowan was standing ten feet away from her, fully dressed and glaring at her.

"Are all Irials as lazy as you?" he snapped. "The wagons are already gathering below."

"Are all Englishmen as vile-tempered as you?" she answered, stretching beneath the covers.

He watched her intently and his pale skin seemed to grow paler. "Get your belongings and come below," he said, then left the room.

It didn't take Jura long to get her few pieces of clothing and her weapons together. The courtyard was loud with prancing horses and shouting men. Geralt, wearing black and on a black horse, was ordering men about. Daire sat on his horse to one side and near him was Cilean.

Jura smiled at her friend but Cilean turned her head away. Jura's smile faded as she accepted bread and watered wine from a servant.

Rowan was in the midst of the men, his horse ready to go, and Jura had to admit that he seemed to be capable of organizing the expedition and the men seemed to recognize his leadership.

There were wagons filled with goods and Jura saw Lora and the boy Phillip sitting on one of them beside a driver.

"Jura!" the boy called, and smiling, she went to him.

"Good morning," she said, offering him a piece of bread.

"Do Lanconian warriors eat bread?" he asked solemnly.

"Always," she answered just as solemnly, and turned to Lora to smile, but the Englishwoman put her nose in the air and turned away. Jura went to her horse, falling in beside Xante as they began to ride.

It took all day to reach the Irial villages. There were other, smaller villages scattered about the Irial land, but these were inhabited by peasants, the lowest class of people, people who fought among themselves, whose family feuds were centuries old. These people had no idea whether they were Irial or Vatell or English for that matter.

But twenty miles from the walled city of Escalon lived the main population of Irials. When a guardsman or woman chose a mate, he/she came from these people. The guards were chosen from these people, and after they were trained, they were sent back to the village to watch and protect the Irials from invasion. In these few square miles was the only serenity an Irial was likely to know. Here children played and women sang and crops were harvested. Here fabric was woven, garments embroidered, and here the sick and old were given comfort and peace. Thousands of the Irial guard had died to protect this place.

Jura rode beside Xante for most of the way but she heard Phillip beginning to complain, so she turned back to the wagon. "Would you like to ride with me?" she asked the boy, and he looked at Lora for permission.

Lora looked as if she were fighting against herself. She turned her head away then gave a curt nod.

Phillip practically leaped into Jura's arms as she pulled him into the saddle before her. For the rest of the journey she told him stories of the old gods of Lanconia, gods who fought and feuded, gods who had more character than the Christian God Jesus who never so much as spoke back to his mother.

"Why do you hold this pup?" Geralt demanded of her angrily as he reined his horse beside hers. "Do you grow soft toward the English?"

"He's a child," Jura said.

"Boys grow into men."

She gave him a look of disgust. "He is no threat to you. He has no pretensions to your throne."

Geralt gave the boy a hostile look and rode away.

"I don't like him," Phillip whispered.

"Of course you do. He is to be King of Lanconia and he will make a very good king."

"My uncle Rowan is the king and he is the *best* king."

"We shall see about that."

It was night when the travelers arrived at the village and the wagons had to be ferried across the river, as did the horses and passengers.

The people, bearing torches, came out to greet them and see this Englishman who called himself king.

Many of Jura's relatives ran forward to greet her. Her status had risen high since she had won the Honorium and married the king.

"What is he like?" they whispered. "Has he given

you a child yet?" "Is he as handsome as Daire?" "As strong as Thal?"

They stopped talking when Rowan walked up behind her and Jura saw the eyes of some of her cousins turn liquid. There was a collective sigh.

Jura smiled at them and even felt a little pride. She turned her smile on Rowan. "May I introduce you to my family?" she asked him politely.

Later, Jura's aunt escorted them to a room in her house. It was a small room and there was only one bed and no window seat.

Rowan seemed very quiet.

"The journey tired you?" she asked.

"No," he said softly. "It was good of you to care for Phillip. I believe the boy is beginning to worship you."

"He is a pleasant child and eager to learn. Perhaps he is more Lanconian than I thought." He was sitting on the edge of the bed and removing his cross garters, and he seemed to be worried about something. It was on the tip of her tongue to ask what was wrong but she didn't. It would be better to stay apart from this man who was her husband only temporarily.

"I assume I am not to sleep with you," she said.

"What? No, I guess not. There are furs. I'll make my bed on the floor. You take the bed."

Jura frowned and removed her boots and trousers and slid into the big, empty bed. She lay awake while Rowan settled himself on the floor in the furs. The air seemed to be charged and she could not go to sleep.

"The moon is bright," she whispered.

Rowan did not say a word and she thought perhaps he was asleep.

"Jura," he said softly.

"Yes," she answered in the same tone.

"Do you ever doubt yourself? Do you sometimes *know* that you are right, but somewhere deep inside you there is a seed of doubt?"

"Yes," she said, "I have felt that."

He didn't say any more and after a while Jura heard his soft breathing of sleep. She puzzled for a long time over what he had meant but could find no answer.

The next morning all the Irials were awake very early. They wanted to see friends and relatives they had not seen in a long while and they wanted a good look at this Englishman who claimed kingship.

Jura stood to one side and watched Rowan pass through the crowds of people, and she saw the way their faces lit as he spoke to them in their own language. There was no display of the quick temper he showed to her, but instead, here was a quiet, calm, intelligent man who made his presence felt.

"He is as smooth-tongued as the devil," Geralt said to Jura. "Be careful that you keep your head on your shoulders. Someone must have his wits about him when the fool tries to plunge us into war."

Jura sipped hot apple cider. "He does not want war; he wants peace."

"What one wants and what one gets are two different things. If we ride into Vatell land, be ready to fight. Brita will be glad to kill him, since his father killed her husband."

"Maybe Brita is sick of war also," Jura said. "Perhaps she would like to see her son again."

Geralt was aghast. "Do you betray your country for this Englishman?"

"No, of course not. He will never be able to unite

anyone, but let him try. Who will follow him? He means to marry Irial and Vatell. What Irial will agree? He'll be stopped before he starts."

Xante was standing near them, and overhearing her words to Geralt, he turned to her. "Look at him. He is surrounded by adoring eyes. They will follow him. Quiet! He speaks."

Jura watched with interest as Rowan stood on a bench and began to speak. All morning she had heard whispers of "Saint Helen's Gate," and so knew the people knew that Rowan had opened the gate. But she also saw skepticism on their faces. They were not going to accept this man merely because of an ancient legend.

Rowan's voice and his perfectly pronounced Lanconian were almost hypnotic. Slowly, every sound in the audience ceased. No one coughed, no one fidgeted, even the children stayed still and listened.

Rowan talked of a country of peace and tranquillity where men and women could ride for long distances without danger from raiding tribes. He talked of good roads. He talked of sharing between the tribes. The Irials could trade their weavings for Vatell jewelry or Fearen horses. He spoke of an end to the deaths of young men, raiders who stole goods from other tribes. He painted a splendid word picture of the Irials traveling safely across Vatell land and Fearen land to reach the Poilen people, who could share their extensive knowledge of herbs and medicine. There were tears in some eyes when he mentioned the deaths that could have been prevented if Poilen medicines had been available.

"We shall *take* Poilen medicines," Geralt said, but quietened when people glared at him.

Rowan said the only way to bring about these glories was to unite the tribes.

"We fight!" Geralt said.

People hissed at him and looked back at Rowan as he waited for silence.

"The Lanconian people must become one," Rowan said softly, and the people leaned forward to hear him.

He told of his plan to unite the tribes through marriage, then, before anyone could ask a question, he asked for volunteers, brave young men and women who were willing not to die for their tribe but to live for it. He grinned and asked what noble souls were willing to sacrifice all and marry some of those tall, beautiful, nubile, young, healthy Vatells?

Jura and Geralt were almost trampled in the stampede of young people who ran forward to volunteer themselves. Jura stood where she was, overwhelmed by the persuasiveness of Rowan's speech.

Not so Geralt. He pushed his way forward to stand before the crowd.

"Do you send your children to be slaughtered?" he bellowed. "This Englishman knows nothing of our ways. He will lead you to your deaths. The Vatells will slaughter the Irials."

Jura watched in horror as Rowan's three knights attacked Geralt and knocked him to the ground. Jura reacted instantly, as did Xante and two other guardsmen.

Jura grabbed the hair of Neile and put her knife to his throat. "Unhand him," she said, and pressed the knife into his skin so that a trickle of blood ran into his collar. Neile released Geralt and began to stand upright. The other English knights also released their hold on Geralt.

The crowd had stopped to watch this new spectacle.

Furious, Rowan came down from his bench to stand beside Jura. "Release him," he said to her.

"He attacked my brother," Jura said. "I should slit his throat."

Neile, being held by a woman, was too humiliated to speak.

Watelin shook off Xante's grip on him. "What he said was traitorous."

Rowan clutched Jura's forearm hard until she released Neile, then he pulled her toward a stone lean-to where they could be private.

"Why?" he asked. "Why did you ruin what I had to say? The people listened to me. You are my wife, man's helpmate, yet you thwart me at every turn."

"Me?" she gasped. "It was *your* men who attacked my brother. Was I supposed to stand by and let them tear him apart?"

"I am your king, and when I am attacked it is treason," he said with patience.

"Treason?" she said, eyes wide. "In Lanconia you have to *earn* kingship. Thal appointed you but we can pull you down. We aren't like your stupid Englishmen who accept the son of the king even if he is a drooling idiot. Geralt has every right to speak, as does *any* man, but Geralt especially, since he is just as much Thal's son as you are. Besides, he was right in what he said."

"The Irials are ready to follow me," Rowan said. "Is it that you and your brother do not want me to succeed? Is that it? If I fail to unite the tribes, the people might want your war-loving brother on the throne. Is that why you work for my downfall?"

"You pompous, overbearing *fool,*" she shouted at him. "Everyone wants you to succeed, but those of us who live here know it cannot be done. The Irials listen to you, oh yes, you make a pretty speech, you almost had me wanting to marry a Vatell, but if you ride to Brita with those young civilians, she will rub her hands with glee—and slaughter all of them. She would love to weaken the Irials enough to be able to take their land. She needs our croplands."

"Then I will ride to her alone," Rowan said. "I will talk to this Brita alone."

"And she will hold you for ransom, and to get you back we will have to pay dearly."

Rowan leaned forward, nose to nose. "Then don't pay the ransom. If I am held captive, consider that I have not earned my kingship."

"And let a Vatell hold *our* king?" Jura shouted back at him. "We will wipe out the Vatells for such an insult. We will—"

She broke off because Rowan kissed her. He could think of no other way to make her be quiet, and Jura responded with all the energy she had built up in her anger at him.

His big hand caught the back of her head and turned her head around to give him better access to her lips, and he kissed her passionately, deeply.

"Do not fight me, Jura," he said against her cheek. "Be my wife. Stand by me."

She pushed away from him. "If being your wife means standing to one side while you lead my people into slaughter, then I will die first."

Rowan straightened. "I have a task given to me by my father and I mean to fulfill it. You may think war is the only way to solve this problem, but there are other ways also. I just pray that these Irials get more from their marriages than I have." He turned to leave.

"No!" she said, catching his arm. "I beg you, do not go through with this. The people trust you. I saw their eyes and they will follow you. Do not lead them to their deaths."

"There is only one thing I want you to beg me for. Other than that, you are my wife. You are to comfort me when I return from battle, to see that I have hot food and perhaps someday to bear my children. I do not plan to run my country according to a woman's counsel." He left the lean-to.

Jura stood inside the dark, cool place for a few moments and tried to settle her raging anger. The man had to be stopped. She knew they would follow him, for they had reacted to him as she had that first day at the river. She would have followed him then if he had asked her to, but now her head had cleared and she could hear him instead of being blinded by his beauty.

She had to do something to stop him. She started out of the lean-to but someone blocked her way. "Cilean?" she whispered in disbelief.

"Yes," Cilean answered. "Could we talk?"

Jura was aware of the noise of the crowd outside and she felt some impatience to be among them. Perhaps she could stop the people from following Rowan.

"Do you still hate him?" Cilean asked softly.

Jura's anger was too close to the surface. "I thought you believed I wanted him for my own, that I betrayed my friend to get him."

"I was wrong," Cilean said. "I was jealous."

Something in her tone made Jura calm down. "Jealous? You love him?"

"Yes," Cilean said simply. "I loved him from the first. He has a good heart, Jura. He is kind and thoughtful and now he is willing to risk all to unite the tribes. He knows he could be killed."

"And he could take a few hundred Irials with him," Jura said. "A noble purpose will not save their lives when Brita attacks them."

"Perhaps she won't. Perhaps God will help King Rowan as He did when he opened the gate."

"What?" Jura gasped. "God does not protect bad leaders, he kills them and their followers off. Cilean, you cannot have completely lost your mind. You cannot believe Brita will allow three hundred Irials to cross her borders and send them greetings—except in the form of arrows."

"I am going with him," Cilean said. "I heard his shouting to you that he would go alone to her first and I am going with him. You know I spent three years as a Vatell captive and I know a way to get to Brita's city through the forest."

"You will be killed," Jura whispered.

"It is a chance I have to take because what he wants to do is right. And, Jura, mark my words, he will try to do it whether I go with him or not. You should have seen him on the way to Escalon. He rode up to those three Zerna boys as if God had put a protective cloak about his shoulders. And he faced Brocain without a guard, and he demanded that Brocain give him his eldest son. And Brocain *obeyed* him. Jura, you should have seen him."

Jura shook her head. "I see him every day and I see

the way he makes no attempt to learn our ways but insists we learn his."

"That's not true. He knows our language, our history. He dresses like us and—"

"He dresses in clothes my mother made for Thal."

Cilean stepped forward. "Jura, please listen to me. Give the man a chance. Maybe he *can* unite the tribes. Think of it! Think of being free to ride without a guard. He talks of trading goods instead of stealing." Her voice lowered. "And think of trading with other countries. We could wear silk like his sister Lora."

"That . . . !"

"Jura, please," Cilean begged.

"What can I do to help? He can go dancing with Brita for all I care. I just don't want him leading my people into slaughter."

"Go with us."

"What?" Jura yelled. "Go sneaking about where I shouldn't be and sacrifice my life to the dreams of some fool of an Englishman I don't even like?"

"Yes," Cilean said. "It is our only chance. If we can get Brita alone and let him talk to her, I think she might listen. I think the man could talk a mule out of its skin."

Jura leaned back against the stone wall. If she went with him, it would surely mean her death. No one could sneak up to Brita's city and capture the Vatell queen without being caught—and tortured.

But what if they won? What if by some twist of fate they were able to get to Brita and allow this silver-tongued king to talk to her? Could Rowan persuade her to send her young men and women to marry the Irials?

"Think how strong we would be," Cilean said. "If

we united only the Irials and the Vatells, we would have twice the strength of any other tribe."

"Don't tell Geralt that," Jura said, and wished she hadn't. It sounded a bit like she wasn't loyal to her brother. "Have you talked to the Englishman yet? Who else would go besides the three of us?"

"Daire, of course," Cilean said. "Brita hasn't seen her son since he was a boy. She won't hurt him."

"Unless she considers him more Irial than Vatell. Who else?"

"That should be enough," Cilean said. "We don't want a crowd. The fewer we are, the quieter we will be. Now, shall we tell Rowan? That is, if we can get him away from the women. Perhaps it's good I'm not married to him because I think my jealousy would overwhelm me."

Jura looked out the doorway. The sunlight on Rowan's hair made him easy to see, but now he was surrounded by pretty young girls who couldn't seem to resist touching this blond king. Rowan had that innocent look men wear when they want to appear helpless so they can get whatever they want from a woman.

"Jealous of a gaggle of silly girls?" Jura said under her breath. "It will take more than that to make me jealous. Come, let us tell him our plan—our last plan on earth—before he starts talking again and persuades a hundred mothers to abandon their babies to follow him."

Rowan's blue eyes almost turned black. "The earth will open up and deliver its dead," he said softly. "The sky will rain blood. The trees will wither and blacken. The stones will turn to bread before I go sneaking into

Brita's camp accompanied by two women and my wife's former lover."

Jura gave Cilean an I-told-you-so look.

"Rowan, please," Cilean said, "listen to me. I know the way through the forest. Daire is Brita's son and Jura is strong and agile and—"

"A woman!" he shouted. They were inside Jura's aunt's house away from curious ears. "Don't you Lanconians know the difference between men and women? A *woman* cannot fight."

"I did a bloody good job when I won you," Jura shot at him.

"Mind your language," he snapped, then looked back at Cilean. "I will take my own men. I know them and they will obey me. You will draw us a map. Daire may come also if I do not have to watch my back for his blade."

"Are you accusing Daire of—" Jura began, but Cilean halted her.

"I will draw no map. What I have I carry in my head. Meeting Brita in secret is your only chance of getting her to listen to you and only I can take you to her. Daire will go because she is his mother."

"But my wife stays here," Rowan said with finality.

"No," Cilean said. "Jura goes with me. Just as you work well with your men, Jura and I work well together."

Jura leaned back on her stool, her back against a wall. She knew who was going to win. Cilean had something Rowan wanted and Cilean wasn't going to give it away for free.

# Chapter Nine

❧

JURA SLEPT ALONE in the small bedchamber that night and she tossed and turned, listening for the door to open and Rowan to enter, but he did not. An hour before dawn she left the empty bed and tiptoed from the house. She was already angry. The Englishman may not sleep with her for whatever strange foreign reasons he had, but she would kill him if he humiliated her by touching another woman.

There were people sleeping everywhere, but look where she would, she could not find Rowan. She woke Cilean and together the two of them began searching for Rowan.

The sun was high in the sky when the women met again. Cilean shook her head. Jura frowned and went in search of Rowan's squire Montgomery. The tall, dark boy was braiding the mane of Rowan's big war horse.

"Where is he?" Jura asked.

Montgomery looked surprised. "The king isn't with you?"

Jura was beginning to grow suspicious. "When did you last see him?"

"Just before I went to bed. He yawned and said he had some hard riding to do and I thought—" The boy broke off, embarrassed.

"Where is his riding horse? That big roan of his?"

"It's—" Montgomery stopped and stared. "I thought it was down there." He looked at Jura. "If someone has taken my master, I am ready to fight."

Jura let out a sigh. "The fool has gone alone into Vatell land. I know that is what he has done."

Montgomery glared at her. "My master is not a fool."

Jura paid little attention to him. "He has yet to prove to me otherwise. This must be kept secret. If the people hear he has ridden alone into enemy territory they will ride after him. We must say he . . . he went hunting. Yes, and you must go with him. He would not go without his squire."

"I cannot lie," Montgomery said stiffly.

Jura groaned. "Not that knightly honor again! You can lie when it means preventing a *war,* damn you! Give me four days. If I do not bring him back in four days, there will be no need to send anyone after us. Can you do this, boy? Are you man enough?"

"Man enough to lie?" Montgomery asked.

"Man enough to take on responsibility. You will have to fight those high-nosed knights of his and I don't know if you can do it."

"I can do whatever is needed."

"Good," Jura said. "This must be kept as quiet as possible. Saddle my horse and I will get a bag of food. Wait! Tell people I have gone with Rowan to be alone with him. Tell them I was jealous of all the women yesterday and he has taken me away to soothe me.

With such an excuse you can stay here and fend off the people for as long as I need." She was on eye level with the boy, and although she felt much older, she was actually only two years older than he and he had the dark good looks she liked so much. She put two fingers under his chin. "And this will be less of a lie for you. Your master and I have indeed gone off together and you will not know where."

Montgomery did not feel that Jura was especially older than he was, and to her surprise, he took her fingers and kissed the tips. "My master is a fortunate man."

Jura, feeling a little confused, snatched her fingers away. "You will behave yourself with my Irials," she said. "I do not want half-English brats nine months from now. Now, saddle my horse so I can ride."

Montgomery smiled at her as Jura left the stables. "Insolent English pup," she muttered.

Jura's first task was an argument with Cilean. Cilean wanted to go with Jura, but Jura wasted valuable moments saying that Cilean's absence could not be explained.

"I must go alone. Just draw me a map as quickly as possible so I can leave at once."

Cilean began to draw but she argued all the while. "How will you find him? He is many hours ahead of you."

"I will think like a blond Englishman. Do you think he is wearing mail and carrying an English banner? Oh, Cilean, pray for me. If he is killed, it will mean war. The Irial people will glorify his memory after his honey-tongued speech yesterday."

"Here is the map," Cilean said, then hugged Jura

hard. "I am sorry I doubted you. Go and find this errant king of ours and bring him back safely." She pulled away. "How will you dress?"

Jura grinned. "As an Ulten. That should keep people away. My aunt has Ulten clothes in storage and I plan to remove them."

Cilean kissed her friend's cheek. "Go with God and come back soon."

Jura rode into Vatell territory cautiously. The old, ragged Ulten garment she wore stank so bad her horse had pranced in anger at first and Jura did not blame it for she could barely abide herself. She had stolen the faded, once-brilliant costume from her aunt's house and dipped it in the muck of a pigsty then rolled it in ashes to get the proper aroma and color of an Ulten costume. Smelling herself, Jura knew why Ultens were the only tribe to be allowed to roam freely. No one coveted anything that belonged to an Ulten, although quite often Ultens were hanged for little or no reason.

Under the filthy garment Jura wore the green hunting uniform of the guards and an arsenal of weapons.

She rode west, staying on narrow paths that wagons and large groups of people could not travel. Whining, she begged food and water from people in front of leaky huts and dried-up vegetable patches. After a day of travel she began to almost understand why Brita had attacked the richer Irial lands to the south.

Late at night she came to a public house. Candles blazed from inside the little wattle-and-daub shack and she could hear raucous laughter and the clank of steel. She tied her horse in the darkness of the surrounding forest and went to the door. A fight surely meant she had found her English husband. She just hoped she had time to save him.

She walked in the door but no one paid her the least attention as they were all watching two Vatell guards play-fighting each other with broadswords. Feeling a little foolish, Jura pulled her filthy hood further over her face and took an empty seat at a table. Immediately, everyone at the table looked about in horror at the smell, then when they saw the hooded figure, they moved away. A skinny woman asked Jura what she wanted to drink and bade her give a copper bead in exchange.

From under the shade of the hood, she looked around the small tavern but she saw no sign of the blond Englishman. Along the walls stood several Vatells almost as dirty as she was.

Jura drank her ale and the fight ended and goods and garments and animals traded hands as wagers were won and lost.

"What is that smell?" a drunken voice yelled.

Jura put her mug down and started to stand. She meant to leave as quickly as possible, but someone put a heavy hand on her shoulder.

"An Ulten boy," someone yelled. "Let's teach him a lesson."

A hand grabbed Jura's hood just as she moved away. Her face was exposed.

"Gor," someone said. "A girl."

"And a beauty."

"Let's teach her another kind of lesson," said a man, laughing.

Jura held a knife in each hand under her concealing garment as the men, about twenty of them, advanced on her.

"Here, now," came a deep voice from behind the crowd. He spoke Lanconian but it was an accent Jura hadn't heard before, very country sounding. A bent-over, burly man with greasy black hair and a patch over one eye, wearing many layers of rags, pushed his way forward. "Don't hurt me daughter," he said, and moved toward Jura.

Instinctively, she drew back from him.

"Follow me, or they'll kill you," he said into her ear, and Jura recognized Rowan's voice.

She was so astonished she followed him without question and the men were drunk enough and had just had enough excitement that they were sated, so they allowed Jura to follow the bent old man out of the tavern.

"You!" Jura hissed as soon as they were outside. "I have come to take you back to safety."

"Safety!" Rowan spat at her. "What do you know of safety? I just saved your virtue and probably your life."

"I could have protected myself."

Rowan cursed in reply. "Do you have a horse? We must ride quickly and get away from this place. Or did you leave your horse in the open so one of these vandals stole it? God's teeth but you stink."

"My horse is well hidden."

"Good, then get on it and ride northwest for one hour then stop. I will meet you there."

"You cannot go back in there. You must return to the Irials and—"

"Go!" he commanded. "Someone comes and I'm not finished here."

Jura slipped into the darkness, found her horse, and

began to ride. It was against her better judgment to leave him alone back there but she knew within her heart how much fear she had felt when the men had touched her. And, also, she had been surprised at Rowan's disguise and the way he had blended into the crowd. In an hour she reached a bend in the river and she knew this was where she was to meet him.

She fed her horse, tethered it in a dark growth of bush, and pulled off the stinking Ulten gown, then climbed a tree and waited for Rowan. He didn't take long in getting there. She watched him dismount then stand still and look around. He turned and looked up at the tree although she knew he couldn't see her.

"Come down," he said.

Jura swung down a branch and dropped right in front of him.

The patch over his eye was flipped up to his forehead. "All right, what are you doing here?"

"I told you, I came to take you to safety."

"You? Take *me* to safety? Tomorrow morning you are to return to the Irials."

"And what do you plan to do?"

"I am going to find Brita and talk to her."

"And how do you plan to find her?" Jura asked.

"If you hadn't interfered tonight, I might have found out where she was. Those two guards were drunk enough and might have been ready after their fight but I had to leave to save your dirty neck. You still stink even without that thing you were wearing."

Jura leaned against the tree and began to unlace her boots. "If the Irials had guessed you rode alone into Vatell land, they would have attacked."

"What are you doing?"

"Undressing. I'm going to take a bath. Your solitary mission could have started a war." She slipped out of the trousers.

Rowan stared at her with eyes so wide she could see the whites of them in the moonlight. "I wanted no argument," he said tightly. "I did what I had to do. Oh God." He said this last as Jura removed the last of her clothes and stood nude in the moonlight, her high-breasted figure gleaming and magnificently structured. "Jura, you torture me," he whispered, his hands going behind his back to grope for the tree to support himself.

"I am your wife," she said softly, then cocked her head. "Someone comes," she said, and flung her body against his. "Hide me from their sight."

Rowan, holding her, was stupefied and didn't wrap his coarse, raggedy cloak about her as he should have. He just stood there with his body pressed against hers, his hands lightly on her back.

She was eye level with him and she waited for him to kiss her but he made no movement, so Jura touched her lips to his. It was all he needed to speed him into action. To Jura's great pleasure, Rowan's hands were all over her at once and he seemed to have a hundred mouths. He kissed her, caressed her, and oh, how deliciously beautiful he made her feel. How wonderful to feel womanly and desirable and adored and wanted and pursued. She kissed him back with all the wanting she felt.

"Beg me, Jura," he said, his voice pleading.

She didn't hear him at first.

"Please beg me," he repeated.

Jura began to hear him and pushed him away. He was limp with desire and malleable in her hands. "Not

in your lifetime, Englishman, will an Irial beg," she
spat at him. She turned away from him and walked to
the river, glad for the cold water to cool her hot skin.
She cursed the man with every word she knew. What
kind of animal was he that he took pleasure in making
a woman beg for his favors? He should be locked away
before he harmed someone—and Thal thought this
idiot was fit to be king!

When she emerged from the river, dried and
dressed, Rowan had a small fire going and two rabbits
skinned, speared, and roasting.

"I have supper," he said softly.

"And what must I do to earn it? Go on my knees
and plead? Or is begging reserved for the marriage
bed? Perhaps to receive food I must bray like a
donkey. Pardon me if I do not know your English
rules of marriage conduct."

"Jura," he said, his voice heavy, "please do not be
bitter. Let me explain that I am a knight. I made a
vow, a stupid vow that has punished me more than
you, but a vow to God nonetheless and I must keep it.
If you would only—"

"Where do you plan to go tomorrow?" she asked.
She didn't want to discuss how awful he made her feel:
desirable one moment and the next thrust away with
all the contempt she had for the Ulten robe.

"*You* are returning to the Irials. *I* am going to find
Brita."

She smiled meanly at him over the fire. "I have the
map. No, you will not find it on me, even if you could
bear to touch my person, for I have committed it to
memory. I am going with you. *We* will find Brita and
*we* will talk to her."

"Why didn't I marry a sweet biddable Englishwoman?" Rowan mumbled. "Here! Take this." He thrust a rabbit leg at her.

"You have made no sacred knightly vows concerning rabbit legs?"

"Only shrews," he answered. "Now eat so we can sleep and leave early tomorrow. We have many miles to cover."

"Maybe," Jura said, and smiled sweetly at Rowan's glare.

She slept quite well that night even if Rowan's getting up twice did wake her.

"Wake up," he said before dawn, and threw the hideous Ulten robe on her. "That should cool my interest in you." He handed her bread and cheese. "Be ready to ride quickly."

"Yes, oh sire," she mocked.

They rode for two hours before Jura told him to halt and follow her down a narrow road leading into the forest. It was a road made for foot traffic and twice Rowan hacked at branches to provide room for the horses.

At noon they stopped to eat cold meat pies Jura had brought with her.

"We should change clothes," she said. She looked at his greasy hair. "An Ulten and a . . . whatever you are, each alone is all right, but we make an unappetizing pair. We will not get near Brita's city dressed like this."

"What did you have in mind?"

"Ten miles from here is the manor house of a rich relative of Brita's. I thought perhaps the man and his wife might not miss a few garments."

Jura watched Rowan's face, and to her surprise, she

found herself thinking that the man's good looks were marred by his artificially darkened hair. Now he was frowning and she wondered if he disliked following a plan made by a woman.

"I would have to know where the clothes are kept and I doubt if it will be easy getting in and out of the house. You must swear you will return to the Irials immediately."

"*I* do not swear things with the ease that you do. Cilean visited this house a few times when she was a Vatell captive, and I know something about it. You will follow me and—"

"I will *not* follow you," he said. "You will remain hidden in the forest until we return."

"We shall see," Jura said, smiling.

The stone of the big manor house was silhouetted in the moonlight and the only sounds to be heard were the soft nickers of horses and the clank of a steel sword as a Vatell guard passed.

Rowan and Jura flattened themselves against the wall and waited, and when the guard passed, Jura motioned Rowan to follow her through a small wooden side door into the larder. Here hung ducks and geese and haunches of venison and freshly cooked chickens and meat pies awaiting tomorrow's dinner.

Jura cautiously opened the door and slipped through into a narrow hallway, at one end of which there was light and the sound of people's voices. She started toward the light but Rowan grabbed her tunic back. He pointed to a steep, dark, stone circular staircase a few feet away. Holding his sword before him, Rowan started up the stairs.

It was easy to find the master and mistress's bed-chamber as it was the only walled-off room on the second floor. They hid in the shadows once as a maid hurried past, then slipped into the room and went immediately to a large chest against the wall.

The Vatells dressed much like the Irials, with cross-gartered boots, their knees exposed below a heavy tunic. Rowan pulled a blue tunic of lightweight wool from the chest.

"No," Jura whispered. "That will make your eyes too blue. They show too much as they are."

"Oh," Rowan asked with interest, turning to look at her, their noses almost touching. "I had no idea you noticed my eyes."

"I have a few times," she murmured.

He seemed to be ready to kiss her when the door latch was raised. As quick as lightning, Jura made a leap inside the big chest and Rowan followed her and closed the lid over their heads. They were pressed together tightly, warm body to warm body and, unfortunately, weapon to weapon. Something was pressing hard into Jura's ribs and she was sure it was Rowan's broadax. She did not dare shift for fear of being discovered.

She lay still and listened as the footsteps, one pair, walked all around the room. A maid, she thought, then held her breath as the footsteps came closer. She tensed her muscles to spring.

When the maid lifted the lid of the big oak clothes chest, out sprang two fierce-looking people, both of them going for her throat.

Quite calmly, the woman fainted.

Rowan and Jura, prepared for a fight, looked at the

crumpled little woman at their feet and began to laugh. It was the first time they had shared laughter.

Smiling, Jura began to grab garments from the chest. "Here, we take these and we better tie her up and put her in here and give ourselves time to get away."

They wrapped the maid in one of her mistress's gowns, stuffed a stocking in her mouth, and Rowan gently laid her in the chest. Her eyes opened and she looked up, frightened, at Rowan.

"Don't worry, sweetheart," he said, "there's plenty of air and someone will find you in no time. Someone as pretty as you will be missed. Just rest; you'll be safe." He bent and kissed her forehead—and just missed Jura's slamming the lid on his head. He barely got his fingers out of the way.

"Sorry," she said. "It slipped. Are you ready to go or do you plan to stay and become a manservant?"

"Ready," he said, smiling at her. "I'm sure you want to lead."

"The most able should lead," she said with a sniff, and went to the door.

They were able to get to the larder without incident and Rowan took two pies on the way out. He was feeling very good after Jura's womanly little fit upstairs. He had almost given up hope that she would ever show any interest in him.

They made it past the guards and ran, crouching, into the forest, jumped on their horses, and whipped them into a gallop. After an hour, Rowan turned off the road and into the forest, reining his horse into the dense growth. They hid there, their hands on the horses' noses, and waited silently. It wasn't long before they heard the noise of many horses and many men riding past them.

When they were gone, Rowan motioned to Jura to follow him and they made their way up the steep embankment to the crest of the hill.

"We can sleep here," he said, and removed the blankets from his horse.

Before they bedded down, they changed into the Vatell clothes, for the riders would be looking for an Ulten and a beggar.

"You'll have to wash tomorrow," Rowan said, looking up at the stars, "or they'll smell you as an Ulten."

"Perhaps you should have taken the maid with you and left me behind. *She* was pretty and sweet smelling."

Rowan smiled broadly in the darkness. "Jura, no woman alive is prettier than you, and even smelling as you do, you are sweeter than a hundred princesses together."

Jura's eyes widened. She didn't know why she had felt so angry at Rowan's compliments to the frightened maid or why she had sniped at him like a simpering girl, but it was amazing how pleasant his words were to her. Daire praised her when twelve arrows in a row hit their mark, and Geralt and Thal never complimented her at all. Of course men had said she was pretty but not in this lavish, gentle way. If they had, she would have held her knife to their throats, but tonight she rather liked this man's words. In fact she wished he would say more.

"You . . . you handled yourself well tonight," she said tentatively. "And you got yourself into Vatell territory without being recognized. It was good that you darkened your hair."

"You thought I wouldn't?" he snapped. Just like a woman, he thought, you give her a compliment and she insults you. He turned on his side away from her. He'd had about enough of her insinuations that he was incompetent. The woman was emasculating! "Tomorrow you go back to the Irials."

Jura grimaced and didn't reply. This Englishman was very strange.

But the next morning they did not have time to argue. Jura woke fully alert, her senses knowing that something was wrong. Slowly, she reached out her hand to Rowan, asleep a few feet from her. He opened his eyes the instant she touched him and read the warning in her eyes.

To her consternation, Rowan leaped to his feet and began to shout. "Damn you, woman, always after me, a man can't even sleep."

Jura saw that he grabbed his sword as he stood. She also took hers and aimed it for his throat. "After you?" she yelled up at him. "You are a poor thing for a woman to want. I have had lovers twice your age who were better than you."

"I shall show you who is the better lover," he said, and leaped on top of her. "Roll to my right," he said into her ear. "Hide in the forest and wait. There are two of them."

When Rowan moved, Jura did indeed roll to his right, but she came up to her feet, her sword held firmly with both hands, and she positioned herself at his back as she had been trained.

Two men, thieves by the look of them, came toward

Rowan, knives drawn. They looked hungry and ready to commit any crime to take what little Rowan and Jura carried with them.

"I am your king," Rowan said, "put down your weapons. I will share what I have with you."

"You'll not give *my* horse away," Jura said, still behind him, watching the forest for more thieves.

"King?" a thief said, and snorted laughter before he attacked Rowan.

Jura listened to the sounds of battle behind her and kept her head turned a bit so she could see when or if Rowan needed help, but he was a good fighter, very good. And she was surprised to see that he fought like a Lanconian.

One of the thieves fell and Rowan went after the other one while Jura still stayed close to his back. She had been trained well and they worked together as if they were dancing. When he moved, she moved.

She heard the second thief scream in pain, but she didn't turn her head because, just as she thought might happen, a third thief came tearing from the forest, a sword raised above his head and coming straight at her. She parried his blow and steel rang against steel.

"Run, Jura, run," Rowan commanded, and she cursed him for trying to confuse her. She was trained to obey orders but this was a bad order.

She fought the man with all her strength, not even hesitating when his steel cut into her upper arm. The man was frenzied as his sword raised and lowered, and Jura took each blow on her own sword. Then she counterattacked and began to push him back toward the forest with angry, aggressive blows of her own.

From the corner of her eye, she saw Rowan, finished now with his own fight, come toward her, but he stopped and watched instead.

Jura pinned the thief against a tree, ready to ram her sword into his belly.

"No!" Rowan said. "He is Lanconian."

"He is Vatell," Jura said, but she hesitated and didn't kill the man.

"Here," Rowan said, holding out a heavy meat-filled pie to the man. "Take this and take your friends. They are only wounded. Remember that your lives are a gift from the king. The king of all the Lanconians."

The thief looked at Rowan the same way Jura felt, as if Rowan were crazy, and it was good to put miles between them. He snatched the pie and ran into the forest while the other two men, groaning, limped off.

The sun was beginning to rise now and Rowan looked at Jura's bleeding arm then led her to sit on a nearby rock while he brought linen and fresh water from his saddle carriers. Tenderly, he began to wash and bandage her arm. It was a shallow cut.

"I have not seen that before," he said softly. "I mean the way you stayed by my back. Feilan said nothing to me of women who guard a man's back."

"Perhaps he took it for granted. What does an Englishwoman do? If you had been here with your sister, what would she have done?"

"Lora would have hidden in the forest as I told you to do."

"And she would have been taken by the third thief or he would have killed you when he attacked your back. Together, we made an impenetrable column with eyes all around."

Rowan was frowning. "I see that but I do not like it. The men should be trained to guard each other's backs."

"Men are the stronger fighters, and quite often a woman only guards, she does not fight. It would be wrong to waste a strong arm merely to protect."

Rowan finished the bandaging but he was still frowning. "I thank you for your protection this time but next time you must—"

Jura kissed him. Her action surprised both of them.

He drew back from her, his eyes dark with longing. "Jura," he whispered.

She knew what he was going to ask: she was to beg him. Angrily, she stood and went to her horse. "If we are to reach Brita, then we must ride." Every bit of her fury told in her voice and her manner as she mounted her horse and rode away, not looking to see if he followed.

They were on higher ground now, always traveling up into the mountains that formed the northern borders of the Lanconian territory and the air was cooler and thinner. They were also off the path Cilean had told Jura about and it was taking longer to reach Brita's fortified city.

Rowan rode beside her but she did not look at him.

"What does this Brita look like?" he asked.

Jura kept her chin up. "I have never seen her and I have never asked anyone about her appearance. She is Daire's mother, so she is old; she has led armies against Thal and the Fearens. When I was a child, I heard she even attacked the Zernas, so she must be scarred from battles. I do not imagine she is a beauty if that is what you are seeking."

"Jura, can't we—" Rowan began, but Jura urged her horse away from him.

She could forgive much of his strangeness because he was an Englishman, but she could not forgive his flirting with a maid one minute and rejecting her a few hours later. At midday they stopped to eat by a stream and Jura looked at her reflection in a still pool of water. She had never been concerned with her looks before, only with her prowess with a weapon, but she had seen the looks in men's eyes and knew they found her desirable. So why did her English husband reject her? Was it because she wasn't blonde as his sister was? Did he only like pale-skinned women?

At dusk they camped. They did not light a fire because now they were very close to Brita's walled city.

"It would be too much to hope that you remain behind tomorrow," Rowan said, his eyebrows raised in question as he looked at her in the fading light.

"Someone must watch your back," she answered. "I thought we would ride into the city tomorrow: believe we can get in without question. It is good you speak our language. We will identify Brita and the first time she rides out, we will take her. There is a peasant's hut a day's ride back; we can keep her there while you talk to her. We will have to watch that the peasants do not betray us, though."

"Is that *all* the decisions you have made?" Rowan asked in a low voice. "You have not also perhaps decided that I am not allowed to participate? Perhaps I would be too much in your way."

"You are the one who tells me to stay in the forest," she said, not understanding what she had done now to make him angry. "Do you have another plan that is better than mine?"

"No," he said through clenched teeth, "it is the same plan I had except that I was to ride into the city alone but—" He stopped.

"What is the difference whether I say the plan or you do? I think it is good that we agree on something."

Rowan kicked at a rock with his toe. "You are a woman," he muttered.

"Not enough of one," she said under her breath, and turned away. Winning a man seemed to be easy. All she had to do was outwrestle, outshoot, outrun, outjump fifty or so other women, but what in heaven's name did it take to please a man after one won him?

They slept a few feet apart, and during the night Rowan's restless tossing woke her. Instinctively, she moved beside him, and in his sleep he reached out for her and pulled her to him, clutching her to him tightly He felt so good to her, so strong, so warm, so right. She snuggled close to him and slept.

In the morning she woke before he did and quickly rolled away from him. She couldn't bear another of his "beg me" talks.

They rode into Brita's city as soon as the gates were open. It was not a rich city and it was very different from Escalon. Here were houses and tiny, narrow shops and men and women running to and fro. But there was an air of poverty about the place, the city smelling of excrement that hadn't been hauled away and rotting meat carcasses. She and Rowan, in their rich clothes, were stared at by raggedy peasants.

They stopped to buy mugs of buttermilk from a street vendor.

"And where does Brita live?" Rowan asked.

*"Queen* Brita," Jura said, smiling at the vendor. "We have business with her."

"There," the man said, pointing to a stone house butted up against the north side of the stone wall that surrounded the city. It was a large but ordinary house, not nearly as large or as rich as the house where Rowan and Jura had stolen the clothes they wore.

"She hunts today," the vendor said, "and you may see her ride past with her guard. There! The door opens now and there comes her guard."

Rowan and Jura nodded thanks to the man and moved into the shadow of a building as they waited for the queen and her guard to pass.

No matter that the Vatell tribe did not own good grazing or cropland, their queen did not skimp on the magnificence of her guard. All twenty men who rode with her were richly dressed in fine blue wool, and their weapons were of high-quality steel that Jura knew had not come from Lanconia. Their horses were tall, spirited, beautiful animals that looked well fed and well exercised.

But Brita put the men to shame. She rode in the middle of these handsome, erect men and she was like the sun surrounded by twenty moons. She was tall, slim, and absolutely beautiful. She wore a long gown in the English style that fitted about her waist very tightly and it was made of rich, cream-colored wool that set off her dark hair and eyes to advantage.

As she rode past, the city came to a halt as every man, woman and child, and it seemed, every animal, paused to look at her. There was a hush when she had left the gates.

"Old, is she?" Rowan said to Jura. "No wonder men follow her. I might follow her myself."

Jura glared at him but he was smiling in an insipid way at the gate where Brita had just disappeared. "Are we going to go after her or not?" she hissed at him.

"This is one task I shall love," he said, grinning idiotically and not seeing Jura's angry glare.

They mounted their horses and rode out of town to a low ridge where they could look down on the city and the plain below. Brita and her men did not go far from the city walls as they rode into the surrounding forest to begin their hunt..

"I will follow her and—"

"We will follow her," Jura said. "We will separate her from her men and then take her. I can throw my cloak over her and—"

"You will follow me and do what I tell you. Now come on. We will ride around the east side and watch her, then take her when we can."

In the end it was Jura who made it possible for Rowan to capture Brita. The queen had separated from most of her men, and with only two guards near her, she was pursuing a big, tusked boar. Jura thought she was ridiculous wearing that white dress while hunting, but Rowan wore an odd expression as he watched her.

"Distract the men," Jura said to him, "and I will lead the boar away. Brita will follow the animal."

Jura saw the expression on Brita's face, that sense of pursuit, the elation of it, the exhilaration. Her guardsmen held back, watchful and listening. Their heads went up when they heard a man's cry of distress from behind them and all but one of them left their queen to investigate.

Brita heard nothing but the blood pounding in her

ears as she charged ahead after the boar. Jura took her spear from the back of her horse and leaped to the ground. For all that Brita did not look her forty-some years, Jura knew she must be getting old to take so long to slay the pig. Brita stood in the animal's path, then when it ran around her to avoid her, she stuck a lance into its neck. The pain-crazed animal turned and charged Jura, as she knew it would.

Jura grabbed the lower branch of a tree and swung up as the bleeding boar went tearing past and not far behind him was Brita in her spotless white gown.

Jura lost no time jumping onto her horse, and in minutes she had the remaining guard chasing her, and it was easy to lose him. She smiled to herself as she rode toward the direction Brita had taken. No Irial guard would be so easily lost.

She had a glimpse of Rowan as he rode south toward where they had camped last night, and before him in his saddle she could see the white of Brita's gown. She did not seem to be struggling very hard against Rowan, nor did he seem to have her bound and gagged.

Frowning, Jura galloped after the two of them. She hadn't gone far when two of Brita's guard saw her, and Jura had a long, exhausting ride trying to escape them. It was nearly dusk when she reached the little peasant's hut. She was shaky with fatigue and hunger and she was concerned that Rowan had escaped unharmed, that the devious Queen Brita had not put a knife into him.

There were candles blazing inside the peasant's hut and Jura feared the worst. Expecting to find Rowan hanging from the ceiling and being tortured by Brita and her men, she cautiously slipped around the side of the building, her sword in her hands, a knife between her teeth, and peered in through the single window.

She could not believe what she saw.

Rowan sat on a stool with an ancient lute in his lap, his hair once again golden, while the dazzling Brita sat on the floor at his feet, her knees drawn up and looking up at him adoringly. A peasant couple and three children sat opposite them, staring at these two lovely people as one would look at a pair of angels.

"Play another one," Brita said to Rowan, and her voice was as husky as the smoke from the charcoal brazier in the room.

He smiled at her. "Yes, my queen, whatever you request."

Jura was so aghast at this scene that the knife fell from her mouth and clattered on the stones of the wall.

Instantly, Rowan was on his feet, his sword taken from where it was leaning against the wall, and he was out the door. He caught Jura before she reached her horse.

"Where have you been?" he demanded.

"Where have *I* been?" she yelled back at him. "I have been leading two guardsmen away from you. I have been protecting you and your . . . your . . ." She was too angry to speak.

"Brita sent word to her men. I thought they were all told that she wanted to stay with me. I thought perhaps you were bathing before meeting a queen." He looked her up and down. "That's not a bad idea, Jura. You are dripping sweat."

Jura brought her sword up, fully meaning to chop

off any part of his body she could reach, hopefully his head.

He caught her arms. "Jura, what is wrong with you? If I had known you were in danger, I would have come to you, but I had no idea. Brita sent her men home. Come, please don't be angry. Brita has agreed to stay here with me for a while and we can talk of uniting the tribes. It is what we want. There is no reason to be angry. Come and meet her. She is intelligent and educated and I find her exceptionally pleasant company. You will like her."

"You certainly seem to like her," she said stiffly.

"Now is not the time for jealousy. It is one thing to be jealous of a maid but you cannot be jealous of a queen like Brita. Come. No, maybe you should bathe first."

She jerked away from him. "So, the smell of me displeases you," she said. "I got this smell from protecting you, but you do not need protection, at least not from swords and arrows. Tell me, am I to bow to this old queen? Am I to beg her for her favors as I am to beg you?"

"Jura, I do not understand you at all. If you want to meet her smelling as you do, that is all right with me. I just thought—"

"You never thought at all!" she shouted at him, and ran away into the forest.

She hated herself for how she was acting, hated the new emotions that were raging inside her. Until this Englishman with his foreign ways had come to Lanconia, she had understood herself. She had known her place in life, where she was and where she was going. She had also understood men. Lanconian men valued strong, sensible women. Thal had shown her maps and asked her opinion of proposed campaigns, and when he thought her answers childish he had told her so—usually at the top of his lungs. Daire had expected her to be strong and fearless, and the two battles they had been in together, he had expected her to protect his back.

But what did this Englishman want from her? He was angry if she protected him, angry if she kissed him. He didn't want her to ride beside him. He didn't want to hear her ideas about what they should do to capture Brita. He said he wanted her to hide and cringe in the forest yet here he was fawning over a woman who had terrorized two generations of men. Jura thought that she had done a bit of her own terrorizing today but all she was told was that she stank.

She grimaced as she thought of Brita in her white dress. The stupid Englishman was taken in by her, but Jura knew the woman's history. She may have said she called off her men, but two of them had chased Jura for hours. What other lies had she told?

No doubt she had told her men to gather an army and attack and kill this Irial king.

Jura left the forest and went back toward the house. Tonight she would stay outside and guard the peasant's hut, and she would be able to give the fool of an Englishman a warning when the Vatells attacked.

# Chapter Ten

❧❦❧

JURA WOKE WITH a start as her body fell forward. She was leaning against a tree and she had managed to stay awake most of the night, but her fatigue had been too much for her a few hours before dawn.

"You're safe," said a voice near her.

She turned startled eyes toward Rowan. He was lounging on the ground near her, looking as if he had been asleep.

"How long have you been here?" she snapped, rubbing her eyes.

"When you fell asleep, I moved beside you."

She straightened, trying to ignore the catch in her back.

"Look," he said, nodding toward the peasant's hut where the plump wife was emerging from the door and scratching. "They are awake and we are safe. I told you you should trust me. Brita is interested in my plan to unite the tribes. We talked for hours last night."

She looked at him and saw the early-morning light touching his golden hair. His eyes were as blue as lake water. "You have washed the grease from your hair to

175

help you talk? Have you found out what she wants so much that keeps her from trying to kill two Irials?"

Rowan grimaced. "Jura, please meet her. She is an intelligent woman and I think you might like her."

Jura realized she was being childish; after all, this woman was Daire's mother, and she had always loved Daire, so perhaps she would like her. She stood. "I will meet her."

Rowan stood also and smiled at her. "You won't regret this," he said confidently.

Jura kept her back completely straight as she entered the hut where Brita sat on a small stool on the opposite side of the brazier. She looked up as Jura entered.

Jura felt that she knew this woman instantly. Brita was a woman who had lived always in a man's world. Jura had, of course, heard Brita's story and she had often wondered how a woman could gain control of an entire tribe and, even more difficult, retain that control, but as soon as she saw Brita's glittering black eyes, she knew. Jura saw the ambition and the force behind those eyes. Once Jura had asked Daire why his mother did not fight Thal for the return of her oldest son, but now Jura saw that Brita would not endanger her throne for anyone, even her own son.

And Jura also saw that Brita considered Jura her enemy. The hairs rose on the back of Jura's neck as she looked at this beautiful woman, and she wondered what she had that this queen wanted.

"So," Brita said in that husky voice of hers, "you are the woman who left my son at the altar and betrayed her best friend in order to win an English king."

Jura's first reaction was to defend herself and explain, but she did not. "Yes," she answered. "It is better to be the queen of the Irials than of the starving Vatells."

Behind her, she heard Rowan groan but she kept her eyes on Brita. They understood each other and it was now open war.

"A maiden queen from what I hear," Brita said softly as she looked Jura up and down, smiling at Jura's wearing of the deep blue Vatell guardswoman tunic and trousers, a bow and arrows at her back. She was in sharp contrast to Brita in her beautiful white gown with a gold necklace set with heavy emeralds lying across her abundant bosom. "Perhaps your husband does not desire so mannish a woman. Perhaps he would do better with a true woman."

So, Jura thought, she wants Rowan. "He was easily won and easily lost," she said, then turned to leave. Rowan was blocking the doorway, and she had to push past him to get out.

She walked about a mile through the forest to a small stream, then tore off the hated Vatell clothes and plunged into the cold water to swim and wash the stink from her body. In all her life she had never been so unhappy. Even when both her parents had died so soon after one another she had not felt so lost. Then Daire had been there to take care of her and he had always been there—until now. Now this Englishman had come into her life and made her miserable. He complained about everything she did. If she saved his life by protecting his back, he told her she should have run into the forest.

He made her feel undesirable and unwanted.

She got out of the water and, wet, put the Vatell clothes back on.

"There you are," she heard Rowan say, but she didn't look up at him as she wrapped her cross garters about her legs.

"I have been talking to her," he said gloomily, "and you were right. The woman wants an alliance between the Irials and the Vatells, but not as I had planned. She wants to marry me. She wants me to put you aside and marry her. If I do this, she will allow the Vatells to marry the Irials." He frowned at Jura. "You should not have gone so far from the hut. There is danger in these woods."

"And the hut is safe?" she asked. "I have been thinking that you also are right: I do not belong in this Vatell land. I should not have come. I will leave as soon as I have eaten." She started back toward the hut but Rowan grabbed her arm.

"You cannot travel alone across this land. Any man who sees you will attack you."

"Why?" she screamed at him. "Why would a *man* attack me? I am a maiden, remember? It is known to everyone that I am not wanted." She jerked her arm from his. "Go back to her. Tell her you will marry her. I will free you and the Irials will be glad to see the tribes united by a royal marriage. You said marriage was the way to unite the tribes. You can set an example as the first."

He was stiffening with every word. "And you will have Daire," Rowan said flatly. "He is the man you have always wanted."

"Yes, Daire," Jura said, and the familiar name and the love and comfort it made her feel brought tears to her eyes. She turned her head away. "Go back to her. Tell her she will get what she wants. She will have her blond Irial king and you will begin to unite the tribes."

"You cry for him," Rowan whispered. "You offer tears for this man Daire."

"Why not?" she yelled in his face. "I have always loved him. I will never love you who talks to me of vows and begging, who does not understand what a guardswoman is trained to do. Go to her. Maybe she can make a man of you."

Rowan's jaw hardened. "Maybe she can. Yes, you are right, this marriage will be good for Lanconia. I should have thought of it at first rather than calling the Honorium in hopes that—" He paused and looked at her. "I have allowed my heart to lead me so far but no longer. The king of the Irials and the queen of the Vatells shall marry." His eyes narrowed. "I wonder if the prince of the Vatells shouldn't marry the princess of another tribe instead of merely the adopted daughter of the old king."

He didn't stop Jura's hand when she slapped him. She was strong and the slap resounded through the forest, but Rowan didn't so much as turn his head. They stood looking at one another for a long moment.

"We will ride tomorrow," he said. "Brita will gather young Vatell men and women and we will bring the Irials to the border. The marriages will be performed there."

"And I will take Daire then, married or not," she said. "I will be a maiden no more."

He stared at her for a moment, the left side of his face livid with her handprint, then he turned back toward the hut. "Do not leave alone," he said over his shoulder, "or I will hunt you down." He walked away.

Rowan did not walk far from her, just far enough that she was no longer in sight, and then he leaned against a tree and rubbed his aching jaw. He felt like crying himself.

It seemed like from the moment of his birth he had known that he was destined to be a king and he had willingly sacrificed everything for that kingship. But there was only one area of his life that he had withheld from old Feilan's constant criticism and that was his choice of wife. Rowan knew that the comfort of a wife could make up for much unpleasantness in life and he meant to have a wife he could love. That is why he risked the Honorium. He hadn't wanted to offend the people of Lanconia but he had wanted Jura above all else. Except for a few moments during the Honorium when it looked as if Mealla might win, Rowan had been sure that Jura would win—she would win because she wanted him as much as he wanted her.

But that had not been so. She had not wanted him at all, and the night he had found that out he had wanted to die.

And since then things had gone from bad to worse. He didn't understand her at all. Every attempt he made to protect her seemed to enrage her. Was he to show that he cared for her by tossing her a sword and asking her to risk her life fighting to help him? That didn't make sense. She went from one harrowing escapade to another, never even noticing that Rowan was so worried about her safety that he could barely concentrate on the task at hand. She screamed at him every time he tried to ensure her safety. Nothing he did pleased her.

And now she wanted him to marry someone else and thus free her to marry Daire.

He had been so angry at Jura because of her attitude about Brita. Brita was charming and had ordered her men home, placing her life in Rowan's hands. He had been immensely flattered by the trust she placed in him and he meant to honor that trust with his life.

Then Jura had arrived and had once again stated that she thought he was a fool and had refused even to meet Brita. She had stormed off into the darkness, acting as if she were immune to attack and could single-handedly fight off an army. He had had to excuse himself from Brita and make sure Jura was safe.

The stubborn little cat had sat up all night and watched the hut. He wavered between thinking she was an idiot and being grateful to her. What if she were right and Brita's acquiescence had been a farce and her men were to attack during the night? When morning came and Jura began to doze, Rowan knew his instincts about Brita were right. She wanted peace as much as he did, and he resented Jura's insinuations that Brita was untrustworthy. He had been angry at Jura for not trusting him, for always doubting him, for always believing he was English and not Lanconian.

Then there had been that awful scene in the hut when the two women had fought a verbal battle that he feared would sour negotiations between the two tribes forever. This time he did not follow Jura when she ran off into the forest but had stayed with Brita to plead for her understanding and forgiveness. He meant to say that Jura was young and hot-tempered, but before he could speak, Brita dismissed the peasants so that they were alone—and she proceeded to run her hand up his thigh.

Somehow, Rowan managed to control his shock.

Brita was beautiful, oh heavens yes, she was stunningly beautiful and no doubt vastly experienced in bed, but he did not feel lust for her. It had been the same in England when women had offered themselves to him. He had been pleased and flattered by the women's attentions, but he had never felt driven to carry them away and make mad love to them.

Only Jura had driven his senses into ecstasy. Only Jura had made him mad with the wanting of her.

Brita had whispered to him in a seductive way that she would marry him and they would unite the tribes and they would rule Lanconia together and they would spend their nights in wild pleasure. She even mentioned a few things Rowan had never heard of.

But she didn't tempt him. All Rowan could think of was not seeing Jura, of not being near her, of not hearing her taunting him. He looked at Brita and her beauty made him feel nothing, and he wondered if he could even perform with her, much less spend all night trying to please her.

He had left Brita and gone to Jura to tell her she was right about the Vatell queen, but then Jura had said she *wanted* out of their marriage. Jura, his Jura, who yelled and fought, had shed tears at the mere mention of the name of the man she loved. Rowan remembered too clearly how he had felt the night he had heard her say she hoped he would never touch her. He had made his vow to God then gone home and brooded for weeks.

But when he saw her again, he had been overcome with the power of her. He wanted to touch her, kiss her, hold her, caress her. But she was so cold to him, never trusting him, always against him, while he lay awake at night just looking at her.

And now she wanted to end their fragile marriage. She wanted to get away from him completely.

So be it, he thought angrily. He wasn't going to force her to stay with him, and if she wanted to go back to another man, he wasn't going to stop her. He would marry Brita and he would somehow make himself content.

He moved away from the tree and started back to the hut. He must tell Brita that he would marry her.

"You are a fool of an Englishman," Jura hissed. "You know nothing of our ways."

"Can you say nothing else to me?" Rowan said back to her, glaring.

They were in the woods before the hut saddling their horses and making ready for the ride back to the Irial border. Behind them were a hundred Vatell guards who looked at Rowan and Jura as if they were snake spit. And behind the guard were a hundred and fifty young men and women. Brita had given no persuasive speech to her people but had ordered her guard to gather suitable men and women and bring them. Many of them sported bruised bodies and the women's faces were tearstained.

"Brita will not help you in your plan to unite the tribes," Jura said. "She hopes to join forces with the Irials and conquer the whole of Lanconia, and when all is hers, she will turn on the Irials. I tell you that she hates the Irials. Thal killed her husband."

"She will have a new husband now," Rowan said coolly, "and a lusty one will drive away her memories of a dead one."

"If she does not displease you and you make no vows to God," Jura said. "You brag of your vigor but I have seen none of it. Perhaps I should pity Brita, but I am more concerned with what you will do to our country. Too many people trust you. And now you are fool enough to trust her."

"Perhaps you are merely jealous," he said.

"Of what? I have been married to you and I know the loneliness of that marriage. Perhaps I should warn Brita that you are without substance." She swung into the saddle of her horse and looked down at him. "You are useful to her now, so you are safe, but watch your back for her blade when she thinks you are of no more use to her."

Jura rode to the edge of the clearing and turned and watched the Vatells as they also watched her. Brita, this time in a gown of yellow wool with a circlet set with rubies about her head, emerged from the peasant's hut and mounted her horse. Rowan rode to her side and Brita threw a look of triumph toward Jura as she extended her hand and Rowan kissed it.

Jura turned away and urged her horse forward. She dreaded the long journey home and she dreaded the looks on people's faces when Rowan announced he was setting her aside. It would be easy for him to do. All he had to do was say she was unpleasing to him, and if Jura were examined and found to be a maiden, he would have no problem in having the marriage dissolved.

But Jura knew that if Rowan set her aside Daire would not be able to marry her. She could marry a lesser man but not a prince like Daire, for she would be tainted goods. But she would not tell Rowan that. Better that she had some pride, and if he did not want her, let him think another man did.

\* \* \*

Rowan rode beside Brita while Jura rode behind them surrounded by Vatell guardsmen, the quiet, subdued Vatell people in the rear.

Brita was looking at Rowan as if she were starving and he were a royal banquet, and he found her stares unnerving.

"How did ugly old Thal breed something like you?" she said seductively, looking at his hair as if it were gold.

"My mother's people were quite fair," he said quickly. "Your son, Daire, will no doubt come to the wedding festivities. You must be looking forward to seeing him."

"I am looking forward to seeing all of you. That will be our wedding night also."

"And Jura's to Daire," Rowan said under his breath.

Brita laughed. "She will not be allowed to marry my son. My son is a prince. Perhaps, if he is strong enough, he will succeed me. He will not put a woman on the throne beside him who has been once rejected by a king. Why, the girl is so undesirable she cannot get a lusty man like you to bed her. She is a useless female."

Rowan opened his mouth to defend Jura but he thought better of it. He smiled at Brita. "But Daire loves her and she him. They were children together and I think they mean to have each other." He tried to keep the resentment out of his voice.

Brita gave him a calculating look. "Do you care for this woman who you refuse to bed? It is Irial law as well as the law of all Lanconia that if a woman is set aside because she is not pleasing to her husband then she cannot marry a man of the highest rank. My son is a prince and has never been married. Jura cannot become his wife."

"Jura does not know this," Rowan said.

Brita laughed. "Of course she does." Her face changed. "Do you mean to go back on our bargain?" She halted her horse, and there was much noise and confusion as the people behind them also stopped. "If you mean to keep this woman, tell me now," she said, her eyes sparkling hatred. "I do not mean to surrender my people to some English king and his Irial bride. Either I am to be queen of all Lanconia or I return now to my own city."

In that instant, Rowan knew Jura was right: Brita meant to rule all of Lanconia and she meant to do it alone. A woman who left her own son in the hands of the enemy would have no qualms about killing a husband who stood in the way of her goal.

He smiled radiantly at her and reached out to take her hand and kiss the palm. He looked at her through his lashes and lowered his voice. "Have a child when I can have a woman?" he asked. He watched as Brita calmed and he realized how great her vanity was. Jura was half Brita's age and, to Rowan's eyes, twice her beauty, but Brita was ready to believe that a man would choose her over Jura. Perhaps Brita's experience and power would appeal to some men, but Rowan did not want to compete with his wife.

Brita smiled and urged her horse forward. "We will make a good pair, you and I. Perhaps we will not wait until the wedding night to taste of each other."

Rowan smiled at her but the smile did not extend to his eyes. "Tell me how a woman as beautiful as you came to command the Vatells." He guessed right in thinking that the woman would love to talk about herself. She droned on with a hundred, "And then I's" and gave Rowan time to think.

So! Jura could not marry Daire and she well knew it.

"Magnificent," he murmured to Brita.

If Jura could not marry Daire, then she wanted out of her marriage to Rowan for another reason, either to give Rowan his freedom or because she truly hated him. But Rowan could not believe she hated him. She could not react to his touch as she did if she hated him.

"You are as intelligent as you are beautiful," he said to Brita.

Was it his vow to God? Rowan thought. Surely she understood knightly vows. Every Englishwoman understood them. Englishwomen wanted knights to make vows to them.

But Jura was not English.

Rowan almost halted his horse when he thought of this. If Jura did not understand his vows, why did she think he did not bed her?

Brita put her hand on Rowan's arm. "So strong," she murmured. "We will do well in bed together. There is nothing . . . wrong with you, is there? You can pleasure a woman in bed, can you not? It is just that wife of yours who displeases you and not all women?"

Rowan blinked at Brita a few times. "I can bed a woman," he answered.

"No injuries? Not even in your English tournaments?"

"No," Rowan said softly. "No injuries." He wanted

to tell her, as he told everyone, that he was Lanconian, but suddenly he felt more English than Lanconian. He had made an English vow to a Lanconian woman.

Brita kept talking but Rowan didn't listen to her. More than anything in life he wanted to go to Jura and talk to her but he dared not offend Brita. He and Jura were two Irials amid a few hundred Vatells and he was not stupid enough to anger their leader.

At noon they stopped to rest and eat. The young Vatell men and women, some of the women still crying, were given coarse bread and water while Brita and Rowan were served a feast on a white cloth. Rowan could hardly eat. He looked for Jura but she was nowhere to be seen.

After the meal he excused himself as if to make a private trip into the forest but he was no sooner in the forest than he fell to his knees and began to pray.

"You have helped me, God," he said in little more than a whisper, "and now I need You again. I want Your forgiveness. Lord, I am merely a man, a foolish man who makes foolish mistakes and I have made one now. I have sworn to You that I would not touch my wife unless she begged me. But I have also sworn to love, honor, and cherish her until I die. I can't keep both of my vows and, Lord, I ask You to release me from the first stupid vow, the one made by an angry boy, not by a man meant to be a king. Lord, I humble myself before You. I will do penance. I will rule this country to the best of my ability and I will even bring the Ultens to Christianity, but I beg You to release me from this childish vow."

When Rowan finished his prayer and opened his eyes, the forest seemed unnaturally quiet, as if he were completely alone in the world. Then he heard a noise to his right, a branch breaking, and he went toward the sound.

Jura stood there, her knife drawn, waiting for him. "Oh, it is you," she said, and wiped her bloody knife on the grass.

"What are you doing?" he asked, smiling at her. He was very glad to see her, for her bloody knife seemed much less dangerous than Brita's glittering eyes and her never-ending stories about herself.

"I have killed six rabbits and I am sneaking them to those farmers." She stood up straight and looked at him. "Or do you plan to tell Brita that I am doing this evil thing? These woods are hers and she hangs poachers."

"I will not tell," he said, still smiling as Jura shoved the dead rabbits into a bag.

"Why are you smiling? Do you anticipate your marriage to her already?"

Rowan reached out and grabbed her to him. He hadn't held her in a while. She was too much temptation to him and he knew touching her would make him forget his vow. "You are my answer from God," he said. "I asked God to release me from my vow and here you are, alone, where I am. It is the answer to my prayer."

She pushed at him. "You are mad. And you seem to have an extraordinarily intimate relationship with God. Does He talk to you at night in little voices? Or perhaps you see Him now and again?"

Rowan chuckled and held her against him. "I am released from my vow. Jura, we can be man and wife."

She quietened in his arms then pulled her head away to look at him. "You are to marry Brita and I am to marry Daire."

"You cannot marry Daire and you know the law as well as I do now. Did you hope to help Lanconia by getting rid of me or did you just want out of our marriage?" He began to kiss her neck.

"Release me. I cannot think when you . . ."

"When I touch you? When I make love to you?" He was moving his hands up and down her body, that wonderful body that he had dreamed about. During the Honorium he had thought of nothing else but holding her and caressing her. He wanted to kiss away her bruises.

Jura had her head back and her eyes closed. "Leave me and go to Brita," she whispered huskily.

"I do not want Brita. I have never wanted Brita. I have always wanted you and only you. Tonight, Jura. Tonight I will come to you. We will make camp and an hour later I will come to you. You will not be a maiden after tonight. And, most important of all, you will stay married to me." He managed with difficulty to pull away from her. His body ached for hers. Her lips were soft, her eyes soft.

"Do you jest with me, Englishman?" she asked quietly. "You will lose Brita if you come to me."

"I have never wanted her. Jura, believe me, I want only you."

"I do not know if I can trust you."

"You can. I swear to you that you can trust me with your life. Now go and give your rabbits away. I do not want to anger Brita's army and get ourselves slaughtered before tonight. Go, my love."

Jura's confusion showed on her beautiful face but she obeyed him as she grabbed her rabbits and left him.

Rowan stood there smiling rather fatuously and

thinking of the approaching night when he heard a
step not far away. Instantly, he slipped behind a tree
and watched. He saw a flash of brilliant yellow then
nothing else.

He leaned against the tree. Brita, he thought. She
had followed him and no doubt seen him with Jura.
His senses had not been alert when he was touching
Jura and he had not been aware of Brita sneaking
through the forest to spy on them. She had been too
far away to hear them but she must have seen them.

Suddenly, Rowan grew fearful. What would a
power-hungry woman like Brita do to a child like Jura
who was in her way?

As silently as he could, he began to follow Brita. As
he moved around a tree, he halted then hid. Brita was
talking in a secret way to one of her guard. The man
nodded and disappeared into the trees while Brita
went back to the camp.

Rowan followed the guard. The man slipped
through the trees along the edge of the camp and
watched the people in the camp. He stopped and
crouched and Rowan moved to see what this man saw.
Jura was in plain view as she moved among the Vatell
people.

Rowan watched in horror as the guardsman drew a
bow and arrow and took aim at Jura. Rowan did not
think of the consequences of what he did; he only
acted. He drew his knife, threw it, and sank it into the
back of the man's neck.

The Vatell guard fell dead without a sound.

Rowan knew he had to get rid of the man's body
quickly. He pulled his knife out of the man, picked up
the body, draping it over his shoulder, and ran toward
a small stream. He managed to hide the body under a

rotting log. After checking that no part of the dead man was exposed, he went back to camp.

Brita was waiting for him, and although her lips smiled, her eyes glittered angrily. "You were gone a long while."

He grinned boyishly. "I saw my wife," he said honestly, hoping to diffuse her with the truth. "I had to soothe her."

"And *how* did you soothe her?"

He moved closer to Brita. "The way I always soothe women. With my arms and my lips. Is that not the way you like to be soothed? Tell me now so I'll know when we are married."

"*Are* we to be married? If you spend your time with your wife, perhaps—"

Rowan leaned forward and kissed her. He could feel the woman's excitement and he would have been flattered except that he knew she wanted him as a king and not as a man. "Jura is the sister of a man some say should be king. If she is angered, or worse yet, if she is harmed in any way, Geralt would raise an army. I do not want us to be killed before we have even tried to unite the tribes."

Brita frowned. "Perhaps," she said, "but I do not like to share what is mine." Her head came up. "I must see to something," she said, and hurried away.

Rowan closed his eyes for a moment. No doubt she was going to see if her guardsman had killed Jura as she had ordered. He wondered what she would think when Jura was alive and the guard was nowhere to be found. No doubt she would know exactly what had happened or at least she would suspect.

How right Jura had been, Rowan thought with a sickness in his stomach. She had warned him from the beginning of Brita's treachery, but he had been so sure that he had known what he was doing that he had gone alone into Vatell land. Now his own life and Jura's were in danger. They were sitting in the midst of their enemy and leading them toward the unsuspecting Irials.

Jura was right: Rowan had led them to this by his arrogance and superiority.

Now he had to get them out of this. He had to quell Brita's suspicions long enough to get them closer to Irial land, then he and Jura could escape. Or perhaps he could somehow hold off Brita until after the Irials and Vatells had married, but however he did it, he must make Brita think he wanted her if he was to keep Jura safe.

His insides clutched together. And that meant he could not meet Jura tonight and spend the night with her. He had to stay within sight of Brita or she might send someone else to kill Jura.

Wearily, Rowan mounted his horse. It was time to ride.

# Chapter Eleven

❧❦❧

JURA MADE SURE Rowan saw her leave the camp that night and she did not go far, but he did not come to her. She moved to sit where she could watch Brita's tent. Rowan had entered but he had not left.

She tried to control her rage by telling herself that she never expected him to keep his word, but it didn't help her much. At dawn her eyes were red and her heart felt as if it had turned to stone.

She mounted her horse to ride and twice she felt Rowan's eyes on her, but she didn't look at him.

At midday she saw Rowan dancing attendance on Brita, popping a morsel of bread in her mouth. When Rowan looked up and saw Jura, she turned away.

That night was their last night before reaching Irial land. Jura tried to keep her mind empty of thoughts as she settled into her blankets to sleep. She was awakened in the middle of the night by one hand held over her mouth and another one clamped on her right hand, in which she already held her knife.

"It is me," Rowan said into her ear.

Jura increased her struggles and was pleased when

she heard a painful exhale of breath from Rowan, but the next moment she lost consciousness as Rowan's fist clipped her jaw.

She woke to find herself lying on the bank of a stream, Rowan pressing a cold cloth to her face. She started to rise but he pushed her back to the ground.

"Jura, please be quiet. Does your head hurt?"

"From your soft blow?" she asked, lying, for her head was pounding. "What do you plan to do now? Rid yourself of me permanently? Perhaps your beloved Brita has decided I am too much of a risk."

"Yes she has," Rowan said solemnly. "She saw us together yesterday and she sent one of her guard to follow you. He had an arrow aimed at you when I sank a knife into the back of his neck."

Jura blinked at him in the darkness.

"I could not come to you last night," he continued, "for she had me watched."

"So you stayed and fed her and kissed her and—"

Rowan kissed her mouth to keep her from talking, as his hand moved down to her breast. "I have a plan," he murmured, his mouth against her neck. "I am going to take Brita to Brocain. I think they might like each other."

He had untied her belt and was easing her tunic over her head. "Brita's army fought Brocain's once and Brita won," Jura said, but her mind wasn't on her words. "Do not do this to me," she whispered.

"Jura," he whispered, "don't you realize that I love you?"

"Love?" she asked, startled. "If this pain is love, give me hate."

Rowan pulled her tunic over her head and began to

kiss her breasts. He knew he could be missed at any moment, that Brita might wake and see that the cot she had had placed near hers in the tent was empty, and she would send her guard searching for him. But right now his need to give to Jura overcame his fear.

Jura cried out in pain as he first entered her. She was a virgin and tight with anger, as well as being hindered by her trousers pinning her legs together. She pushed at him but he seemed oblivious to her pain.

There were tears in her eyes when he collapsed on her body.

"Get off of me," she said, shoving at his shoulders.

He drew back, rolling off of her as he adjusted his clothes and Jura angrily pulled hers on.

"Jura," he said, "it will be better."

"It could not be worse," she snapped, her voice strained. The lower half of her body ached with pain. "Had I known what this was like, I would have given you to Brita at sword point."

"Damn you!" he said fiercely as he stood. "I have risked both our lives by coming to you tonight and now you are no longer a maiden. I will not marry Brita." He bent and grabbed her chin in his hand. "I swear that I will make you love me, Jura. If I have to chain you to me, you will love me and you will enjoy what we did tonight."

"Never," she said, looking up at him with fury in her eyes.

They didn't speak as Jura adjusted her clothes and went back to the camp, Rowan not far behind her. She didn't sleep much that night, and the next morning she was so sore, it hurt to sit her horse. She watched

Rowan with Brita with much less concern than she had the day before.

It was late in the day when they reached the river that was the border to the Irial land. Jura waited, surrounded by Vatells, while Rowan came toward her.

"We will cross the river alone while the Vatells wait here," he said without softness.

Jura answered him in kind with a cool nod and urged her horse ahead to follow him. They rode alone together without speaking as they forded the river. Just on the south side, they were met by a group of angry Irials who surrounded these trespassers wearing the Vatell clothes. But as soon as they saw Rowan's golden hair, they lifted their swords in salute and rode with them toward the Irial village.

It was night when they reached the village and, tiredly, Jura slipped from the saddle.

"Come with me," Rowan said, grabbing her arm.

"I am hungry and—"

"You can eat later, now I must meet with my men."

"Your Englishmen are probably sleeping by now."

"My *Lanconian* men," Rowan emphasized, pulling her with him.

Daire was just coming out of a stone house, his broad, muscular chest bare, and Jura would have run to him if Rowan hadn't kept such a fierce grip on her arm.

"Follow me," Rowan commanded Daire, and then kept walking as if he expected to be obeyed. When he saw Cilean, he ordered her to follow him also. He led the three of them into Jura's aunt's house.

By now the village was beginning to waken but Rowan told Jura's family to go back to their beds. He lit a candle in the farthest room of the stone house and turned to Jura, Cilean, and Daire, who were seated.

"I have Brita and a hundred and fifty Vatells waiting for me across the river," Rowan said. "I have brought them here to marry with the Irials. Brita agrees to marry her tribe to the Irials but only on the condition that she marry the king."

Cilean's eyes opened wide as she looked at Jura, who was studying her hands in her lap.

Daire was on his feet instantly. "I will take Jura. I will rule the Vatells and she will be my queen."

Jura smiled at him gratefully.

Rowan put himself between the two of them and looked Daire in the eyes. "I will not marry Brita. I will not set aside Jura." His brows drew together. "Jura is no longer a maiden and I will not discard her."

Daire sat down on a stool near Cilean and he looked despondent.

Rowan walked away. "I think I can put Brita off until some of the marriages take place, then I will take her to Brocain and he can marry her."

"You want to marry my mother to that brutal, scarred old man?" Daire shot at Rowan.

Cilean put her hand on Daire's arm. "Brocain has a wife. She was twelve last year. He won't give up his child for a woman of Brita's years." She thought for a moment. "But Yaine has no wife," she said, referring to the leader of the Fearens.

"He must be lusty and *very* healthy to satisfy that woman," Rowan said.

"My mother is a queen," Daire said. "You cannot order her to marry one of those Fearen runts."

"Your mother ordered Jura's death," Rowan said,

then his jaw tightened as he saw the fury in Daire's face. He turned away. "I am taking Brita to this Fearen leader and I need help."

Jura looked up at this. Was this the same man who rode into Vatell country alone?

"I am going to have to take her by force, but I must make it look as if she is willing to go. I cannot start a war because of this woman. She has strength and that strength must be diluted."

"She might unite with Yaine against the Irials," Cilean said.

"But I hope to have the Irials and Vatells mixed at that point," Rowan said tiredly. "She may well have a much smaller army to lead by then. She has come with her guard, and I hope some of the Irial trainee guardswomen will marry them. A man will think twice before angering his wife—as I well know." He rubbed his hands over his eyes. "Daire, I want you and Cilean to go with Jura and me as I take Brita into Fearen land."

Cilean looked at Jura. "You want two women with you?" Cilean asked.

"Daire and I need our backs protected," he snapped, then his head came up.

Cilean smiled at him. "Yes, I understand. I will go with you, but will Yaine accept us? Or do we wear disguises?"

"I plan to send a messenger, a Poilen or Ulten. I will tell Yaine that I bring him a royal bride."

Before anyone could speak, the door burst open and in ran Lora, looking beautiful in a robe of deep garnet-red velvet, her fair hair hanging down her back. "Rowan," she cried, and ran to him to put her arms about his neck. "I was so worried about you. Montgomery said you had gone for a love tryst but I knew that wasn't so. What have you done? Are you hurt?"

Rowan was smiling tenderly at her as he smoothed her hair back and kissed her cheek. "I went into Vatell territory and I have brought back Brita and her people to marry the Irials. You shouldn't have worried so."

"But I did. You had to do something like that alone with no one to help you and you had the added burden of a woman to protect."

Jura came out of her seat at that, but Rowan spoke first.

"Jura was no hindrance," he said, and hugged Lora to him as he looked over her shoulder at Jura. "She even helped me at times."

"Uncle Rowan?"

Everyone in the room turned to look at a sleepy Phillip, dressed in his long white gown and nightcap, standing in the doorway and rubbing his eyes. "You are home," the boy said.

Rowan released his sister and knelt to open his arms to his nephew.

Phillip started toward his uncle, but when he saw Jura sitting to one side, he smiled and went to her. She picked up the boy and cradled him in her arms. He smiled and fell asleep.

"Of all the—" Lora began, but Rowan stopped her.

"Let him be," Rowan said. "I for one would like to go to bed. We shall make plans in the morning." He started to take his nephew from Jura but she held the boy fast.

"He will stay with me tonight," Jura said as if daring Rowan to contradict her.

Anger showed in his eyes because he knew Jura did not want to spend the night in his bed. He straightened and left the room, pulling Lora with him.

Cilean went to Jura. "I see that things have not changed with you two. I had hoped . . ."

"There is no use to hope. He is English and he will never learn our ways."

"Hmmm," Cilean said. "Before he left he wanted no woman with him, but now he wants two women to guard the backs of the men. It seems that he is learning some of our ways."

Jura stood, carefully holding Phillip so as not to wake him. "Do you have a place the child and I can sleep? Tomorrow the Irials will meet Brita and everyone will need strength for that."

Cilean nodded and led her friend to another house where a bed awaited her.

Jura woke in the morning to Rowan roughly shaking her. "I am leaving now to get Brita and the Vatells. As my wife you must be there to see them marry."

"And see the beginning of their misery," Jura mumbled, holding on to Phillip as the boy began to wake.

Rowan left her alone while she dressed. Lora came to get Phillip and did not speak to Jura.

As soon as Jura left the stone house, she felt the tension in the air. There was no one in sight and the village had a strange deserted air about it, as if God had decided to take all the people away with Him to heaven. Jura took a piece of bread from a table and ate it as she walked toward the river.

What she saw was an eerie sight. All the Irials, freshly washed and in clean clothes, were lined up along the riverbank. No one was speaking, not even a child was crying or a dog barking as they watched the arrival of the Vatell men and women.

The Vatells rode horseback, sometimes double, or came in wagons or little carts. Jura had seen them crying for nearly a week at the hideous prospect of having to marry the Irials, but there were no tear-stained faces now. The Vatells were also washed, their clothes still damp from cleaning, their hair slicked back from early-morning bathing. They sat erect on their horses or wagons and they were looking intently at the people standing across the river.

Jura moved forward to stand just at the back of the Irials.

"See the one in the third wagon," a woman near Jura whispered. "If I were choosing, I would choose him."

"No," a younger woman whispered, "the one I want is there on that black horse. See his calves? There is strength in that body."

Smiling, Jura began to walk along the back of the long row of people. The people were beginning to talk and all the talk was of bedding.

Jura thought the day seemed to be growing warmer than usual. In fact, little beads of sweat were beginning to form on the back of her neck and on her upper lip. For some reason, she began to remember vividly that day she had first met Rowan, that day when she had been wearing only her tunic and he had worn only a loincloth. She had sat on his chest and his hands had traveled up her legs, up toward her breasts. And his mouth had—

"Jura!"

She came out of her daze to turn and look at Cilean.

"You are far away," Cilean said softly. "And who would you choose?"

Jura looked at the people now fording the river. Rowan rode beside Brita. A few weeks ago she had hated his blond hair and white skin but now he stood out like a single star in a black sky. He not only had different coloring but he was broader and thicker than the Lanconians. Once she had thought him fat and ungraceful, but she knew his body to be the product of years of muscle-building exercise and that there was no fat on him. She also knew how his skin felt under her fingertips.

Cilean's laugh made Jura blink.

"He may displease you elsewhere but he does not displease you in bed," Cilean said knowingly.

Jura turned away. "He is a clumsy oaf," she said, but she felt damp with perspiration. "Has food been prepared for these people? We have had a long march and they are hungry and tired."

"Yes," Cilean said, laughing. "They look as hungry as our people. Rowan says the tribes are to spend the day together and near sundown we will choose mates."

"We?" Jura asked. "You plan to marry tonight too?"

"If I see someone I like. There are a few guardsmen who look interesting, but I want to go with Rowan to Yaine and I do not relish leaving a new husband behind. Come, let's get these people to work. The morning fires haven't been lit."

Jura was glad for the distraction. She did not want Rowan to see her watching him, and when he rode past she was ushering people away from the river and toward the houses.

It was a strange day. Never before had Vatells and Irials spent time together in peace. There had been conferences between leaders, even, once, it was told, generations ago, the Vatells, the Irials, and the Fearens had united to fight the Huns. But at the end of the battle the Fearen king's son had killed the Vatell king's brother and their victory had turned into a bloody battle among themselves, with the tribes of Lanconia hating one another with renewed rage.

Now there were both tribes together in the Irial village. It was awkward at first, with the Vatells standing in a clump together, watching, a little afraid, not knowing what to do. The Irial women were beginning to cook while the men stood guard behind them protectively.

"This has to stop," Jura heard Lora say. She was not far away, near Rowan, as always. "Rowan, you must translate for me, my Lanconian isn't good enough yet. We must get these people together."

Rowan looked up and met Jura's eyes. His blue eyes were dark, the lids heavy looking, and Jura could feel her body once again growing warmer.

"Jura will translate for you," Rowan said.

Lora grimaced. "Perhaps Xante will—"

"*Jura* will translate for you," Rowan emphasized.

Jura didn't like being forced to do her sister-in-law's bidding, but she knew Lora was right, that something had to be done. She doubted that a useless, soft thing like Lora could help the situation but perhaps she herself could think of something.

An hour later, Jura revised her opinion of Lora. Lora began organizing and ordering people about with the authority of the toughest captain of the guard. She sent Vatell women to help the Irial women cook. She sent Vatell men and Irial men out to get firewood. And when she saw a handsome young male Vatell and a pretty young female Irial staring at one another, she sent them fishing—without poles or hooks.

"But how will they catch fish?" Jura asked.

Lora looked at her sister-in-law, her eyes twinkling.

Jura began to laugh then leaned toward Lora and said conspiratorially, "That trainee, the one with the red border on her tunic, the one who fought so hard for Rowan, might like that Vatell guard, the one there near Brita."

"Oh," Lora said, "the one with the broad shoulders and those legs?"

"I've seen better," Jura replied. "About a three-hour walk up that mountain are some very sweet berries. I think they need collecting."

Jura smiled happily when she saw the little cat of a trainee go off with the handsome Vatell guard.

After that, Lora and Jura began to relax together. Jura's life had been so different from Lora's. Jura had spent her time with men, doing men's things. She knew how to sharpen a lance blade to a razor-sharp edge but she knew nothing of cooking and running a household. Whereas Lora had known only the gentler aspects of life, and when her cousins terrorized her, she went to Rowan. Jura would have removed the skin of any man who tortured her.

Lora was frightened by Jura's lack of womanly skills and Jura was contemptuous of Lora's uselessness. But what they began to see that day was how each woman had her own skills. And they were drawn together by the common bond of women everywhere: the need to talk to each other.

As the two worked together, Jura began to enjoy herself. Old Thal would have sneered with contempt if Jura had even mentioned romance, but Lora seemed to glow in the romance of their matchmaking.

"Look at those two," Lora said. "Perfect together, aren't they?"

"She is a weaver," Jura said. "Perhaps we can send them to look at her loom."

"Oh, yes," Lora answered. "You are very good at this, Jura. I would never have imagined you to be a matchmaker. Tonight there will be a clear sky and a big moon and all those newly married couples. They will hold hands and walk along the river. It reminds me of my own marriage."

Jura was staring vacantly into space and thinking that it might be nice to be courted by a man. Daire had given her twenty new arrows when he had asked her to marry him. At this moment she thought she would rather have flowers.

"We'll have Rowan play his lute and sing tonight," Lora said. "He knows some beautiful songs."

"Play? Sing?" Jura said. "Oh, yes, he played for Brita."

Lora gave her sister-in-law a sharp look. "He has not played his lute for you? He has not sung you love songs in the moonlight?"

"He said once I was prettier than a maid we had seen."

Lora was quiet for some time as she studied Jura. "Perhaps I have misjudged you. Why did you not want to marry my brother?"

"Cilean was meant to be queen. She will make a better queen than I ever will."

Lora put her hand on Jura's arm. "I'm not so sure of that."

They did not hear the approach of Rowan. "You girls look as if you are enjoying yourselves," Rowan said in that special, superior way that men have when they are amusing themselves at a woman's expense.

Lora whirled to face him. "Your wife risked her life to win you and you have not so much as played your lute for her," she spat at her brother. "Yet you played it for that Brita. Look at that harlot! She sits there surrounded by the most handsome men and you court her as if you planned to marry her. You should beg Jura's forgiveness. Come, Jura, we have work to do."

Jura allowed herself to be pulled away by Lora and she felt good, oh, very, very good. This Lora carried weapons on her belt too. It was just that the Englishwoman's weapons weren't made of steel. Jura looked at Lora with new respect.

By late midday there was a feast spread on long tables in the center courtyard of the village and the atmosphere was one of excitement and laughter. The sense of anticipation was overwhelming. The children, sensing that something was about to happen, were screaming and laughing and chasing each other, and no one paid them any mind except to keep them from falling into caldrons of soup. The Irial adults watched fondly as the young people eyed one another and giggled senselessly if they should happen to touch.

And there was a lot of touching that day. Girls bent over boys so their breasts touched shoulders. Boys reached for things and their elbows "accidentally" came into contact with breasts. Everyone dropped everything so that there was much bending together, or one bending and coming up slowly to look long at the body of another. There was teasing and laughing and playful slaps, and by the time the feast was ready, everyone was warm from more than the sun.

"Are you available?" asked a tall, healthy, extraordinarily handsome young Vatell guard of Jura. "If our queen marries your king, you will be free." He leaned close to her to whisper and his breath was on her neck. "I can make you forget that Englishman."

Jura smiled at him, her lips close to his.

But before she could answer, Rowan grabbed her arm and pulled her away. "What are you doing? I thought you were with Lora."

"And *you* were with Brita. Have you planned your marriage ceremony?"

He had her by the arm and was pulling her toward her aunt's house. "We must talk." Once they were secluded in a room, Rowan turned to her. "I have told Brita I cannot put you aside until after the marriages tonight. God's teeth, but I hate lying. I will do penance for this. I think I may have a temporary solution to our problems: your brother."

"Geralt? What has he to do with this?"

"While you have been may-daying and matching one lust-filled wench with an equally lust-filled male, I have been observing. Your brother is taken with Brita. I don't know if her beauty interests him or her power. For all I know he plans to join with her and slaughter me. No! Don't protest. It is only conjecture. I want you to tell me if you think he could interest a woman of Brita's appetites."

It took Jura a moment to understand what he was asking. "Do you mean, is my brother a *man?"* she said through closed teeth. "Can he give pleasure to a woman? More than you can," she half yelled. "He has had many women and none of them have complained."

Rowan looked shocked. "Jura, what—" he began, then stopped and stared at her. After a moment, he turned away. "For once, let us not fight. I have told Brita I will not bed her tonight but the woman is . . . persistent. I thought I might do well to supply her with some eager young man."

"You control too much, Englishman," Jura said.

He looked back at her. "I can perhaps control a country but I do not think I can control my wife. Tonight there will be a . . . a strain in the air. There will be many couples in the midst of their wedding nights and Brita will cause trouble if she is not occupied." He stopped suddenly. "This is my concern. I will go find your brother."

When he had left the room, Jura sat down heavily on a stool in a darkened corner. What had started off well between them that first meeting by the water, had now turned to this.

She did not look up when the door was opened. "Jura," Lora said, but Jura did not look up.

Lora looked at the proud Jura slumped in a corner and guilt overwhelmed her. She had not welcomed this woman as Rowan's wife, had made no effort to understand her Lanconian ways. But while Rowan and Jura had been away, she had spent time with Cilean and she had heard the truth of what had happened at the Honorium. Jura had tried to make it so that Cilean could win, but Cilean had fainted and Jura had won by default.

Lora had sought out Daire and asked him about Geralt and Jura and realized that Jura had reasons to believe Rowan should not be king. Jura knew nothing of how Rowan had trained nearly all his life in order to be a good king.

And Lora had wormed from Cilean the truth about where Rowan and Jura had gone. She had fretted and worried every minute they were gone, angry at Jura for being a burden to Rowan. But then he had returned, both of them safe, and Rowan had even said that Jura helped him. Later Lora had made Rowan tell her how Jura had protected his back.

Lora's opinion of Jura was beginning to change. And then, of course, there was Phillip's adoration of Jura. The boy followed her everywhere and Jura never lost patience with his questions, was never curt with him.

Then Rowan had forced Lora to spend the day with her sister-in-law and Lora found herself liking Jura. Jura seemed to have none of the jealousies that the women Lora had known in England did. Jura ignored the way Rowan hovered near Brita, the way he smiled at the woman, even the way he looked at the pretty Vatell and Irial women.

While she and Jura had been matching couples and contriving ways for them to be alone, Lora had thought of matching Rowan and Jura. Of course they were already married, but she had seen no evidence that they shared any secrets or intimacies. They had gone away together as strangers and returned as strangers.

As the day was drawing to a close and the couples were pairing themselves off in preparation for the mass marriages, Lora saw Rowan angrily pull Jura away from the crowd. It was not the gesture of a lover but the act of an angry father with a wayward, defiant child.

Lora's matchmaking qualities came to the surface. She found Xante and told him to have Rowan's campaign tent erected five miles down the river, away from everyone else, in a quiet, secluded place. Then Lora had waited until she saw Rowan storming out of the stone house and she had gone to find Jura.

And now her heart went out to this proud woman who looked so dejected and forlorn.

Lora didn't waste any time. "Come with me," she ordered.

"What?" Jura asked, blinking.

"Come with me."

"Is someone hurt? Someone needs me?"

"Yes, your husband needs you. Lanconia needs a queen. You need children of your own before you completely steal mine, and you need what I have to offer," Lora said.

"I don't understand."

"You will. Now come along. We have work to do."

Jura allowed herself to be led from the room, out of the house and into another house where Lora was staying. Lora had taken over the simple farmer's stone dwelling, and trunks and boxes were piled to the roof. She called for young Montgomery to stop flirting and come and move the heavy trunks for her.

"I am going to dress you in the English fashion," Lora said.

Jura backed toward the door. "I'll not wear one of your tight-waisted gowns," she said. "If we were attacked, I could not fight."

"The only one who will attack you tonight is your husband," Lora said, then turned at a sound from Montgomery. "I didn't give you enough work to do that you eavesdrop on women's talk?" She went toward Jura. "Daire asked you to marry him, didn't he? What caused him to propose?"

Jura smiled warmly in memory. "I beat him in an archery contest."

Both Lora and Montgomery gaped at her.

Lora recovered first. "There is a basic difference between English courtship and Lanconian courtship," she said softly. "I don't believe an Englishman would ask a woman who beat him in an arms' skill to marry him."

"But it is necessary for a woman to be strong."

"It is also sometimes necessary to be soft," Lora answered gently. "And tonight you will be soft. Montgomery!" she snapped. "Have you uncovered that trunk yet?"

The boy, obviously fascinated by the women's conversation, opened an oak, iron-bound trunk. Lora looked through it until she pulled out a heavenly, beautiful gown of deep, dark sapphire-blue velvet.

"It is my longest gown and I believe it will fit you perfectly."

Jura backed away from the gown as if it were poison, but then a ray of the setting sun touched it and she moved closer. She had never seen such fabric and the woman in her ached to feel it against her skin. "I could not wear . . ." she began, but hesitated, then looked at Lora. "Your brother would like this better than my being a good shot?"

"Jura," Lora said with serious intensity, "when I have finished with you, my brother will fall to his knees before you and beg you to forgive him for any unkind word he has ever said to you."

Jura snatched the dress from Lora's hand. "Let us begin."

Lora ran Montgomery from the room and began to dress Jura.

Jura was used to the loose-fitting tunic and trousers she wore as a guardswoman, and she had worn gowns for ceremonial occasions, but she had never worn anything like this English gown. First, there was a tight-fitting dark gold tunic that laced up each side. Lora called the fabric Italian brocade. Over this went the rich, thick blue velvet surcoat that had the sides cut away to show the deep curve of Jura's waist and hips.

Lora unbraided Jura's dark hair and it fell in ripples made from the braids to her waist. About Jura's forehead, Lora placed a simple circlet of pure gold, and on her feet were soft leather slippers instead of the tall boots Jura usually wore.

Lora stood back and looked at her sister-in-law critically. "Yes," she murmured, "yes."

"I . . . I look all right?" Jura asked. "As good as Brita?"

Lora laughed at that. Jura had no idea of her beauty or the power it gave her. To Jura, power was being able to shoot well, ride well, to stand close to a man in battle. But this beauty of hers was a new power altogether.

"Brita is a chamber pot next to you," Lora said, making Jura smile. "I want you to go out that door and go straight to your husband. Don't rush, but let everyone see you, and when you get to Rowan tell him that you will be waiting for him in his tent after the marriages. Don't tell him where it is, let him find out, and don't say anything else except that you will meet him in his tent. If he tries to talk to you about what is good for Lanconia or what must be done with this Vatell queen, merely tell him to bring his lute—then *leave*. Understand me, Jura? Do not let him treat you as a man."

"As a man?" Jura whispered. "I do not think I understand the English mind."

"And he doesn't understand a Lanconian guards-woman. I don't know how you two met before the Honorium, but I'll wager it wasn't when you were beating the men in war games."

Jura smiled in memory. "No, it was not."

"Now go out there and let my brother see you. Remember that you are beautiful. No, better yet, let the eyes of the men tell you you are beautiful. Go on," Lora said, pushing Jura. "The marriages will begin soon and Rowan must preside over them. Xante will escort you to Rowan's tent and my brother will come to you as soon as possible."

"And then what?" Jura asked. She wanted to postpone leaving the house as long as possible. She felt very strange in the tight garments that tangled about her feet, and she was afraid she would trip and fall. And she felt almost naked without her weapons. No knife rode on her hip, no arrow sheath hung at her back. No sword, no shield, no lance filled her hands.

"I will have a supper sent to you and you will sit in a chair with Rowan at your feet and he will play and sing for you. Jura, do not look so frightened. It is not a battle you are going into."

Jura gave a weak smile. "I would rather fight four Zernas at once than do this."

"Go!" Lora ordered, shoving her forward.

Jura swallowed hard and left the little stone house. She knew Rowan would be near Brita and the queen had established herself on a carved chair at the eastern boundary of the public square where she could see and be seen by all. Right now it seemed like a long way away. Jura kept her eyes straight ahead and walked with a purpose.

People began to stop and look at her, and at first she thought they saw her as ridiculous, but as she saw their eyes, she began to gain confidence. The women, even the prettiest women who had had their choice of suitors, were frowning at Jura, while the men . . . The men were gaping.

"That is Jura," she heard whispered as if they had never seen her before.

Jura's shoulders went back and a little smile spread across her face. It was rather nice to be looked at this way, she thought as she slowly made her way toward where her husband must surely be.

He was not far from Brita but at least he was not hovering over her as he usually was. Instead, Geralt was sitting by Brita, his black eyes devouring her. He glanced up at his sister but he did not notice any difference in her appearance and quickly looked back at Brita. But Brita turned, stared, then gave Jura an appraising look, as one would try to judge the strength of an enemy. Her eyes followed Jura as she walked toward Rowan.

Rowan was intently conversing with Daire and was unaware of the commotion Jura's approach was causing.

Daire looked up, saw Jura, then looked back at Rowan. But then Daire's face changed and he turned slowly and stared at her. He had not looked at her like this the day she had beaten him at an archery contest. Then he had been proud of her, but this new look was something altogether different, and it made Jura feel quite, quite good.

Frowning at Daire's distraction, Rowan followed his glance.

Jura's lack of confidence disappeared instantly when she saw Rowan's face. His eyes bugged and his mouth dropped open. He looked to be paralyzed as he watched her come forward.

Jura was astonished as she found herself not walking with her usual purposeful stride, but in a slower way that made her hips move from side to side. Suddenly she felt more powerful than she ever had in her life, much more powerful than when she carried a lance and a battle-ax.

Rowan continued to gape in a very flattering way as she approached him.

"I will meet you in your tent after the ceremonies," she said, her voice low and husky.

He nodded and she smiled, then turned to leave.

"Jura," he called, "where is the tent?"

She looked over her shoulder at him. "Find it," she said. "And bring your lute. I may want you to play for me."

Her heart was pounding as she turned away, but she was smiling. Behind her she could hear Brita demanding that the attention be returned to her, but Jura felt that she had won.

All she had to do was continue her act tonight, she thought with a gulp.

# Chapter Twelve

❧

THE INTERIOR OF Rowan's tent was a sumptuous affair, the walls hung with heavy samite silk, and now there were carpets from the faraway Holy Lands on the ground. English furniture, two chairs, a little table, candle stands, and a bed filled the space. Jura found her face blushing as she looked at the large feather mattress draped with a beautiful embroidered cover against the far wall.

She sat in the tent and waited for the arrival of her husband. Servants came with food and placed it on the table as they gave Jura knowing looks.

"How go the ceremonies?" she asked.

"The bushes and beds are filled with lovers," the man replied, smirking. "And Prince Geralt has claimed that Vatell queen's bed." They left her alone.

Jura was not sure she liked her hot-tempered brother placing himself under the influence of so treacherous a woman as Brita. No man seemed able to handle her. But then Jura thought that perhaps Rowan was handling her rather well. She had said she would not allow her people to marry the Irials unless Rowan married her, but here she was with her people married and she was not united with the Irial king.

Jura was thinking so hard about this that she did not hear Rowan approach the tent. He must have left his horse some distance away.

"Is that smile for me?" he asked softly.

She looked up at him and her smile broadened. "You have done what you said. The Irials and Vatells are married and Brita has only a prince in her bed. Perhaps there is hope for you as king."

Rowan laughed. "I have had to risk much to earn that compliment." He walked toward the little table where the food waited. "May I pour you a glass of wine? This looks to be some that I brought with me from the Frankish lands."

She accepted a tall, golden mug set with rough-cut rubies from him. She tried not to gape at the mug and to act as an Englishwoman might. "Nothing went wrong at the ceremonies?" she asked.

"No." He grinned. "Though I think there was some bedding done before the vows, thanks to you and Lora sending couples off alone." He sat on a carpet on the floor and leaned against the foot of the bed. There wasn't much room in the tent and of necessity everything was very close.

Jura took a deep breath. She didn't know how to be friendly with this man. They had done nothing but fight since they had met. "When we guardswomen have trained very hard, we rub each other's shoulders. Perhaps I can do the same for you," she said tentatively, afraid he might reject her.

Rowan smiled at her with great warmth, and there was gratitude in his eyes. He leaned back and held out his hand to her as she went to him.

She knelt beside him for a moment, still holding his hand, and looked into the deep blue of his eyes. For the first time in a long while, she felt herself drawn to him. Right now Lanconia, Daire, Cilean, her brother's right to the throne, all of it seemed a faraway dream. When she moved, the velvet undulated about her body, and now the candlelight was gleaming on Rowan's golden hair.

"You must remove your tunic and lie facedown," she said, trying to keep the tremor from her voice.

His eyes turned hot and the lids lowered as he looked at her eyes then her lips. He set his wine aside then unbuckled his belt and pulled his tunic over his head. He wore nothing beneath and the candlelight shadowed and highlighted the heavy muscles of his chest. There was a scar across one shoulder and she lightly put her fingertips on it.

Rowan smiled at her. "I wasn't giving Feilan my full attention and he thought he'd teach me a lesson." He clasped her fingertips, then brought them to his lips. "You are beautiful, Jura," he said as he kissed her fingers, then put her thumb inside his warm, wet mouth and ran his tongue over it. He made little nibbling kisses to the inside of her wrist and began to work his way down the inside of her forearm, pushing her sleeve back as he went. "I thought you were beautiful the first day I saw you but now . . ."

"As pretty as your Englishwomen?" she whispered, watching him. "As pretty as the woman you should have married?"

He laughed deep in his throat. "There is no Englishwoman to compare with you." He put her arm down in her lap and looked at her. "If you are to rub my shoulders, perhaps you should remove some of your own clothing."

Jura could feel the blood rushing to her face. She had undressed before him repeatedly, but somehow, now, in the soft candlelight, it seemed different. And, too, she knew that if she undressed now it would lead to another painful episode like the last time. But, somehow, she wasn't afraid. There was just that feeling of excitement that she always felt before a battle.

Taking a deep breath to calm herself, she slipped the outer layer of velvet over her head and she was left wearing only the very tight silk garment. Years of exercise had given her layers of muscle that molded her hips and made her waist tiny and her breasts high and proud.

Rowan, looking up at her, gave a groan that was so heartfelt that Jura smiled. It was frivolous the way this Englishman valued physical beauty but it did feel good to have him look at her so. It was almost as if her skill with a lance didn't matter.

"Jura," he whispered, and held out his arms to her.

It was the most natural thing in the world for her to go to him. To deny him would have been to deny a drink to a man dying of thirst.

He kissed her lips tenderly, not hard or fiercely, but as if he had all the time there was. He played with her lips and touched them with the tip of his tongue. By the time he finished, Jura's body was so fluid he could have tied her in knots. She lounged against his arms, her entire weight supported by him, her eyes closed.

Slowly, she opened her eyes and looked at him. His lids were lowered slightly and his lips were softened from their kiss. She had never seen a man look like this before and certainly not this Englishman who usually frowned in displeasure. But now there was desire in his eyes but gentleness too, and a kind of contentment, as if he wanted to be nowhere else on the earth but here with her. Jura's heart began to beat a little faster. This Englishman said he loved her. Could that be true? Could this expression on his face be love?

He caressed her face with his fingertips, then with his whole hand, his palm against her cheek, his fingers entwined in her hair, then kissed the corner of her mouth, then her eyelids. Jura lay still in his arms, accepting his gentle caresses, but her heart was beginning to beat faster with each second. Who would have thought that this big man who cursed and fought and raged could touch a woman so softly?

He kissed her lips again but this time she kissed him back. She put her arms about his neck and pressed her silk-clad breasts tight against the warm, bare skin of his chest.

"Jura, my love," he whispered against her neck, his lips hot against her skin.

Her pounding heart was beginning to rise in her chest, making its way toward her throat until she wondered if she might suffocate. His fingers touched the laces at the side of her gown, and as skillfully as he might play a stringed instrument, he untied the knots and loosened their hold.

She gasped when his big, warm, callused hands slipped inside the silk and clutched her bare waist. He squeezed her as a playful boy would, and to Jura's disbelief, she laughed in delight like one of the empty-headed girls who aspired to be a guardswoman—one of the girls who was always turned down. But Rowan wasn't disgusted by Jura's giggle as a Lanconian warrior most assuredly would be. Instead, he grinned, his blue eyes twinkling with merriment. "*Jura* ticklish?" he said. "The great warrior Jura *ticklish?*"

She tried to get away from him, but she couldn't move from his hands that held her so firmly about the waist. His fingers began to move, and try as she would, Jura could not control her laughter. She pushed at him but she may as well have tried to push an oak tree down. Torturously, his fingers began to move inside her dress and Jura kept laughing. Helplessly, she fell backward onto the carpet.

When she heard the dress tear, she cried out in protest, but it didn't sound like a serious protest and Rowan's hands kept making her laugh.

Suddenly, he stopped tickling her and looked down at her. Somehow, Jura was nude, or at least nearly so, for the gown was split from neck to knees. Her breasts, even as she lay on her back, stood up high in excitement and pleasure as Rowan, on his knees, straddled her thighs.

His face changed from teasing to serious as he looked at her, his blue eyes almost black, a vein at his temple extended and pounding, the muscles of his chest rigid and pronounced. His nostrils flared slightly as he looked down at her. Then, smoothly, he picked her up into his arms, tearing the last of her dress and hose away, and carried her to the bed.

Jura's body felt alive as it never had before, but she was also a little afraid. "Your sister will not like her gown being torn," she whispered.

He didn't answer as he put her on the bed, then stood over her and stared down at her body. His eyes traveled slowly from her bare toes, up her legs, to her breasts, and at last to her face. By the time he finished his long perusal of her, Jura's heart was pounding in her ears.

He sat beside her, his broad, gleaming, muscular back to her, and began to remove his clothing. He didn't seem to be in a hurry, but more as if he had waited all his life for this moment and planned to enjoy it to its fullest.

He turned back to her, his big body completely nude and stretched out beside her, his heavy, hairy legs against hers, his powerful arms around her, pulling her to him, stroking her back, his hands sliding down to her buttocks. "I mismanaged the first time, but I will do better this time," he whispered before kissing her lips again.

This kiss was different, not so gentle but with more yearning and longing in it—and more heat. Jura's skin was so hot she felt as if she had a fever. She did not want him to leave her, but he did as his head began to move downward, down her neck, across her shoulders, down her arm, where he nipped inside her elbow, then he raked her palm across his teeth and Jura's body contracted with pleasure. He brought his head to the center of her throat, his tongue licking at the hollow there. His hands caught both of hers and held them at her side, pinned to the bed as he began to make love to her breasts. Jura began to moan, her head turning from one side to the other. She could feel sweat forming on her body as she tried to release herself from some of the intolerable heat building in her body.

His head moved downward, his wet tongue touching her stomach, running along the taut muscles, licking at her hipbones.

He released his hold on her hands and slid his hands under her buttocks to lift her as his tongue slid into her womanhood. Jura gasped, her eyes flying open. "Rowan," she moaned.

"Yes, my love," he said, and moved upward to her lips.

Her legs opened to receive him and he slid inside her easily, with no pain, only the most divine pleasure. Jura arched her body, her head rolling back at the sheer ecstasy of this new sensation. Slowly, he pulled himself almost out of her, and Jura dug her fingers into the skin of his arms in fear that he might leave her, but he just slid back into her again in that exquisite, torturously slow way.

She opened her eyes to look at him, and the expression on his face made her skin tighten. It was a look of such supreme, all-consuming pleasure that Jura's heart beat faster.

It did not take her long to catch on to the rhythm of this new sensation of lovemaking. She lifted her knees to better accommodate his deep, slow thrusts. In and out. Again and again. Slowly, gently, smoothly.

It was just moments or perhaps it was days, but Jura began to crave something else or perhaps it was just more that she wanted. She did not know what it was. "Rowan?" she whispered in question.

He opened his eyes to look at her and the fire there made her heart pound.

He changed. Instantly, he changed from gentleness to a wild animal as he roughly grabbed her leg and shoved it around his waist. Jura wrapped her other leg about his waist and lifted her hips as he began to thrust hard and fast. She met his thrusts with an equal force of her own, using her years of training and power to slam together powerfully, building into a crescendo of passion and desire.

When at last she exploded, there were stars in the blackness before her eyes and a roaring in her ears. She cried out as her arms and legs clutched Rowan with all her strength, holding on to him like a log in the sea. She strained against him as he shuddered, his body seeming to be racked with spasms.

For a long while they lay together, clinging with the strength of two strong animals, their bodies plastered with sweat, their limbs intertwined.

Rowan was the first to move his head so he could look at her. "I did not hurt you?" he said with a smug little smile.

Jura did not take offense. Her body felt too good to be offended at any words in the world. "I had no idea," she whispered. "I did not know there was such as this."

He kissed her cheek. "To be quite honest, I didn't either. No wonder men . . ." He trailed off.

"Men what?" she demanded, one eyebrow arched.

"This is why men run from one bed to another. Such pleasure is . . ." He closed his eyes. "Such pleasure is—"

"Mine," Jura said coolly.

Rowan looked at her, smiled, and hugged her to him.

They untangled their arms and legs from one another and snuggled close, their sweaty bodies sticking together.

Jura had never felt this way in her life. It was as if

something had always been missing and now was filled. She turned her head slightly so she could see Rowan's profile in the candlelight. Rowan, she thought, not "Englishman," but Rowan, her husband, a man with a name. She put her hand up and touched his cheek and he kissed her fingertips, his eyes closed, his body completely relaxed.

"Tell me of your life in England," she said softly. She had never cared much about his history or about his thoughts but now she wanted to know more about him.

He turned to look at her as if he were studying her. He smiled at her in a way that made Jura feel a bit soft inside, a softness that had nothing to do with passion.

"There is a cold dinner waiting for us," he said. "Shall we eat while we talk?"

Rowan put his knight's loincloth on, and Jura, having nothing else to wear, put on his big embroidered tunic. It left her long legs bare, and when she saw Rowan glancing at them, she made sure they showed at every opportunity. And the tunic kept slipping off one shoulder, but Jura did not bother to straighten it.

The food was indeed cold but, to her, she had never tasted anything better. They set the dishes on the carpeted ground, and between the free-flowing wine and Rowan's eyes looking at her with great intensity, she felt giddy. His voice—why had she never noticed the golden tones of it before—further intoxicated her.

He told of the responsibility of being king that he had always lived with, how he had rarely been able to please old Feilan or his father.

"You worried that you weren't pleasing Thal?" Jura gasped. "But he talked of you as if you were a god. The son *my* mother gave him was nothing to him. He taunted Geralt with you."

"But he sent instructions to Feilan that I was to do more and more. When I was sixteen and I thought Feilan and I were going hunting, instead, four Lanconians attacked me at once. We fought for hours while Feilan stood and watched."

"You did not kill them or they you?"

Rowan grimaced. "I realized later that they toyed with me, one protecting the other. I cut a few of them but they merely bruised me. Merely, ha!" he said. "I limped for weeks after that, and I was so angry at Feilan that I could barely speak to him. He was a hard, loveless old man."

"But he praised you to Thal," Jura said. "Thal always held you up as an example to Geralt."

"Who now hates me."

"With reason. He is a Lanconian prince while you are—" She stopped because Rowan jammed a large piece of bread into her mouth.

"One night, Jura," he said, with the eyes of a lost puppy begging to be taken home. "One night of peace, please."

She could not help laughing as she bit off half the bread then, on impulse, put the other half in his mouth. "All right," she said, smiling, "you may be king tonight, but tomorrow you must prove to me that you are fit to rule."

"Fit to rule," he said, and his eyes darkened. "I will show you who is fit to rule." He began crawling toward her on his hands and knees like some great predatory animal.

Jura started to laugh, but then his loincloth "accidentally" came unfastened and he left no doubt as to his intentions. Jura's mouth was suddenly dry and this time there was no fear. When she flung the tunic from her body and opened her arms to him, she saw the momentary surprise on his face, but she did not understand it. She had not been raised to be coy, to cover her true feelings with pretense and playacting. She wanted him as much as he wanted her and she did not pretend otherwise.

After his first shock, Rowan smiled happily at her eagerness. There was no reason to go slowly this time, and his passion for Jura was raging. He had looked at those bare legs of hers for two whole hours and he had thought of nothing but mounting her again, but he had been cautious, for an Englishwoman, at least the ones he had known, liked to pretend virginity with each coupling.

But Jura was Lanconian, not English, and she said what she thought, acted upon what she believed, and went after what she wanted. He need never worry about her deceiving him. She would tell him to his face that she believed him right or wrong.

After their first coupling, which he had stupidly bungled, he was afraid she would never want to bed him again, but it looked as if she were about to change her mind, he thought with some smugness.

"Here, my eager darling, let me teach you a few tricks," he said, smiling at her. He picked her up and set her down on his manhood and smiled with pleasure at the look of surprise then grateful pleasure on her face. At least *here* was one area where she was not calling him a fool. Here was one place where he had all the knowledge and she had none.

Within seconds, Jura changed his mind on that. She was strong and clever and lusty and creative in ways Rowan had never dreamed possible. His encounters with women had not been frequent, as old Feilan had believed war training was more important than bed training, and, too often, Rowan's encounters had been with jaded women who wanted to say they had been to bed with the handsome prince. They had forced Rowan to do all the work.

"Jura," he whispered as his hands stroked her long, hard thighs as she moved up and down on top of him. He thought he might die from the ecstasy she was causing him.

Suddenly, he could stand no more, and never breaking contact, he threw her to her back on the carpets and finished with a few deep, desperate strokes, finishing with deep shudders that seemed to come from within his soul. He held Jura so tightly she cried aloud.

"You are breaking me," she said, struggling to make him loosen his grip.

He chuckled. "I will bend you to fit into my pocket and I will take you out only when you are the Jura-by-the-water."

"I am always that Jura," she said, fitting her body close to his.

He gave a jaw-popping yawn. "Perhaps you are used to sleeping on the floor but I am for the bed." He picked Jura up as if she were a child, ignoring the protest she began, but soon stopped, and took her to bed. He pulled her into his arms, drew a cover over them, and was instantly asleep.

Not so Jura. Her mind and body were too full of

new sensations to sleep. When Rowan's breath was deep and his body relaxed in sleep, Jura eased from the bed, picked up his tunic from the floor, drew it over her head, and left the tent.

The night air was cool on her face and bare legs, and she turned her face to the moon. Smiling, she hugged her arms about her body. At last, she was truly no longer a maiden. This is what she had felt the day she had first met Rowan after she had been swimming. And this was what she had never felt with Daire, she thought. If only she could feel with Rowan the safety and serenity that Daire made her feel.

A cool wind blew across her, making her shiver, and she went back into the tent. In the candlelight she looked at Rowan sleeping as bonelessly as a baby, one palm upward trustingly. She must have made a noise, for he stirred, his hands reaching out for something. Me, she thought with a smile, then blew out the candles and climbed into bed with him.

She woke with something tickling her nose. She jumped when she opened her eyes to see Rowan bending over her brushing a piece of her own hair against her nose. For a moment she was startled at the sight of this man in her bed, and when she remembered, she blushed.

Rowan smiled knowingly. "Good morning, wife," he said, and kissed her softly. "And what entertainment do you have planned for me today? I'll wager you'll not outdo yesterday with your velvet dress and leading me to this den of earthly pleasures. Had I known you'd react so to Brita, I would have seen that she attended our wedding."

Jura was not used to being teased. "I did not

plan this," she said indignantly. "Your sister said I should try to look like an Englishwoman in order to . . . to . . ." She gave him a weak smile.

"To what?" he asked innocently.

"Brita had nothing to do with this. If you want to follow that old woman about like her pet dog, that is your choice." She started to roll away from him to get out of bed, but he held her fast.

"Brita is not old. She is a beautiful, powerful woman, and power like hers appeals to a man, especially a king like me."

"She is not so beautiful as I!" Jura half yelled, then saw by Rowan's face that he was laughing at her. Her voice lowered. "Brita is the better off, for I saved her last night from a boring evening." She gave a yawn. "Perhaps she found herself a lusty Lanconian lover, someone as handsome and virile as Daire."

"Daire!" Rowan gasped. "Why, I could break that scrawny, ugly, little—" He broke off when he realized she was giving him some of his own back. "I know how to punish you for that," he said, looking fierce. The next moment he was on her, tickling her until she was squealing with laughter and writhing between his legs.

The writhing made him forget that he was "punishing" her, and in a moment they were kissing as hungrily as if they had not seen one another for a year. The kissing led to a long lovemaking, then both fell into a short but deep sleep.

The rumbling of Rowan's stomach woke them both.

"I do not want to leave here," Rowan said, holding her close to him. "Out there rages the world. No doubt Brita has already declared war on the Irials, and it is my fault for not seeing to her."

His tone was so gloomy that she kissed his nose then her head came up. "Someone comes."

Instantly, Rowan was out of the bed, pulled a cover over his shoulder to cover his nakedness, and grabbed his sword. "Stay here," he ordered Jura. "And I mean that."

He left the tent to await the arrival of the lone horseman, who, when he saw Rowan, increased his pace.

It was Xante and he looked at Rowan—nude but for the wool blanket over one shoulder and trailing behind him, his sword drawn—with amusement. "It is good I am not an enemy," Xante said. "You took long enough to hear me."

"What is wrong?" Rowan asked, his voice heavy and sharing none of Xante's humor. "How am I needed?"

Xante paused a moment before answering, his jaw working. "You are not needed. Your sister has sent you food and clothing for Jura." He raised an eyebrow at Rowan. "She seemed to think Jura's clothing would not last the night." Xante gave a big smile at the reddening of Rowan's face.

Rowan cursed his fair skin and the Lanconian smugness as he took the baskets from Xante. "Brita is all right? She is not angered because I was not with her last night?"

"Young Geralt entered her tent last night and has not yet come out. We Lanconians seem able to do some things on our own, brother."

"Brother?" Rowan asked.

Xante's face turned hard, as if preparing for Rowan's disapproval. "I married your sister last night," he said almost defiantly.

Rowan's grin almost split his face. "It seems we English are not so incompetent. She has you delivering goods and messages the morning after your marriage. Could you not keep her in bed this morning?"

It was Xante's turn to look sheepish, then he smiled. "There is enough food there for two days and there is no need for you to come back. Everyone is . . . interested in each other. There will be many children nine months from today. I bid you good morning, for I have my own children to beget." He waved his hand in farewell and turned his horse away.

Jura came out of the tent wearing Rowan's tunic, a small eating knife in her hand. "So now you have the captain of the guard on your side," she said thoughtfully. "I wonder if Geralt knows of this."

Rowan put two fingers to her lips. "Peace for as long as possible, remember? Do not speak of your brother today, please. Let us eat and make love and swim and sing."

Jura smiled at this. "Can we actually do what we want today? No uniting of tribes nor any other state business?"

"We shall be lovers and do what lovers do. Shall I play my lute and sing for you?"

"I'd rather you showed me that trick you have of throwing a knife. I have tried it but I cannot move my wrist as you do. It would be very useful in battle to be able to throw a knife and kill a man so cleanly and quickly. I could—" Once again, Rowan put his fingers over her lips.

"An hour's knife practice, an hour of singing, and the rest of the day making love," he said.

Jura looked thoughtful. "That seems like an equal

division to me," she said seriously, her eyes twinkling. "Shall we eat first or bathe first?"

"Eat," he said, reaching for her, but laughing, she eluded him and grabbed the basket of food. When his blanket fell away and she saw that he wanted more than food, she ignored him as she sat on the ground and began to eat. But all through the meal she stretched her legs often and bent so he could see down the front of the loose tunic.

It was a heavenly day to both of them, the first they had shared as people, not as enemies. Rowan reluctantly showed Jura how to throw a knife, but he soon realized that she had a natural aptitude for using a weapon and after an hour's practice she was nearly as good as he.

"You should teach my men," he said grudgingly.

"Not that Neile," Jura snapped. "I do not like that man."

Rowan started to correct her but, instead, he said nothing. Perhaps Neile was offending other Lanconians as well as Jura.

For both of them the day was too short. Although they had been married for some weeks, they knew very little about each other, and so much anger had been between them that they could not easily trust. But each of them had been reared to do nothing except train for war. Rowan had had Lora to teach him some of the gentler ways and he had come to believe that was a woman's place in life. Jura had no idea what Rowan expected of her.

They spent the day tentatively trying to please the other, neither of them knowing what the other expected in a marriage mate. Jura wanted to have an archery contest—after all it was what had made Daire ask her to marry him. But Rowan did not like that idea. He wanted to show Jura how to play a lute or to sing some English songs. Jura knew she had a musical sense that was made of lead and she did not want to appear to be a fool in front of him. It seemed that neither of them was willing to do what he knew the other one excelled at.

So they ate and made love and they talked. Rowan listened with some wonder at Jura's story of her childhood. He had been so horrified at the idea of a women's guard at first that he had dismissed the women, but now he listened more openly because he had seen the way Jura protected his back.

"But when did you dance and play?" he asked. "When did you ride out in the fields to look at the spring flowers?"

"The same time you did," she answered.

They made love again that night and slept twined in each other's arms. It wasn't quite dawn when the sound of a horse, coming at a run, woke them. Jura and Rowan rolled out of bed instantly, both pulling on a tunic while they ran toward the tent door. Rowan ordered Jura to stay behind, but she made no move to obey him. She stood beside him, sword in hand, and waited for the rider.

It was Geralt, his dark face black with rage—and across his saddle, hands and feet tied, mouth gagged, was Brita.

# Chapter Thirteen

∽✥∽

"YOU JAPING FOOL," Rowan bellowed before Geralt spoke. Rowan caught the halter of the horse then pulled Brita into his arms. The Vatell queen's eyes were on fire with fury.

"What did she do?" Jura asked her brother.

"It does not matter what she did," Rowan yelled. "You have ruined us with your stupid little-boy temper."

Geralt grabbed his sword as he dismounted and Jura put herself between her husband and her brother.

"You will not fight over this," Jura said. "We will talk and see what can be done."

Rowan hefted Brita in his arms. The rage and anger on the woman's face spelled the end of all his dreams for a united Lanconia and all because of the childish temper of this half-brother of his. Geralt wanted power only for power's sake, not because he meant to do some good with the power.

"I heard her planning to attack the Irials," Geralt said, his voice full of hatred for Rowan. "She slipped from the bed we shared last night—the foolish woman thought I was asleep." He glared at Brita. "It will take more than what an old woman like you can give me to make me sleep," he spat at her. "I followed her. She went to one of her guard and ordered him to find your tent and kill both of you. I killed the guard and then, when this viper slept, I took her."

Jura looked to Rowan. "My brother has saved your life and mine as well. You should not have doubted him."

Rowan was aghast. "He has caused a war because he could not keep a woman in bed with him and I should not have doubted him?"

"You—" Geralt shouted, and advanced on Rowan, sword drawn.

Rowan was about to put Brita down and go after Geralt, but again Jura stepped between them.

"We must *prevent* war!" she yelled. "If the Vatells find their queen gone, they will murder the Irials as they sleep. We must work with what has been done— and it must be done quickly."

Rowan stood holding Brita, ignoring her squirming in his arms, her noise made through the gag, and glared at his half-brother. He was seeing dreams and hopes crumble all because of this boy's uncontrollable temper. No doubt Geralt was angry because Brita could leave his bed and felt the woman was insulting his masculinity.

"Rowan!" Jura shouted, trying to get his attention because all he seemed able to do was glare at Geralt with hate in his eyes. "We must make plans."

Rowan could think of nothing except his anger. Slowly, he turned to look at Jura. "You side with him."

"There are not sides to take," she said. "Geralt thought he was saving your life, and it looks like he was." She turned to her half-brother. "What did you do with the guard's body?"

"I pushed it off Foran Cliff."

"Get it," she ordered, but Geralt didn't move. "Go get the body and fasten it to sit a horse. We will take this queen back to the village and she will tell them she means to ride with us to Yaine."

Brita gave a sharp "Ha!" through her gag.

"Go!" Jura screeched at Geralt. "We need to act quickly before someone suspects."

Geralt rode away, toward the village, while Jura walked past Rowan into the tent. "We must dress," she said, "and put her down."

Rowan, still carrying Brita, followed her into the tent. "Damn you, Jura, you'll not start giving orders again."

She was wrapping her cross garters about her legs. "I should have stood there and let you two fight one another over *her*?" She looked up at him. "Do you enjoy holding her?"

Rowan tossed the tightly bound Brita onto the bed and put his hands on Jura's shoulders. "Could we not be at peace, you and I? Must you always take the side of others against me?"

"I told you I did not choose sides. What is done is done, now we must solve it. We must do something to keep the Vatells from realizing that their queen is held captive." She picked up Brita's feet and removed her belt.

Rowan straightened. "All right, I will take her back to the village and she will tell her men that she rides with us to the Fearen village. We will bring back Fearens to marry into the Vatells and Irials." Again there was protest from Brita.

Jura leaned over the woman on the bed, put her face close to Brita's, and said in a silky voice, "We will have arrows aimed at you, and if you do not say what we want and you somehow escape, I will come after you, and one day, while you sleep, I will creep into your bedchamber and cut the end of your nose off. Never again will you fascinate a pretty young prince." She smiled coldly at Brita and touched the woman's nose with her fingertip.

Rowan threw up his hands in exasperation. "Go get Daire," he said. "The Vatells will believe she rides freely with us if her son stands beside her. We will say Yaine has agreed to see us, and two hours from now we will ride toward Fearen land. And may God be with us."

Jura finished dressing and left the tent to go to her horse. Rowan came after her and caught her arm.

"It didn't last long, did it? Our peace, I mean."

"My brother probably saved your life," she said. "He kept your vicious, lying queen busy so she wouldn't notice you had lied about marrying her, and he killed a Vatell guard who was being sent to kill you. If someone had seen Geralt do the killing, he would be dead now, you and I might also be dead, and there would be a war started. He risked much for you, yet you condemn him."

"You see killing as the only solution. You Lanconians live your lives training for war. I wonder if you are capable of living in peace. You plot and plan against each other so much that—"

"If you despise us so much, why don't you return to

your perfect, peaceful England?" she shot at him. "We do not need you to constantly tell us that we are wrong, that everything we do does not live up to your knightly standards. We have survived centuries without you and we can continue to survive."

"All you do is *survive!*" he said with anger. "Each tribe of Lanconia lives in a prison. You have no roads, no outside merchants, no trade between tribes; you have nothing but weapons and warfare. And you fight me, your own king, at every turn. We had two days of peace and now the Vatell queen lies tied and gagged."

"Geralt should have let the guard come for you," she said, her eyes black with anger. The man was English: he thought like an Englishman, he talked like an Englishman, he reasoned like an Englishman.

Rowan took a step backward. "You do not mean that," he whispered.

"Hear me well, Englishman: I will always choose my country over any single life. I would die now if it would help my country. My brother, who you insult, is the same. You have taken a throne which should be his, but he killed to save your life because he too wants peace between the tribes. We see, more than you ever could, the impossibility of the task, but we are risking our lives to help you, yet you despise us for it."

"I despise your tempers," Rowan shot back. "You think with a battle-ax in your hands. Geralt was angry because a Vatell queen dared threaten the life of an Irial. Geralt thinks only of the Irials, not of what is good for all of Lanconia. He would be a good king of one tribe, but he does not consider himself part of all the country. He should have come to me and warned me. He should *not* have kidnapped the Vatell queen and risked war." Rowan leaned closer to her. "Or perhaps your brother would like this peace to fail. The people would no doubt turn on me and kill me if I had brought the Vatells here and they attacked. Geralt would be king then."

He caught her hand before she slapped him. "Go," he said. "Get Daire and Cilean. We will ride into the Fearens as soon as possible."

Rowan watched her ride away, then went back into the tent. Brita lay on the bed, her eyes watching him as he walked across the room. He drank deeply of wine to fortify himself. He cursed Geralt for his stupidity. Rowan had meant to try to persuade Brita to travel to Yaine's country in peace, and, more important, he was waiting for his messenger to return with the news that Yaine would receive the new king.

Now Geralt had forced Rowan to accelerate his plans and now Rowan had an enraged queen on his hands. And, Rowan thought sadly, a wife who once again hated him. He had proved nothing to her, had made her see nothing of his way of thinking. Still, she assumed her jealous brother was doing what was good for Lanconia and that her husband was an outsider who understood nothing.

Rowan cursed as he put down the empty wineglass. He would have to take Geralt with him into Fearen territory. Jura might believe the man to be interested in his country's good but Rowan didn't trust him. There was something more than anger in Geralt's eyes, something that was greedy and repulsive, and Rowan's instincts told him that Geralt wanted the peace between the Irials and the Vatells to fail. Cynically, Rowan wondered if Geralt had tried to get Brita to join forces with him against Rowan and the woman had refused. Brita would never settle for a boy prince;

she would want only a king who could match her in strength.

If Rowan was right about Geralt, he could not afford to leave him behind so that he could break the fragile peace between the tribes. Rowan had hoped to remain in the Irial village for a month or more and preside over the peaceful union of his people—and over the peace in his own marriage—but now he would have to leave the tribes to themselves.

"Damn him!" Rowan muttered. Geralt had ruined everything, and now the hot-tempered boy would have to go with them. If Rowan was right about Geralt, he would have to watch his back.

His back, he thought with a grimace. Jura would never protect her husband's back from her brother's arrows.

He turned back to Brita. "It's time to go." He pulled the gag from her mouth.

She spat in his face. "My guards will kill you for this. I will never go with you and my people will never believe that Irial son of mine. He was fool enough to be taken by Thal, so what do I want with a coward like him?"

"From what I heard, Daire was just a boy when he was taken and he attacked Thal himself."

"He lost, though," she said. "He was not a true son to his father. My husband was a magnificent man, a Vatell, not an Irial like that puny boy you sent to my bed."

Rowan was untying her hands. "Whatever you think of us, you are going to help us now."

"You think the threats of that nothing whore you married frighten me?"

Rowan wrapped the neck of her gown in his hand.

"She is more than you will ever be," he said, "and if her threats do not frighten you, let me tell you that if you are not a convincing liar to your people and make them believe you *want* to go with us to Yaine, I will remove more than your nose. I will remove your head."

She glared at him, but she made no more threats while he finished untying her. "What has Yaine to do with me?"

"I want you to marry him," Rowan said, pulling her from the bed.

Brita began to laugh. "You are more a fool than I thought. Me marry that brigand? If I did, I would rule the Fearens as well as the Vatells and I would destroy you."

Rowan began pulling her out of the tent and toward his horse. "Perhaps Yaine believes he will rule the Vatells."

"I will kill him if he dares try to take my power," she seethed.

Rowan picked her up and dropped her into the saddle. "Good, maybe you two will fight each other for control and I will be the winner. I hear Yaine has a pretty daughter, perhaps she can marry Daire."

"You bastard!"

He mounted behind her and took the reins. "My parentage is well documented. I think 'fool' is a better choice of name for me. That I may be, for all I know."

He kicked his horse forward and hoped Brita could not feel the pounding of his heart. If this woman made one wrong move, he would have to kill her, and any hopes he ever had of peace would be lost.

Jura rode out to meet him with Cilean and Daire behind her. "We are ready," she said, her eyes cool.

"Where is Geralt?" Rowan asked.

Jura pointed to the ridge just behind them. Geralt sat on his horse beside a Vatell guard—a dead Vatell guard that from this distance looked alive.

Brita's announcement that she was leaving with Rowan to go into Fearen country was met by disbelief and protest from her guards. The protest was what saved Rowan. She was angered that her guardsmen seemed to believe she could not take care of herself.

"I taught you how to fight," she said to one twenty-year-old guard. "Do you tell me now that I know nothing of weapons?"

"You are our queen and we value you," the young man said, "and it is a long way to Yaine's village."

"You are saying I am too *old* to make the journey?" she half whispered. "I am too *old?*"

"Forgive me, my queen, I did not mean—"

Brita turned to Rowan. "We will ride now and I will meet this Yaine and we will see who is old." She swept from the room, leaving her guard standing in stunned silence behind her.

Jura rode third in line up the narrow, rocky mountain path. Rowan was first, then Brita, Geralt behind Jura, then Cilean and Daire at the back. Jura watched Rowan's back even while she watched Brita for any sign of foul play. It had been a harrowing few hours since Geralt had delivered a bound and gagged Brita to the tent.

Jura smiled at the thought of that tent and the two nights they had spent there. But then she wiped the smile from her face, for she could not afford to allow bed pleasure to influence her decisions regarding her country.

Geralt had been rash and impetuous in his kidnapping of Brita, but Jura did not see what else he could have done, except, perhaps, do as Rowan said and give warning first. Jura shook her head to clear it. She didn't know who to believe. But Geralt was Lanconian and Rowan was not.

They rode for hours, putting as much distance between themselves and the Irial village as possible. No one spoke since the horses moved in single file. They would spend two days on Vatell land before reaching Fearen territory, but they did not travel in the open because, except for Brita, they wore clothes of the Irials. The Vatells in the southern part of the country would not have heard of the new peace and Rowan did not want to risk their lives to someone shooting them as intruders.

It was nightfall when they finally stopped, and only Brita looked tired. She had led a soft life over the last few years and the softness was telling on her.

Brita started off alone in the darkness, but Rowan caught her arm. "You do not leave our sight."

"I am a queen and—" She paused and her expression changed from haughty to seductive. "You will go with me?"

He released her arm. "Jura, go with her, see that she stays near us."

Jura left the horse she was unloading and went to accompany Brita into the darkness.

"He will not give me to Yaine," Brita whispered the moment they were out of sight of the others. "He will want a queen beside him while you are—"

"Young and healthy and capable of giving him children," Jura said tiredly. "You can use your wiles on someone else. If my husband had wanted you, he would have taken you. Can you not see that he wants, above all else, to gain peace for Lanconia?"

Brita was quiet for a moment as if judging her adversary. "To rule all of Lanconia : . . Even I had not thought on so grand a scale. How does he plan to kill those of us who had power before him?"

"He does not plan to kill anyone as far as I can tell. The man has an irrational distaste for death. He does not even kill the Zernas."

This bit of news shocked Brita so much that the coaxing little whine dropped from her voice. "He thinks to unite Yaine and me and that there will be no deaths?"

For a moment, Jura felt a kinship with Brita. "He is an Englishman and he has a head made of stone. He also believes God talks to him. I do not understand him at all, but Thal made him king and Rowan has the power until . . . until—"

"Until someone kills him. He is not long for this world," Brita said with finality. "It is good I did not marry him."

She was once again Jura's enemy. "He did not want to marry you. Now let us get back. Tonight you will be watched, and while my husband hates death and my brother ties women up, I have been wanting to try a new knife trick I have just learned. I will kill you if you try to run."

Brita did not reply to this as she made her way back to the camp. She sat to one side while the others built a fire and began preparing the simple meal. She watched this Rowan who was called King of Lanconia but was in truth king only of the Irials. He watched Jura constantly and Brita thought him a fool. He had fallen in love with the girl and thus made himself vulnerable. To be in power one must never love. She knew that all too well. Daire's father had taught her that lesson. She had loved a young man, loved him with all her heart—and Daire's father had ordered him killed. What had enraged Brita so much was that her husband wasn't jealous, he was merely teaching her a lesson. When one loved, one was weakened. Brita had learned from that and she had never loved again, not her husband, not her son who was taken from her, no one.

Now she saw how this Rowan's eyes followed Jura and she saw where his weak point was. He would never accomplish his goal because he was weak.

She looked at the other people in the group. The woman Cilean she dismissed. She was a "good" woman, fair, kind, loving—worthless. The woman Jura had possibilities as a source of conflict. She did not yet know she loved this Rowan and her mind was therefore clearer. And she had no compunction about killing. She had been trained to kill. Brita knew she would have to be on guard against Jura.

Brita looked at her son Daire a long time. He was a handsome young man and she could see some of his father's physical features in him, but she saw none of his father's detachment. Nor did Daire seem to have any of his mother's ambition. Brita did not think she could get her son to join her against this English usurper. No, Daire was as much Irial as he was Vatell.

At last her eyes rested on Geralt, and there she saw what she wanted. He was a man filled with hatred. Brita had to hide a smile when she thought of the simplicity of the boy—for boy was what he was. He had come to Brita on the night of the marriage ceremonies looking rather like a puppy pleading to be liked. He had swaggered a bit and bragged a bit, but he couldn't conceal his fear of rejection.

At first Brita had been furious that Rowan had presumed to send her this boy as if she were a mare in heat and any stallion would do, and then she had looked at Geralt and seen the lust in his eyes and she had thought perhaps she could get information from him.

She had allowed him to think he seduced her. He was an energetic if unskilled lover, and later Brita realized he needed a mother more than a woman. Geralt began to pour out his heart to her when she cuddled him and made sympathetic little sounds. He told of his hatred for Rowan because Thal had always held Rowan up to Geralt as an example of what he should be.

"And he had never met him!" Geralt had shouted. "He compared *me* to a boy he had never met. This Rowan was better than I was because of his weak, English mother. But I was the rightful King of Lanconia and I would have been chosen except for . . ." He had looked away.

"Have some more wine," Brita had said. "Why was the Englishman chosen over you?"

Brita had listened with some awe when told of St. Helen's Gate that Rowan had opened.

Geralt had talked to her most of the night until at last he had fallen asleep. Brita had listened to his talk with only half an ear because she was thinking that if Rowan were dead, this angry young man would become king. How easy it would be to marry this man and be his queen. She would be queen of the Vatells and the Irials, and they could destroy the Zernas and Fearens. The other two tribes, the Poilens and the

Ultens, could gradually be forced out of Lanconia, and eventually Brita would be queen of it all.

But the boy had awakened and followed her, killed one of her best guardsmen, and ruined her plans. He had been rather appealing in his anger when he had tied her up. If he had just allowed her to speak, she knew she could have persuaded him to listen to her, but he reacted like a little boy betrayed by his mother. Only this boy was a large, strong man.

He had made the mistake of taking her to Rowan. Damn that Rowan! He may be hardheaded and believe he is connected to God, but he certainly was clever. Brita had meant to find some way to tell her guardsmen she was being taken against her will, but she had allowed her vanity to get in her way. When she returned, she would teach that guard of hers who was old. She smiled in anticipation.

But now she had to do something to get the young Prince Geralt back on her side. If she could find the right words, the two of them could rule Lanconia together. Perhaps they could take old Yaine, or perhaps she could marry Yaine, take the power and fill the land with Vatells, and then dispose of him.

But first she needed help getting rid of Rowan and that pesky Jura. Geralt would have to help her.

Jura woke an hour before dawn, nodded to Cilean who stood watch, and quietly made her way down the steep slope toward the stream at the bottom. She wanted to bathe some of the travel dirt from her body before the day started. She undressed and washed in the dim light, and she had just her tunic on when she heard a noise behind her.

She reached for her knife.

"Please don't throw it," said Rowan from the darkness, and she could read his thoughts from the tone of his voice. Immediately her skin began to warm.

She let the knife fall to her side and watched as he slowly rose from his seat on the bank. It was obvious that he had been sitting there for a long while, absolutely silent, as he had watched her bathe. The knowledge of this, for some reason, excited her.

He came toward her slowly, his big body and his dark blond hair reminding her of a story she had once heard from a man who had traveled far south and seen lions. Muscles in his big shoulders moved as he came toward her. His eyes were dark, but what little light there was glinted on them. She could feel her own breath coming deeper as her own muscles seemed to expand.

When he was only an arm's length from her, she opened her arms to him and he held her against him. His hands slipped down to her bare buttocks and he lifted her so that her legs straddled his waist. She clung to him as he walked with her, stopping when her back was against a tree, and when she was braced, he lifted her and set her down on his manhood.

Because of her position, she could not move very well so he moved her as if she were a doll. His hands gripped her waist and lifted her up and down while her back jammed against the rough bark of the tree, her head back, her hands on his shoulders, her fingers biting into his skin.

Their coupling was almost violent as he thrust into her with might and Jura received him with desire and wanting as she held on to his waist with all her muscles in her powerful legs.

When at last they finished together, he collapsed against her, pressing Jura between the tree and his heavy, limp body, but she did not release her hold of him.

After some minutes, he lifted his head from her neck to sweetly kiss her lips. "Good morning," he whispered.

She smiled at him. "Good morning to you."

He still held her against the tree as he moved his hands to stroke her bare legs.

"You were watching me?" she asked. "I did not sense you. If you had been—"

He kissed her to stop her words. "I was not. I told Cilean to let no one leave the camp except to come down here where I could watch them."

"But I could have protected myself without—" she began, but he kissed her.

"Shall we bathe again? I would like to join you in the water."

Jura could feel herself blushing. It seemed odd to be so intimate with this foreigner. When he moved her from the tree, she uncrossed her ankles, but he did not let her get down as he held her for a while and stroked her back under the tunic and her bare legs. Then he moved his head back and smiled at her in a way that seemed almost more intimate than their fierce coupling.

"Duty calls," he said sadly. "The others will be awake soon." He let her down and gently pushed her toward the water.

She removed her tunic and once again stepped into the water. Behind her she heard Rowan sigh as if his heart were breaking and Jura smiled in satisfaction.

He entered the water behind her and dove under to wet his hair.

The sun was beginning to rise now and, as always, the first rays seemed to seek out Rowan's golden hair.

"You . . ." she began tentatively, "you seem to know many ways of . . . of joining for a man and woman. You have had many teachers?"

Rowan smiled happily at her, pleased whenever she talked of anything besides war and politics. "A few," he said smugly. "A prince, even a prince of a country as remote as Lanconia, is sought after in England."

"Ah, the women wanted you because you are a prince."

"Were," he said. "I'm king now, but, no, they wanted me for my person."

"I see. They admired your skill on the training field. It is so here. Daire is an excellent fighter."

"No," he said with annoyance in his voice. "The women admired me for . . ." He hesitated.

"For what?" she urged.

"For my looks," he said quickly. "Jura, some women find me to be pleasing to look at."

"You are as tall as a Lanconian, but your paleness is difficult to adjust to. But perhaps all Englishmen are colorless."

"I am not colorless," he snapped, then shook his head. "Jura, will you always make me feel less than a man? Will you always find other men better looking, better fighters or less of a fool than you think I am? Will you ever follow me without question, merely because you believe in me?"

"I do not think so," she said after a moment's thought. "One must always think for one's self. We

Irials are taught to think for ourselves. Would you follow me without hesitation? You have not done so yet."

"Of course not, but you are a woman," he said angrily.

"Do I have less of a brain than you?" she snapped. "I will follow you when I believe you to be right. I will not follow you merely because the sun touches your hair rather prettily."

Rowan looked as if he were about to make an angry reply, but his expression changed and he smiled. "So you do think me handsome," he said softly.

"Handsome does not matter," she answered.

"Oh? Then why did you allow me to caress you that first day we met? I do not think you had ever allowed another man to touch you so. Even your precious Daire. I see the way he looks at you. He no doubt chose you because you could handle a weapon better than any other woman."

"It is how I won you," she said, and started toward the bank.

He caught her arm and they stood together, un- clothed, on the bank. "You are afraid to let yourself love me, aren't you, Jura?" he said softly.

She tried to pull away from him. "That's ridiculous. We had better get back. The others will be awake now and we must travel."

He still held her arm. "*Why* are you afraid to love me? Are you afraid you will lose yourself in me?"

She turned to stare at him. "How romantic your thoughts are, Englishman. Is this part of your knightly training? You are right: I do not want to love you, but it is because you do not have long to live. You walk into situations that your English mind cannot understand, and so far your innocence, or perhaps it is God, has protected you, but you cannot last long. If Yaine does not kill you, someone will soon."

Rowan looked at her as if she had slapped him, but then he began to smile. "I will never accustom myself to your direct speech." He released her arm so she could dress. "I am going to surprise you, Jura, because I am going to live. I am not only going to live but I am going to accomplish what I have set out to do. Before I die I am going to unite the tribes of Lanconia."

She had just slipped her tunic over her head when he pulled her into his arms. "You may deny what you feel for me but they are empty denials," he said. "Your body has always recognized me as its partner; only your mind is not as smart as your body." He began to kiss her, his hands on her back. "You were to marry your Daire—who you respect so highly—but I do not believe he ever kissed you and made you feel as I do. Your mind will come to me, Jura. It is only a matter of time."

She turned her head away from his kisses, but she was not strong enough to move out of his arms. "You should not be king," she whispered. "You are only half Lanconian. I do not understand you. None of us understands you. You should return to your own country before your meddling starts a war."

"And take you back to England with me?" he asked. "Take you to a place where a woman is valued for her household skills and not for her ability to outwrestle other women?"

She gave a great push and moved away from him. "I would stay here. I am Lanconian." Even as she said it, she felt a sudden ache. To never see him again, to never see him smile, to never again see that look that told her she had done something that seemed strange to him. To never feel his arms around her again.

She turned to look at him. He wore only the loincloth of an English knight, and the sight of his big, muscular body with its covering of blond hair made her want to touch him. Suddenly, she straightened. She had to control herself. She had to force her mind to govern her body. She was a guardswoman, not some silly cow maiden who fell in love with the first pair of broad shoulders that she saw. Nor could she afford to follow this man blindly. It was not just herself involved, but an entire country. What she and Cilean, Daire and Geralt did on this trip would affect all of Lanconia. If they acted stupidly or hastily, they could cause the deaths of many people. Whatever she did, she must keep her mind clear. She could love this Rowan but not with the blind love he spoke of. She could never follow him merely because he said, "Come." She must watch and wait and see what he planned and she must never, never allow what they did in the dark to influence what she thought during the day.

She resisted the urge to touch him. "We must return," she said softly, and turned away to finish dressing.

He kissed her once before they returned to the others but she managed to control her reaction to him and keep her head cool.

"It will be easier to conquer Lanconia than to conquer you," he said with a sigh. "Now go on, get up the hill. I fear to leave our brother with Brita too long or she may persuade him to put a knife to my throat as I sleep."

"You misjudge him!" Jura snapped as she began the

climb. "He has been trained from childhood, as I have, in the policies of Lanconia."

"I know hatred when I see it in someone's eyes. Will you protect my back from your brother's knife? Who would you choose if it came to a choice between the two of us?"

Jura stopped at that question for she had no idea what her answer was. Rowan kept climbing and after a moment she followed him. Of course it would not come to a choice, for Rowan would no doubt get himself—and perhaps the rest of their group—killed before he reached the Fearens' city. Once again, Jura felt a little ache inside her breast at the thought of the loss of Rowan, but she managed to control it. She must steel herself for the time when he would be gone.

# Chapter Fourteen

As THEY RODE that day, each step taking them closer to Fearen territory, each person grew more watchful. The road became steeper and in places so narrow the horses shied at having to travel it. They were traveling east toward the rising sun, with the mountains that hid the villages of the Poilens and the Ultens to their left in the north.

No one spoke as they stayed alert for any noise not of their own making. Twice Jura saw Brita looking at Geralt in a hungry way and thought with disgust of the woman's appetites. One day Brita wanted Rowan and the next she wanted Geralt.

Perhaps it was Rowan's words that made her doubt her brother, but she looked at Geralt with appraising eyes. He sat stiffly on his horse, never once glancing in Brita's direction, but something in the way he carried himself made Jura think Geralt was very aware of Brita's gaze.

Jura looked up to see Rowan's eyes on her. He gave her a level gaze that for some reason embarrassed her and she looked away. The man was treacherous! He knew that his words had made Jura watch her brother and now he was making her doubt him.

They camped that night in the crook of the river that was the boundary of the Fearen territory. They did not build a fire but ate cold food then put their blankets onto the rocky ground and settled down to sleep. Geralt had the first watch.

No sooner had Jura gone to sleep than suddenly she was awake. The river was noisy and masked a great deal, but her senses told her something was wrong. She eased onto her elbow and looked about. Brita and Cilean seemed to be asleep and she looked toward the deep shadows in some rocks where Geralt hid and guarded. Rowan had moved his blankets away from the others and she could not see him. She looked at Daire and knew he was awake.

Daire lay where he was but his hand moved to point toward Rowan's place in the trees then toward the narrow trail leading into the Fearens' land. Jura felt her heart begin to beat faster. For some reason the Englishman had ridden alone into enemy territory.

Jura eased out of the blankets, signaled Daire to stay with Brita and Cilean, then crept toward the horses. She knew Rowan would ride directly toward Yaine's city, so she mounted bareback and began to ride, slowly and softly at first then with more speed and vigor the farther away from the camp she got.

She had not gone far when Rowan shot out of the trees on his horse with the fury of anger.

"Damn you, Jura!" he yelled at her. "You are worse than a possessive mother. Go back to the others *now!*"

"You left without protection," she said, her horse dancing about. "And you are in enemy land. Yaine's men will kill you and they will not question whether you are a king with a noble purpose or not."

He seemed to be trying to calm his temper. "I am looking for the messenger I sent. He was to travel along this back road, the road the Irials use to steal the Fearen horses, and he should have reached us by now."

"The Fearens will not let your messenger live—that is, if he ever reached their king."

"*I* am king. Yaine is— Hell, Jura, I don't have time to argue with you. I know you won't return, so ride with me. And watch my back," he called over his shoulder.

She smiled in the darkness as she began to follow him. Perhaps he was learning some Lanconian ways after all.

They rode along the rocky path for an hour, the moon their only source of light, when Rowan raised his hand to halt. When he dismounted, so did she, and as silently as possible they led their horses down the steep ridge and tied them to a tree.

"I saw the light of a fire ahead," Rowan whispered. "Stay close to me and do not do anything foolish."

"*You* have ridden alone into enemy territory," she reminded him. Even in the darkness she could see his warning look.

For such a big man he could certainly move silently, she thought as she followed him along the ridge. And his eyesight was excellent, since they were some distance from the flat place in the trail where the fire burned.

She and Rowan hid behind trees and surveyed the scene for a while before moving. Three men squatted around the fire, gnawing on the remains of a rabbit. They looked tired and their clothes were torn and patched and repatched, as if they had been wearing them for years.

Jura recognized them for Fearens. They were small men, half a foot shorter than the Irials, but as anyone who had fought them knew, they had a wiry strength that was formidable in battle. They were dark men with brows that nearly grew together and their legs had the characteristic bow of the Fearens. It was said that at three years of age a Fearen child was set on a horse and never again allowed off. They were said to love their horses more than each other and that if an Irial on foot met a Fearen on horse, the Irial should pray for a swift death.

Jura turned toward where Rowan was hiding. He was staring at her and he nodded his head toward the distant trees on the far side of the Fearens' fire. She could barely make out the outline of another person, and as she stared, she thought the person seemed to be tied to the tree. She looked in question to Rowan and he nodded. So, here was his messenger, trussed like a goose for Feastday. She couldn't tell whether the man was alive or dead.

For all that Rowan was an Englishman, Jura was beginning to be able to understand him. Without saying a word, he directed her to the other side of the Fearens' camp while he stealthily made his way through the trees toward the man they held prisoner.

It seemed to Jura that Rowan was gone for a long time and she jumped a bit when he at last moved into the shadows beside her.

"They have Keon," Rowan whispered.

Jura could not see Rowan's face but she knew the anguish he must be feeling. Keon was the son of Brocain, the prince of the Zernas, the boy Rowan had pledged his life to keep safe. She thought it was a foolish thing to have sent this valuable young man into Fearen territory as a messenger, but she did not tell Rowan this. For now she would hold her tongue.

Rowan motioned to her that he wanted to take the three Fearens so he could rescue the Zerna boy, and for a moment Jura thought he meant to try to take them by himself. Jura gave him a level look that told him what she thought of his plan.

He grimaced in resignation, then said, "No killing," under his breath and disappeared into the trees.

She sat absolutely still and waited for him to give a signal that they were to begin. Her heart was pounding as it always did before any contest of skills, but now there seemed to be something else. She was worried that Rowan would be all right. She prayed that now was not the time when he would be killed. She offered a prayer to the Christian God, then, just to be safe, she asked the Lanconian god of war, Naos, to watch out for the well-meaning Englishman.

Rowan did not attack in a subtle way, but stepped forward into the circle of light of the fire, his sword in his left hand, and said, "I am the King of Lanconia, put down your weapons."

All three of the tired Fearens leaped up at once and ran toward Rowan. Jura came from the trees behind them and brought the back of her battle-ax down on one Fearen's head. The man crumpled at her feet, and before she could turn, a second Fearen had her about the waist.

He was strong—very strong—Jura admitted as she struggled against the man's hold on her. His arms were forcing the breath from her body. She brought her heels back and her elbows slammed into his ribs, but the man didn't let go. To her left, Jura could hear the sounds of steel against steel as Rowan fought the third Fearen.

The man holding her kept tightening his grip, and Jura tried to keep her lungs open to breathe but she was failing in her attempt. She was losing strength and she could feel herself growing limp in the man's grasp as the pressure continued. Her eyes closed and she felt nothing.

"Jura! Jura!"

She wakened to find herself on the ground, her upper body in Rowan's arms as he slapped her face and shouted at her. She stirred in his arms and tried to sit up but he held her fast.

"Jura, are you all right?"

"Yes," she said impatiently. "If you don't crush me now." She rubbed her sore ribs. "I could not breathe."

"Why did I allow a woman to help me fight?" he said woefully, still clutching her.

She pushed away from him to sit up. "Because I knocked one man out and kept a second busy while you were still trying to subdue the first man." She rubbed the back of her neck. "If we had just sent arrows into them—"

Rowan stood and looked at the three unconscious Fearens on the ground around them. "They are my people the same as the Irials." He turned away to the tree where the boy Keon was, and Jura followed him.

At first the boy seemed to be dead, but upon closer

inspection he was only sleeping very deeply, for the sounds of battle had not wakened him. Rowan knelt to him. The boy was not tied to the tree as Jura had thought. She also knelt before the boy and the smell was overpowering.

"He's *drunk,*" she said with disgust. "He's not a captive, he's merely a drunken boy."

Rowan shook the boy awake.

Keon rolled his eyes, smacked his dry mouth, then smiled stupidly at Rowan. "My father'll be proud of me," he slurred. "I went to Yaine."

"And Yaine didn't kill you?" Jura asked, aghast.

The boy grinned and closed his eyes briefly. "Said I was brave. I told him about Brita." The boy moved his hands to make a female shape in the air. "Yaine says he'll marry her." He leaned toward Jura, his foul breath making her pull her head back. "They will be a funny pair. He's a little man, but then Brita's not as young and pretty as you, Jura. If you had a sister, I would marry her. I would then be related to my king."

Jura raised her eyebrows at Rowan. "Your king? You mean your father Brocain?"

The boy gave her a crooked smile. "King Rowan. King of all Lanconia. King of—"

"Where is Siomun?" Rowan said impatiently, ignoring the way Jura was looking at him over the boy's obvious hero worship. "I sent Siomun to take the message to Yaine."

"I tied Siomun up. I couldn't stay there with all those Irials. My father expects me to be a man—like you. I had three older brothers and they got killed when my father sent them on raids." He leaned toward Jura. "I attacked this Irial king, but I lived. Now I have to do more. I have to prove I can be as good a man as my father and I have to prove myself to you, King Rowan. Have I done so?"

Rowan put his hand on the boy's shoulder. "You have pleased me and, yes, I believe you to be a man," he said softly.

"So you rode alone into Fearen territory," Jura said, then looked at Rowan. "Your innocence is affecting us all." She turned back to Keon. "Why didn't Yaine kill you?"

Keon's expression changed to one of sadness. "They are very poor. Yaine says everyone steals their horses, so they must move all the time. They cannot plant crops and last winter they were very sick. Many died. They need women." Keon's young face brightened. "My father will give them *all* of our women if they want. We will take the Irial women."

"So Yaine accepts us?" Rowan said.

Keon's head lolled to one side as he nearly fell asleep. "Those three are to take you to Yaine. Did you kill them? One is Yaine's brother. For little men, they sure can drink." He closed his eyes, his head falling forward, and went back to sleep.

Tenderly, Jura eased him to the ground. "I never noticed what a handsome young man he was," she said.

"Not colorless like some of us?" Rowan snapped. "Now, if you can stop mothering that child, we had better see to the Fearens. I thank God I did not have to kill one of them."

Jura smiled at him as she patted Keon's cheek. "He is actually about my age, so I don't guess he is a boy. And he was very brave to go to Yaine alone."

"He is brave when he goes alone, yet I am foolish," Rowan muttered, and left her to see to the Fearens.

Jura smiled at his back, loving his jealousy. For all his faults, this English husband had a way of making her feel . . . well, beautiful. Not that beauty was of any use whatsoever but it was a rather nice feeling.

One of the Fearens was beginning to stir as he rubbed his sore head. Rowan sent Jura off to fetch water while he looked after the men. She returned to see Rowan holding a sword on the men while they glared at him. But Jura wasn't surprised when, as they listened to Rowan's explanation, their faces began to change. Jura thought that Rowan's words just might be able to coax flies off dead meat.

When Jura stepped into the light, the men looked up at her and one kept staring. She knew he was the man who had nearly killed her, and they exchanged looks of gratitude that they were both alive.

Jura sat by the fire, behind the Fearens but where she could see if they went for their weapons, and listened to Rowan talk. Idly, she pulled a leg off a roasted rabbit and gnawed at it, then tore off a chunk of stale bread. The fire, the exercise, the safety, and most of all, Rowan's voice was making her sleepy. She stretched out on the ground, sleepily pulled one of the sheepskins that the Fearens used for horse blankets over her, and went to sleep.

She woke, but not fully, when Rowan picked her up in his arms. For just a moment she fought against him but then she settled against him, snuggling her head against his broad, hard chest, and let herself drift back into sleep. She was not conscious of it but somewhere in her mind she knew she was safe. He had done several things that she knew were foolish, but he had made them work. He had befriended Brocain of the Zernas, persuaded the Vatell queen to allow her people to marry into the Irials, and now the Fearens were listening to him.

She opened her eyes. "Do you *really* talk to God?"

Rowan gave her a look of puzzlement. "I am only a man and I need help from wherever I can get it."

She closed her eyes again and went back to sleep. She didn't wake until it was almost daylight. Rowan lay beside her, sound asleep, his big arms wrapped about her as if she were a child's toy. Slowly, trying not to disturb him, she tried to untangle herself.

"Do not leave my sight," he said, not opening his eyes and tightening his hold on her.

"I *need* to go," she said pointedly.

He still didn't open his eyes. "To that tree there and no farther," he said. "I do not want to fight anyone for you today."

She shut her mouth on a sharp retort and went to the tree. When she returned, he was still lying there, still looking as if he were asleep. "We must get back to the others," she said. "Daire and Cilean will worry, and where are those Fearens and Brocain's son? Do you plan to stay here all day?"

His hand shot out and caught her ankle. "Jura, do you not sometimes want to lie all day on the bank of a pretty stream and watch the butterflies?"

She smiled down at him. "Perhaps, but it cannot be done today. Geralt will—"

"God's teeth!" Rowan gasped, coming to his feet. "I had forgotten that brother of yours. He will kill the Fearens without giving them a chance to explain. Mount and ride!" he ordered her.

Jura had trouble getting her bearings because she had been asleep last night when Rowan had carried her from the camp. She hastily gathered their few belongings, mounted her horse bareback, and went after Rowan.

Minutes later she saw that Rowan's fears were justified. Damnation, but she hated to admit even to herself that he was right.

Geralt was always an excellent fighter, but when his temper was aroused he was fearless. He had managed to capture all three Fearens, no doubt sneaking up on them while they slept, and he was now threatening their lives if they did not tell him how they had murdered his sister.

Jura came into the clearing just in time to see Rowan throw a knife that landed in the dirt between Geralt's feet. Jura knew there was going to be a fight. She kicked her horse forward but it was already too late. Even years later she would not be sure what happened next. The Fearens, who had come in peace, had already been attacked twice in a few hours, and their anger was directed at Geralt. When they saw their chance, they leaped, weapons ready. Young Keon, who was roused from a drunken sleep, looked up and saw the confusion, not really understanding who was attacking whom. To him it must have looked as if his beloved King Rowan was in danger.

Keon ran, sword drawn, and put his body in front of Rowan's. A Fearen lunged at Geralt, missed as Geralt sidestepped, and the Fearen's sword pierced Keon's heart. Had he not been there, Rowan would no doubt have been killed.

For a moment time seemed to stand still. Keon fell to the ground without a sound while everyone stood as if frozen.

Rowan reacted first, kneeling and taking the boy into his arms.

"You will tell my father that I did not die in vain," the dying boy whispered.

"I will tell him," Rowan said softly.

Slowly, painfully, Keon put his hand up to Rowan's shoulder. "I have not lived without purpose. I have died for my king." His lifeless body collapsed in Rowan's arms.

"This will mean war," Geralt said with unconcern as he sheathed his sword.

Jura turned to look at her brother and could see the look of near glee in his eyes. He was *glad* of this boy's death, glad of the war to come, glad that Brocain would now kill Rowan. In that moment Jura knew Geralt cared nothing for Lanconia but merely for himself and his own sense of power.

Jura looked at Rowan as he still held the boy, but she could not read his expression. His face may as well have been carved out of cool marble for all the emotion he betrayed. No doubt he too worries about the war, she thought.

Very slowly, Rowan tenderly picked up the boy in his arms and walked with him into the forest.

"We had better ride," Geralt began. "Brocain will—"

Jura glared coldly at her brother. "You will remain here and you will wait for him, and if you harm anyone, I will kill you," she said through her teeth.

"But Jura—" Geralt began.

She walked away from him, through the trees toward where Rowan had carried Keon. Cilean called her to leave Rowan alone but Jura wanted to find him. They would talk about what must be done now that this Zerna boy was dead.

She walked for some time before she found him and

she did not approach him when she did see him. To her, it was a strange scene. Rowan had stretched Keon's body on a rock, as if it were an altar, and Rowan was on his knees before the boy's body.

Jura stood absolutely still but Rowan did not turn to her as he knelt there, his face in his hands. It took her a while to realize that Rowan was crying.

Her body was paralyzed as she watched him. She had never seen a man cry before, had seen very few women cry, but the sounds coming from Rowan were unmistakable. She did not go to him, did not have any idea what one did with a crying man.

She stepped behind a tree and waited and watched. She did not want to leave him, but she did not understand his reaction to the death of a Zerna boy. Was he afraid of the death Brocain had promised him? Did the prospect of war make Englishmen cry?

Her head came up when she heard Rowan begin to speak. He was talking to that God he seemed to believe was his friend. She strained her ears to hear what he said.

"I have failed, God," Rowan said softly. "I have failed my father, my country, I have even failed my wife."

Jura frowned at this and listened harder.

"I begged to be released from this task," Rowan said. "I told You I was not worthy of it. I am a coward and lazy, just as my old tutor said. I cannot unite this country. It is not mine to unite."

He put his head in his hands and cried again. "Jura saw through me. Jura knew that I would fail. Oh, God, I was not the one to be chosen for this. Better that someone else had been born Thal's son. Now this boy has died for me, to save my worthless soul. I cannot go on. I will return to England and leave Lanconia to true Lanconians. Forgive me, Father, for having failed You." He began to cry again.

Jura leaned against the tree and found that there were tears in her eyes also. She never knew he doubted himself. How could he believe himself to be a coward? He had walked against the Zerna alone. How could he doubt that he was the true king after all he had done in so short a time?

How could she have doubted him? she asked herself. What more must he do to prove himself? Why hadn't she sided with him from the beginning? She prided herself on her logic and clear thinking but she had never thought clearly about Rowan. She had fought him every step of the way.

More tears came to her eyes. Was it because, as Rowan had said, she was afraid of loving him? Had she fought him not out of logic but because of a weak emotion such as love? Had she perhaps loved him from that first tempestuous meeting at the riverside? Maybe then she had known that he had the power to take her soul from her.

Rowan was still crying and suddenly Jura knew she had to do something to keep him from leaving Lanconia. She had a vision of what would happen to her country if Rowan were not there trying to unite the tribes. If Geralt were king, he would plunge the country into war.

And Jura would . . . She thought she might die without this man. How used to his soft, tender ways she had become. How used to his strength. No matter how she ridiculed him, how she fought him, he always had the strength of his belief in himself. Now she saw that he had doubted himself all along. Why hadn't she *helped* him?

She looked around the tree at Rowan and saw the slump in his shoulders, saw the defeat in his body. She had to help him now.

But how? An Englishwoman would no doubt hold him and caress him, and Jura was surprised that that is what she wanted to do. She wanted to put her arms around him and let him cry on her shoulder while she stroked that fine hair of his.

And make him feel worse, she thought. To offer him sympathy would be the worst thing she could do. She had to somehow make him believe in himself again.

Rowan was standing now and looking at the body of Keon. Jura felt tears in her eyes again as she looked at Rowan's ravaged face. He did care about Lanconia, not just the Irials, but all of Lanconia, that he could grieve so over this Zerna boy. Thal had been right to allow Rowan to be raised out of the country. Thal had been right and Jura had been more than wrong.

And now she had to do something about having been so loudly wrong.

Quietly, she slipped through the trees, away from Rowan, then turned and acted as if she were just coming toward him. She made a great deal of noise but Rowan did not turn toward her as he merely stood there, his back to her, looking down at Keon's cold face.

She straightened her shoulders. "What are you doing here?" she demanded belligerently. "We must ride to the Fearens."

Rowan did not turn around, and she almost put her hand out to touch his hair, but she withdrew it.

"What is this?" she asked loudly, gesturing toward Keon's body. "You mourn a Zerna boy? Or is it Brocain's wrath you fear? When it comes to war, we Irials will win."

"There will be no war," Rowan said softly. "I will give myself to Brocain. I hope I can appease him."

Jura winced but said, "Good! Then Geralt will at last be king."

Rowan didn't react.

"As he should have been all along," she said, but still got no reaction from Rowan. "But tell me, before your sacrifice, do we go to the Fearens or not? Do we leave Yaine waiting for Brita?"

"It is no longer my concern. I am not Lanconian."

The sympathy she felt for him was leaving her. She frowned. "That is true. A Lanconian never would have started this absurdity of uniting the tribes. It can never be done."

"Perhaps by someone other than me," he said sadly. "I was the wrong choice."

"Yes you were. Geralt will do a much better job than you. He will have no trouble uniting everyone. *He* will not cause the death of innocent boys." She watched Rowan's face and she thought she saw some sign of life.

He turned to look at her. "Geralt unite the tribes?"

"Yes, of course. He will do a grand job, don't you think? Brita has already seen his power and she knows how strong he is. Yaine has only to see it also."

"Brita has seen Geralt's power?" Rowan asked. "But Brita . . ."

"Oh yes, I can see it in her eyes. She fears my brother."

"She means to have him on a platter. She will marry

that stupid boy and rule all of Lanconia." There was light returning to Rowan's eyes.

"What does it matter to you? You will be dead. You will have sacrificed yourself for this dead boy."

Rowan looked back at Keon's body and his face fell again. "Yes, that is true. Geralt will make an excellent king, I am sure."

"If he wins," Jura said.

"Wins?"

"Being married to a king has given me a taste of power. I shall marry Daire and perhaps we will fight Brita for control of her tribe. Perhaps I shall be queen of all Lanconia yet." She smiled. "Yes, I like that idea."

Rowan turned to look at her and the sadness in his eyes began to change. It changed to hate and the hate was directed toward her. "War," he whispered. "War and power are all you Lanconians think of. You would war on your own brother to gain power. For your own selfish wants you would cause the death of thousands of people. You do not care about Lanconia."

"And you do? You would leave what you have started behind and sacrifice yourself to Brocain?"

"I must," he said softly. "I gave the man my word. A knight's word is his bond."

"You are English," she spat at him. "You are English purely and I am glad you go to die. We need no cowards such as you who cannot finish what they start. Go then. Go to Brocain. Go back to England. Go to the devil for all I care." She turned on her heel and stormed away from him.

She didn't go far, just until she was out of sight of him and then she stopped. Great sobs began to well inside her, and before she knew what she was doing, she sank to her knees and began to cry. It was as if all the tears that had been denied her all her life were coming to the surface. Her shoulders heaved, her hands clenched. She fell forward into the dirt and cried harder. She would die if Rowan gave himself to Brocain, but she could not tell him that. He did not need sympathy, so she had not given it. He had needed her anger, but she had not been prepared for the look of hate in his eyes.

After a while, she lifted herself and went back to the camp. The others were sitting about quietly and looked up with hope in their eyes when they heard Jura. But when they saw she was not Rowan, they looked away.

They need him as much as I do, Jura thought.

Cilean came toward her and Jura turned her face away. "You have been . . . crying?" Cilean asked in disbelief. "What have you done to him?"

Jura could tell no one, not even a friend as close as Cilean, of what she had seen. How could a Lanconian understand a man who cried like an infant? Yet Jura had understood. Did that mean she was not wholly Lanconian?

"Merely smoke in my eyes," Jura said. "He will return soon, I think," she added.

It wasn't long before Rowan returned. His hair was wet, as if he had been bathing, and he ordered everyone to prepare to ride. The Fearens stood apart, and Rowan went to them and talked quietly for a long while. Jura saw him pointing out the different people in the group and, Jura thought, no doubt guaranteeing their safety with his own life.

She watched him closely and she could detect a difference in his eyes, an emptiness that wasn't there before, but he looked as if he were ready to resume command.

She waited until he looked at her so she could smile at him.

But Rowan did not look at Jura.

All day they rode and he never once looked at her. Did he not understand that she had said what she had on purpose to enrage him? That she wanted to spur him out of his misery? Tonight, she thought, tonight she would get him alone and he would touch her again, perhaps even make love to her.

But it was not to be. They camped and Rowan avoided her. She asked him to walk with her into the trees, but he said he had to stay with the Fearens.

"I cannot leave them with your brother," he said, then looked at her with cold eyes. "Or perhaps I should call him the Rightful King." Before Jura could say a word, Rowan left her standing alone.

Cilean saw Jura standing there and ordered her to unsaddle the horses and Jura went about the familiar task blindly.

"You have hurt him," Cilean said.

"I have helped him but he does not know it." Jura looked across the firelight to where Rowan sat sharpening his sword. "I am—"

"—a fool," Cilean said, taking her saddle and walking away in anger.

Jura had her own attack of self-pity. Did no one believe she was capable of at last seeing the light? She sat quietly with the others by the fire that night and took her turn at watch near dawn, but Rowan made no attempt to speak to her privately. He gave her duties and orders like he did the others.

No one else besides Cilean seemed to notice any difference because Rowan was treating her as Lanconian men treated their women: as equals. But Jura had grown rather used to Rowan's protectiveness and the way he thought of her as soft and fragile.

And she also missed their lovemaking.

On the morning of the third day, just before dawn, she saw Rowan slip from the camp and make his way into the trees. Feeling a little tentative at what she was doing, she followed him.

She half expected him to leap from the trees and curse her for leaving the protection of the others, but he did not. He was squatted by the side of a stream, bare to the waist and washing himself.

He did not turn around. "What do you want, Jura?" he asked, his voice as cool as the mountain stream.

She almost turned back to the camp but she made herself go forward to kneel beside him and drink of the water. The sky was just barely pink. "We have not spoken in days and I thought . . ." She put out her hand to touch his shoulder, but he looked at her hand in such a way that she removed it.

"I was not aware that Lanconian men and women talked," he said. "I believe your job is to guard my back."

She frowned, utterly confused by him. "But we are also married."

"I see. So, it is the bedding that you want from me. I am to carry steel in my hands and between my legs and that is all you want."

"If that is what you believe of me, so be it," she said

angrily, and left him alone. Was she supposed to explain to him why she had done what she had? Did he really believe she wanted him dead?

Again, tears came to her eyes, but she blinked them away. Damn him! Why did she love a man who made her cry?

# Chapter Fifteen

ᴿOWAN DID NOT look at her when he returned to camp and Jura stiffened her shoulders as if his ignoring of her was a physical blow. Her head and body ached when she at last lay down to sleep. It was because of Jura's turbulent thoughts that she was awake when the others slept and she saw "them" come into the camp. At first she thought she was dreaming, for the people were more shadow than flesh and blood. And they moved without sound, slipping through the darkness as silently as a fish through water.

With wide, unbelieving eyes, she saw one of the small, thin, dark-clad figures bend and put something over Daire's mouth. But before she could rise up in protest, something hit her on the head and she saw no more.

When she woke, she was aware of pain in her head and her back. Before she opened her eyes, she tried to move her hands but couldn't.

"Jura. Jura."

Painfully, Jura opened her eyes to look at Cilean. They were in the back of a wagon, under a tall wooden

279

frame and on top of lumpy bags of grain, and what felt to be rocks.

"Jura, are you all right?" Cilean whispered.

Jura tried to sit up, but her hands and ankles were tied together behind her. "Yes," she managed to whisper through a dry throat. "Where are we? Who has taken us? Where are the others?" She grimaced as the wagon hit a deep hole in the road and whatever was in the bag beneath her dug into her side.

"I don't know," Cilean said. "I was asleep, and when I woke I was here."

Jura struggled against her bonds. "I have to save Rowan," she said. "He will try to talk his way out of this and they will kill him."

Cilean gave a bit of a smile. "I think we should worry about ourselves now. If they have taken us prisoner, they must have taken the others. I hear other wagons. I think we should sleep now and try to keep what strength we have."

Jura had difficulty sleeping because of her worry about Rowan—and the others, she reminded herself. She prayed to God to protect him. It is too early for him to die, she prayed. He had work to do. And he needed her to protect him. What if he lost confidence again? Who would be there to help him?

She slept at last, but she dreamed of Rowan being dead and, in the dream, she knew his death was her fault because she had never told him that she loved him.

The abrupt halting of the wagon woke her. Rough hands grabbed her ankles and pulled her from the wagon, her head hitting hard bags. More hands untied her so she could stand on the ground.

Ultens, she thought as she stared at the thin little man standing before her, and all the horror stories she had ever heard came to her mind. Stories of the Ultens were told around the fire on cold, stormy nights. Parents threatened their children with Ultens.

No one knew much about them really except that they were filthy beyond belief, sly, thieving, untrustworthy, and as far as anyone could tell, they had no concept of honor. Over the centuries the other tribes had done their best to ignore the Ultens. They lived high in the mountains in the northeast corner of Lanconia and no one had any desire to see their city.

Yet there were rumors about the place. When Jura was a child, an old man with an arm and an eye missing had told of being captured by the Ultens, and he had talked of a city of fabulous wealth. Everyone had laughed at him until he had slinked off into a corner and gotten drunk. Days later he had disappeared, never to be seen again.

Now, Jura stood staring in the darkness at the filthy face of her captor, half hidden under a grimy hooded cloak. The ancient man held out a cup of liquid and a stale chunk of bread to her. Jura took the food, and as the old man pulled Cilean from the wagon, she looked about her. There were four other wagons and about them silently moved more of the cloaked figures, but they pulled no other prisoners from the wagons.

Jura's throat swelled closed. "Where are the others?" she asked the man.

No one said a word but, silently, slicing through the darkness, came another figure and Jura was slapped across the mouth. It didn't take much thought to realize she was to remain silent. She ate her bread, drank the musty-tasting beer, and she and Cilean were allowed to relieve themselves in the trees, then they were shoved back into the wagons.

The motion of the wagon seemed to be endless and the days merged into one another. They stopped twice a day during the three-day journey and Jura and Cilean were given meager rations and a brief moment of privacy, then their bonds were retied and they were returned to the wagons.

After the first day Jura and Cilean didn't talk much, for their hunger, tiredness, and grief were almost too much to bear. Jura was plagued by remorse. If only she had had time to explain to Rowan what she had said. If she could have told him she could not bear the thought of his death. Perhaps she should have held him while he cried. Maybe that would have worked best. If only . . .

"Do you think they killed the men?" Cilean whispered. Her eyes were sunken in her head and she looked as bad as Jura felt.

Jura's throat swelled closed and she could not speak.

"No doubt they want women slaves," Cilean said. "Brita was too old for their use, so they took us."

Jura swallowed but it didn't help.

"Yes," Cilean continued, answering her own question, "I think they killed the men. They would have come after us and these Ultens could not fight our men."

Cilean waited for Jura's answer, but when none came, she kept talking. "We did not hear the Ultens come into camp. Even the Fearens who guarded did not hear them." She closed her eyes a moment. "Brocain will declare war on the Irials when he hears his son is dead. And who will lead the Irials now that both Rowan and Geralt are . . . gone?"

Jura closed her eyes and envisioned Rowan's blond hair. She remembered his smile. She remembered the way he tickled her the night they spent in his tent.

"We will never unite the tribes now," Cilean said. "The Vatells will have lost Brita, Yaine's brother is dead, Brocain's son is dead." She also swallowed. "And our king is dead."

"Stop it!" Jura commanded. "I can bear no more."

Cilean looked at Jura in puzzlement. "Is it grief that makes you so strange? Is it Rowan's death that . . . ?"

"No more, please," Jura whispered.

Cilean was silent for a moment.

"We must keep our strength up," she said, trying to get Jura's attention back on the present. "We have to find a way to escape these slimy people and get home. We have to tell the rest of Lanconia what has happened. We will unite the other tribes to kill the Ultens. We will avenge Rowan's death. We will—" She said no more as she heard the sound of tears coming from Jura. She had never seen Jura cry before.

Jura tried to sleep but could not. Hour after hour passed slowly and painfully, and she had time to remember every moment since she had met Rowan. She thought of how she had reacted to him at their first meeting and later how angry she had been when she found out who he was. She had felt betrayed, as if he had lied to her and played with her feelings.

And she had been afraid. She hated to admit it even to herself, but the force of her emotions concerning the man scared her. She had been afraid she would follow him and betray her country, betray everything she had ever believed in.

"Oh Rowan," she whispered into the darkness as hot tears rolled down the side of her face. "If only I could have told you."

At the beginning of the fourth day the wagons halted and Jura could hear the noise of people around them. Cilean opened her eyes and looked at Jura. Cilean was fighting fear, but Jura looked as if she had given up the battle. They had no idea what the Ultens planned for them, whether it was death or slavery, and Jura didn't look as if she cared one way or the other.

"We will escape soon," Cilean reassured her friend and herself. "Perhaps we can arrange a ransom."

Jura didn't answer.

The women had time to say no more as they were pulled from the wagon and stood in the bright sunlight. As Cilean blinked to adjust her vision, she was surprised at what she saw. Based on the Ultens she had seen, she would have imagined their city to be filthy and poor, a place of squalor with the lazy Ultens lying in drunken heaps. So what she saw surprised her so much it left her wide-eyed and gaping.

They were inside a walled city with neat, clean buildings against the inner wall. There were cleanly swept stone paths with no pigs or dogs running about. There were shops open in the bottom floor of the houses and people bustling here and there. Clean people, richly dressed people.

No, she thought, not people but women. Everywhere there were women, adult women, very few children, and what children there were were girls.

"Where are the men?" Cilean whispered to Jura.

Cilean received no answer before one of the filthily clad guards shoved her forward and motioned to the bags inside the wagon. Jura could see now that the guard was a woman, a small woman nearly a foot shorter than Jura and thin to the point of frailty.

"What have you done with our men?" Jura asked, showing her first signs of life.

"They are dead," the Ulten woman said in broken Irial. "We want no men here." She shoved Jura and Cilean forward.

Jura and Cilean were weak from the long days of being tied and the small amount of food, so they were slow in removing the heavy bags of goods from the four wagons and stacking them inside a long stone building. All the while they worked more of the little Ulten women stopped and watched them and talked to each other in their strange guttural language.

Cilean glared at two women who were pointing at the tall women and nodding their heads.

"I feel like an ox being judged for strength," Cilean said to Jura. She didn't say any more because one of the women held a whip under her nose and made her meaning clear.

It took most of the day to unload the wagons and, exhausted, Jura and Cilean were led away to a tiny, empty stone building that contained nothing but two sleeping cots. The building was surrounded by at least a dozen of the little Ulten women.

"Jura," Cilean whispered from her cot.

Jura sniffed in answer.

"We must try to escape," Cilean said. "We have to get home. We have to explain to people what happened before there is a war. We must get to Yaine and . . . Jura, are you listening to me? I see no way of escape and I am too tired to think."

"Why do you want to go to Yaine?"

"To continue what Rowan started," she said as if

Jura should have known that. "We must find a way to unite the tribes. If for no other reason, we Irials will unite them to kill these Ultens who sneak about and kill the King of Lanconia."

To Cilean's horror, Jura's sniffles turned into full-fledged crying. Cilean had no idea what to do. Tears were not something one dealt with much in Lanconia. She turned on her side and tried to sleep. Perhaps tomorrow she could talk to Jura about escaping.

Jura also tried to sleep but she couldn't stop her tears. Lanconia didn't seem to matter; Geralt didn't matter; Yaine's brother or Brocain's son didn't matter. All she cared about was having lost the man she loved.

"And I didn't even get to tell him," she whispered into the darkness. "Oh God, if only I had another chance. I would be a *real* wife to him." She cried herself to sleep.

Geralt's laughter split the air and reverberated off the white marble walls of the Ulten palace. The three beautiful women before him smiled in delight as they looked at the ebony and ivory gameboard.

"You have won again, master," one woman fairly purred. "Which of us do you choose tonight?"

"All of you." Geralt laughed. "Or perhaps I'll take three new women tonight."

"We are yours to choose," said a second woman.

The beautiful, luxurious Ulten palace was a product of centuries of "borrowing." The marble had been on its way to a cathedral in England when the Ultens had silently attacked during the night, killing all the merchants and their hired guards, and had taken the wagonloads of marble through the mountains to their cities. They had even "borrowed" the stone masons, worked them to death, then tossed their bodies off a mountainside.

The enormous room, long, narrow, tall, was walled with veined white marble and everywhere was evidence of the Ultens' skill at "borrowing." They were the scavengers of every battle. While the participants grieved over their dead, the Ultens moved about and took anything worth taking. They were like ants and could easily carry half again their body weight away with them. They raided cities without the cities knowing they were being invaded.

And they brought whatever they took back to their king and their city, so the palace was filled with wealth that was already ancient: beautiful swords, shields, tapestries, hundreds of embroidered cushions, gold cups (none of which matched), plates, candlesticks, eating knives. There was little furniture as that was more difficult to carry without notice, but there were some low, crude, long tables hidden beneath beautiful Irish linen cloths. The guests sprawled on the cushions and watched the many women walk silently about the room in their soft slippers, hurrying without haste to do the bidding of each man. The three Fearens sat at one end of the room together, frowning slightly in disapproval. They ignored the ten or so women near them and ate sparingly of the food on their plates.

Geralt leaned back from the gameboard and lounged against the pillows, one woman fanning him, another holding his feet in her lap and massaging them, two others gently massaging his calf muscles, another shelling almonds and feeding them to him.

Four other women stood by in case Geralt should think of something else he wanted. He wore an expression of sublime happiness.

Daire sat farther down, engaged in intense conversation with a splendidly lovely woman, and from his expression he was thoroughly enjoying himself.

In stark contrast to the men behind the table, Rowan stood by the windows at the east end of the room, staring down at the people and buildings of the walled city.

Daire excused himself from the woman and went to Rowan. "Still worried about Jura?" he asked.

Rowan kept looking out the window and didn't answer.

"They said they left the women there," Daire said in the tone of a man repeating something for the hundredth time. "The Ultens do not kill. They will steal anything, including the King of Lanconia if they want him, but they are not murderers. They drugged all of us, took us, and left the women there. Why do you doubt them? They have no need of women, as you can see." Daire smiled at the pretty woman waiting at the table for him. "They want only the men." He couldn't control his smile. "We must give them what they want from us and be on our way. Perhaps we can take some of these women back with us."

Rowan gave Daire a cool look. "You are being seduced by them."

Daire's eyes twinkled. "A time or two."

Rowan looked back out the window. "I do not trust this man Marek," he said, referring to the man who called himself king of the Ultens. "And I do not like being held captive, no matter that the bonds are made of silk."

"You have said you wanted to unite the tribes. What better way to do that than to . . ."

"To impregnate their women?" Rowan asked, frowning. "I believe I am better than to be used as a stud." He turned his head away, and Daire, shrugging, went back to his table.

Rowan continued to stare out the window, cursing his helplessness. How could he fight women, especially such lovely, small women as these? Six days ago he had awakened to find himself in the back of a silk-clad wagon with a raging headache. He had shoved open the locked door with a few thrusts of his shoulder and the wagon had halted. He was greeted by six pretty little women who begged him not to be angry. Rowan's anger had calmed somewhat when he saw that the other men were unhurt, but it returned when neither Jura, Cilean, nor Brita stepped from the wagons. The Ulten women said they had left the Irial women at the campsite.

It took most of a day to return to the campsite and it was indeed clean, as if the Irial women and Brita had packed and left. Rowan was still not satisfied. He didn't like being drugged and locked in a wagon. He said he was going after the women.

At that the Ulten women began to cry. They promised Rowan they would do *anything* if he would return with them. They said they had heard how he was uniting all of Lanconia but they knew he would not think of the Ultens, that everyone hated the Ultens, and they needed him more than any other tribe. They said they would even send a message to the Irials from Rowan if he would just return with them.

Rowan the king and Rowan the man were torn apart. As king he wanted to see this elusive tribe but as a man he wanted Jura back. During the long journey Daire had told him that Jura had gone after him after Keon's death, so Rowan knew she must have seen him crying. He knew Lanconians did not cry.

Yet Jura, a Lanconian, had seen him cry and she had not ridiculed him or been disgusted with him. Instead, she had kicked him into once again believing in himself.

And he had not realized at the time what she was doing. His own sense of failure had turned to a rage that he directed at her. Rowan ached for her and wanted to go find the women but Geralt had started yelling at Rowan and saying that if the Ultens needed them they should go with the Ulten women. Rowan said Geralt's thoughts were below his belt, and that had nearly caused a fight. Daire had stepped in and his calm counsel had made Rowan the king win over Rowan the man. Daire said they were close to Yaine, and Jura and Cilean would no doubt take Brita to Yaine, and that Rowan wasn't needed. Also, Rowan could not afford to insult the Ultens as he might never get another chance to enter their secluded mountain village peacefully.

Reluctantly, Rowan went with the Ulten women.

Over the next few days, he, the only man who spoke the Ulten language, talked to the women. He was disturbed by the promiscuous nature of the women and had he been in England he would have forbidden his men to consort with them, but the Fearens, Geralt, and even Daire slept with a different woman each night.

It was while the others were cavorting in the bushes that Rowan got to talk to the two remaining unoccupied women and he heard some of the recent sad history of the Ultens.

Fifteen years ago, a strange fever that was said to have come from the east struck nearly every person in the isolated Ulten villages. The women recovered quickly but man after man died, hundreds of men, in fact. When the fever was gone, only a quarter of the Ulten men were still alive and by the end of the next year it was found that these men could produce only girl children. So for many years now, the Ultens had been a city of women.

"Why didn't you go to the other tribes and ask for men?" Rowan asked. "Surely men would have come with you."

"But King Marek forbade it," she answered simply.

Rowan began to get a picture of the remaining Ulten men loving having a city full of women to themselves, any of whom would go to bed with them in order to get a child.

When they arrived at the city, Rowan's worst fears were reinforced when he saw Marek, a fat, slimy, toothless old man surrounded by beautiful young women. Rowan cursed himself for having been seduced into believing what the women had said, that they wanted him merely to give them children and that they wanted to unite with the other tribes. Perhaps the women believed that, but Rowan saw that greasy old Marek had no intention of sharing his private harem with other men. And Rowan thought that, perhaps, Marek meant for the foreign men to impregnate a few women, then Rowan and the others would be put to death.

If only Jura had been with them, Rowan thought.

Her skepticism and cynicism would have made him think twice about going with the Ulten women. He cursed himself for being a fool—just like Jura said he was. Now, the men with him thought only of how many women they could bed each night, but Rowan saw beyond that. What was planned for them when their usefulness was over? Rowan had to come up with a plan for escape because he sensed that the men would not be allowed to leave peacefully. Marek would not like the information that the Ultens were a city of women living near a palace containing great wealth to leave the Ulten boundaries. Marek had worked hard to make the Ultens seem poor. Whenever an Ulten left the border, she wore rags covered in filth. No one wanted to follow an Ulten to examine the city. And Marek no doubt wanted to keep it that way so he could not allow Rowan or his men to leave alive.

Rowan kept staring out the window, and the more he thought, the more he worried. What had they done to Jura? Why had he been so trusting? Why had he believed the tears of some pretty women? If *men* had drugged him and locked him in a wagon and he had found out the women were not with them, he would have drawn a sword and removed a few limbs of the men and forced them to tell what they had done with Jura and Cilean and Brita. But like a sheep being led to slaughter he had docilely gone with the Ulten women and left Jura on her own.

*If* she were on her own, he thought grimly. If they had not killed the women, for unlike Daire, he believed the Ultens capable of more than stealing. They wanted male children, so they captured a king and a couple of princes to use for stud service. They took whatever they wanted.

His face turned hard. I will give these women to the Zerna men, he thought angrily. Let us see if the conniving she-devils can manipulate Brocain's men.

While he was thinking with so much fury, he became aware of some commotion in the street below. It was some distance away, across the rooftop of another building, but he could see some angry activity. One of the little Ulten women raised a whip and cracked it, hitting another person who was half hidden by the building.

As Rowan watched, from the shadows came a third woman, a tall woman, with a black braid flying out behind her, who leaped onto the smaller woman with the whip.

"Jura," Rowan whispered, and almost climbed out the window to go after her, but some bit of sense made him stay where he was. With a pounding heart and his face showing his anguish, he watched silently as a dozen Ulten women leaped on Jura and knocked her to the ground. A moment later the Ultens led Jura and Cilean away, out of Rowan's sight.

He leaned against the window casing and took deep breaths to calm himself. There was more treachery here than he thought, and he, fool that he was, had walked directly into it.

Tonight he must, somehow, escape these women and go to Jura. And he must figure out a plan to get all of them away from the Ultens safely.

# Chapter Sixteen

❦

Sore?" Cilean asked Jura softly.

Jura shrugged in answer but the truth was, her shoulders and back hurt a great deal from the whip strokes of that afternoon.

They were alone in the little stone house again, this time their guard outside doubled because of what had happened that day. Cilean had fallen under a heavy bag of grain, and when one of the Ultens had cracked a whip over her, Jura had leaped for the woman's throat. Jura had received a dozen lashes with a whip for that and Cilean had chided her for taking the punishment. They had been worked especially hard the rest of the day and only now, so late, were they allowed to rest.

But Cilean's anger, reawakened, kept her awake. "We have to escape. I saw two women talking by the gate today when they should have been watching. If we could find a way to distract them, perhaps we could—"

She broke off at the look on Jura's face and she turned. Standing in the doorway, lit from behind by torches, was a ghost—a thick, wide, golden ghost.

Jura blinked to clear her vision but the ghost remained there.

"Jura?" the ghost whispered.

Cilean was the first to recover. In spite of her exhaustion she leaped from the cot and flung her arms around Rowan.

Sometimes Rowan was angered by the way these Lanconians treated him. He was their king but he got no "Your Majesty's," merely argument and challenges about his decisions. But at this moment he was glad for their sense of equality. He'd rather have a woman's arms about his neck than all the fawning in the world.

He hugged Cilean back, feeling as if he were touching someone clean for the first time in days. How good it would be to hear the honest opinion of a woman instead of the meek subservience of the Ulten women.

"You are well? Unhurt?" Rowan asked Cilean.

She released her clasp on his neck but still kept her arm around his waist. "Tired and bruised but not hurt. It is Jura who was hurt today."

Rowan stared across the darkness at his wife, who still sat on her cot. Cilean slipped away from him. "You have nothing to say to me?" Rowan said softly to Jura.

"Why are you alive?" she asked in an angry tone, her heart pounding in her ears.

Rowan did not take offense as he smiled and stepped toward her. "You *are* glad to see me."

"We were taken captive and made into slaves," Jura said angrily. "They use us as oxen to unload wagons full of stolen goods. I had thought that you were dead or else you would have come for us, but you are not dead." She said the last as if it were an accusation.

Somehow, she felt betrayed by him. The last time she had seen him he had been looking at her with hatred, and for days she had done little but cry because she thought he was dead. But here he was, not only alive but free as well.

Rowan kept walking toward her, and when at last he was in front of her, he put his hand on her shoulders.

Jura leaped off the cot and flung her body against his, holding on to him with all her might. "You are not dead. You are not dead," she kept repeating in wonder.

"No, my love," he whispered, stroking her sore back. "I am not dead."

After a few moments, he pulled away from her. "We must talk. Come, Cilean, sit here by us. I want to have you both near me. We haven't much time."

He put an arm around each woman, as if he feared they might disappear, and began to explain what had happened to him and the other men in the last few days.

"You *believed* them?" Jura asked, incredulous. "These women slipped into our camp and put their hideous potion over our mouths and hit me, and you believed them when they said they had left us quietly sleeping? You are a—"

Rowan kissed her mouth. "I have missed you, Jura. However I got us into this, I must get us out."

"You?" Jura said. "You are the cause of this. If you hadn't—"

"She thought you were dead," Cilean interrupted, "and she has done nothing but cry since we were taken. I have never seen her cry before and now she does nothing else. She talks of nothing but how much she regrets never trying to help you unite the tribes and never being able to tell you that she loved you."

"This is true, Jura?" Rowan whispered.

Jura turned away. "One says things in grief."

Rowan put his fingertips under her chin and kissed her tenderly. "I tried to make a decision as a king. I went with the Ultens because King Rowan wanted to unite them with the other tribes, but Rowan the man came to regret that decision. I was a fool, Jura, just as you have told me a thousand times."

She looked into his eyes. "But you meant well," she whispered and he kissed her again.

"As you did the day Keon was killed," he whispered, and was amazed to see tears in Jura's eyes. "You gave me strength when I would have failed my country and you let no one see me in my weakness."

"Rowan!" came an urgent whisper from the doorway. It was Daire, and Cilean went to him but he motioned her away. Immediately, she became a guardswoman again.

"We must go," Daire said. "Even Geralt is failing."

"Failing?" Jura asked, pushing away from Rowan and starting to rise. "Cilean and I are ready. We will leave with you."

Rowan cleared his throat nervously. "We cannot take you," he said. "There are too many of them and too few of us. I could visit you only because the Fearens and Geralt are, ah, keeping the guards, ah, busy. Jura, do not look at me like that. I will get you out of here, but you cannot expect me to wage war on a city of women, my own Lanconian women."

"Women!" she gasped, standing and glaring at him. "These delicate little women have Cilean and me pulling rocks out of pathways, digging water mills out of mud, hauling great bags of grain, repairing stone walls. We are being used as *horses* while you men are . . . are exhausting yourselves trying to impregnate them."

"I am not, Jura," Rowan said pleadingly. "I swear to you that I have not touched one of them. I am sure they will let us live as long as I the king do not give a woman my child."

Jura's eyes bulged in rage. "How much you are sacrificing for us!" she half yelled.

Rowan tried to take her in his arms but she twisted away. "Jura, please trust me."

"Like you trusted the Ultens? You went off with these little women and left Cilean and me and Brita to rot."

"That's not true," he began, "I—" Rowan was confused and pleased by Jura at the same time. She was hissing at him like a jealous woman. No coolheaded guardswoman was attacking him. She was an angry wife who thought her husband was sleeping with other women. She really did care more for *him* than for Lanconia.

"Rowan!" Daire said urgently. "We must go. Marek will hear of this if we do not go soon. He will have all of us killed."

Rowan moved away from Jura with regret. Never had he wanted her so much as now. He was tempted to abdicate to Geralt and get out of Lanconia. He'd take Jura with him back to England. Even as he thought this, he knew it wasn't possible. "Give me two days," he whispered. "I will have you out of here in two days."

He left, and in the stillness he left behind, Cilean

tried to talk to Jura, but she was too angry to listen. She felt betrayed one minute and the next she knew Rowan should have gone with the Ultens and left the Irial women behind. She was too confused to sleep. If she had married Daire, she would never have expected their marriage to stand in the way of what was good for Lanconia. So why did it enrage her when Rowan chose Lanconia over her?

Before dawn she went to the doorway to look at the silhouette of Marek's great palace, and the thought of Rowan inside and perhaps lying with another woman made her furious. But the way she was thinking was *English,* not Lanconian. And this was not the way it was supposed to be. She was supposed to think first of Lanconia, not of herself.

She leaned her head against the coolness of the stone doorway and tried to think clearly. But she could not. All she knew was that she wanted Rowan back. She did not want to wait until he grew tired of his Ulten women or until her arrogant brother had had enough. She was willing to make a wager that Geralt had never given a thought to what had happened to Cilean and Jura, much less Brita, who had humiliated him. Geralt had never had much compassion for others.

When Jura had thought Rowan was dead, she regretted that she had never had a chance to help him with Lanconia. Now she was being given that chance.

"Jura," Cilean said softly, "have you been awake all night?"

Jura turned bright eyes on her friend. "We are going to get ourselves out of here," she said. "And we are going to use Rowan's English weapons: words. We are not going to kill and maim, we are going to do worse.

We are going to tell these women what old Marek has kept from them, that there are men, hundreds of men, out there, and that each woman can have her own man and all the male children she wants."

"But we don't speak the Ulten language," Cilean said, "and Rowan said he'd get us out in two days. Shouldn't we do what he wants?"

"We're going to *help* him," Jura said firmly.

There was only one of the women guards who spoke the Irial language and it took Jura a while to get her to listen. She kept telling Jura to get back to work. But at midmorning every woman in sight came to a halt as Marek came down the street, lounging in a carriage, four beautiful young women hovering near him. Marek was old, fat, dirty, toothless, and ugly.

Behind him in two other carriages came Rowan, Daire, Geralt, and the Fearens. Jura could feel the quiver of excitement run through the women as they looked at these strong, healthy, virile men. Jura clenched her fists at her sides as Rowan went by. A pretty little Ulten was practically sitting in his lap.

"How weak those men look," Jura said as if suppressing a yawn.

The little Ulten who spoke Irial looked at her in surprise.

"In my country we women wouldn't look at such men, we would send them away," Jura said as if greatly bored. "Can we return to work now? I would rather work than look at such weaklings as those."

Jura could feel that she had the woman's attention, and when she heard the woman whispering to the others, she knew it was going to work.

Not long afterward she and Cilean were back at hauling rocks from a field when the Ulten woman began asking questions about where Jura lived, and, specifically, about the men there.

Jura wiped the sweat from her brow, leaned on her pike, and began to talk of marriages between one man and one woman. She had to pause while this was translated and to allow the women to gasp over this idea.

By sundown she and Cilean were sitting under separate trees in the shade and drinking cool fruit juices while spinning stories about the hundreds of available men in the rest of Lanconia. The Ultens especially loved to hear of the strong Zerna men who had only ugly, big women.

Jura answered all their questions, even the ones about how the Irial men could possibly like women as tall as Jura and Cilean. "They manage," Jura said with a forced smile.

That night she slept more easily than she had since being captured.

In the morning there were over a hundred women waiting for her and Cilean outside the building, and they did nothing all day except talk. Most of the women were young and did not remember when there had been men available, so Jura's talk seemed like a fairy tale to them.

On this second day Jura did not just talk of the men of other tribes, but began to talk of the Ulten men and how unfair it was that the women had to worship them and obey them because of their scarcity. Jura told them of her own defiance of her husband, not mentioning that Rowan was her husband. The women had her repeat a few episodes in disbelief.

"And he loves you still?" one woman asked through an interpreter. "You do not have to be perfect to keep a man? He does not cast you out if you are not kind and loving and sweet-tempered at all times?"

"You can say what you actually think without fear of punishment?"

"You can get angry at a *man?*"

"Yes," Jura answered. "And your husband is faithful to you or you have the right to complain in court. *You* can cast *him* out."

By nightfall, Jura's throat was raw from talking so much, but from the expressions on the women's faces, she knew she had made an impression. As they walked back to the town, Ulten women everywhere were pointing and nodding at them and talking seriously among themselves. Jura smiled to herself. Perhaps Rowan's way of fighting had some advantages to it. She didn't think she could have caused more commotion if she had attacked the city with an army of guardsmen and women.

With a jaw-snapping yawn, she wondered what the morrow would bring.

Rowan was just waking when the first noises sounded outside the palace. He had not been able to go to sleep until quite late for worry about how to get them out of this situation. The other men seemed content to remain with the Ulten women for the rest of their lives, but Rowan, much to his disbelief, was finding the women's fawning annoying. Tonight he had had a great deal of difficulty persuading the women he wanted no bed partner. He smiled to himself, knowing that it wasn't that he wouldn't love the attentions of one of the women, but the fear of Jura's wrath was more than he liked to contemplate.

"Winning Lanconia is easy but winning Jura is next

to impossible," he muttered, then went back to trying to solve the problem of getting all of them out of their silken prison without having to hurt a woman or offend greasy old Marek.

At the first sound of women's voices raised in anger, Rowan did not react. After having spent time with the volatile Irials and then Brita, a woman shouting in rage was a commonplace occurrence. But then he remembered that he was in a land where women were in a to-the-death competition for men and they competed with soft words and languorous smiles.

He sat up in bed. "What has Jura done now?" he asked aloud, and knew without a doubt that whatever the women were angry about was caused by Jura.

In moments he was dressed, hurriedly wrapping his cross garters about his legs, then running along the corridors to the rooms of the other men, who were each wrapped about one, two, or in Geralt's case, three women. He ordered the men into the great room *immediately*. Only Geralt gave him trouble.

"You'll be there or I'll come for you," Rowan said, slamming the door and beginning to run, Daire and the Fearens on his heels.

What looked to be an army of women was streaming into the palace, each face angry, and in their hands they carried whatever they could use as weapons: rakes, shovels, hand axes, long bone needles, clubs of various sizes. They were such small women and armed so poorly that they were almost an amusing sight—but Rowan did not laugh.

Rowan grabbed the arm of a woman near the front, a beautiful dark-haired wench. "What has happened?" he asked in the Ulten language.

She sneered at him. "We have been lied to," she

yelled. "We were told that *all* men died of the sickness, that the only ones left were here in our city, but Jura says that is not so."

Rowan groaned as he released the woman then turned to translate to the other men.

"Jura!" Geralt snorted. "I should have known she would ruin paradise."

Rowan grabbed his half-brother's tunic front. "Your sister has been in slavery while you were eating figs. Now we have to stop this or we'll have a war on our hands."

Geralt twisted from Rowan's grasp. "Let them kill old Marek. What do I care? I will rule the Ultens. You have taken the Irials from me, so I will take the Ultens."

It was Jura, Cilean behind her, who pushed her way through the crowd just in time to hear her brother's words. "You are not fit to rule yourself much less a tribe," she yelled at him. "You think only of yourself, not of your people or your country. You are not loyal to the Irials or anyone else in Lanconia. You could not even spend the night with Brita without starting a war. You may think so highly of yourself that you believe these women would love to follow you, but right now they are too angry to think." She looked at the other men and they were now surrounded by angry Ulten women as they surged through the palace. "They are furious at Marek for lying to them over the years, and their blood is up. They may not stop at killing one man but may decide to kill *all* men. We have to get you out." Jura turned to leave, but Rowan caught her arm.

"You did not side with your brother," he shouted to her.

"My brother is Irial, not Lanconian," she said,

somewhat annoyed. "Is there another way out of here? Please, Rowan, do not try to talk your way out of this. These women seek blood."

He took a moment to caress her cheek, then turned back toward the wing of bedchambers. "Follow me," he ordered, and only Geralt hesitated. Rowan grabbed the young man's shoulder and pulled him with the others.

Like a reluctant boy, Geralt fought. "Unhand me, you usurper. The women will not harm me. I am their master."

Quite calmly, Jura picked up a vase from a nearby table and brought it down over Geralt's head. He crumpled gracefully to the floor.

Rowan looked at her in disgust. "Now how do we get him out?"

"You must carry him. Come on, we haven't much time to lose. I think the women are looting the palace."

Rowan, without arguing, took an order from a woman and heaved the tall Geralt over his shoulder, then once again took the lead as he went down a corridor. There was no other door besides the front one, but in the last few years of safety the Ultens had become lax and had built a granary near one of the palace windows.

"Daire!" Rowan said. "Take that marble and put it between the buildings."

It took four men and Cilean and Jura to put the long thick slab of marble between the two buildings, forming a slide. It was precariously positioned and the slippery surface made it dangerous.

"I will go first," Jura said, but Rowan pulled her back.

"*I* will test it. Take care of your brother. He is waking."

Jura only gave a quick glance to Geralt as he sat on the floor and began to rub his aching head as Rowan slid across the marble slab to the safety of the other building. When he was across, one by one, the others followed him.

Geralt refused to go with them. "I will stay here. This is where I belong," he told Jura. "I will not be second to that Englishman."

"He is more Lanconian than you are," she said. "Thal knew what he was doing."

"I am betrayed on all sides," Geralt said grimly. "Go with him. I will stay here and bring order out of this chaos."

Jura was already on the marble slab but she didn't release the windowsill as she watched her brother straighten his shoulders and head back toward the women.

"Jura, come on," Rowan shouted behind her.

She made a decision. "I must go after him," she yelled to Rowan, then threw her leg back over the window.

Rowan allowed himself a few precious moments of cursing, then he untied his boots and went up the inclined marble. The only way he could hold on to it was with his bare feet. Behind him the others begged him not to go, but he ordered them to leave the city as fast as possible.

There was no sign of Jura or Geralt in the corridor but there were several Ulten women removing tapestries from the walls. They paused and glared at Rowan in hatred. Yesterday he had been a god and today he was demon.

He gave the women a tentative little smile and hurried past them. It wasn't difficult to see Jura and Geralt, since they were a foot taller than the Ulten women. Jura was bodily protecting her brother and trying to talk to the women, but no one understood her.

"Marek is getting away with the gold!" Rowan shouted in Ulten, but got no response. "Marek is taking the children!" He had to repeat himself a few times as he pointed toward Marek's quarters in the north end of the palace, but he was able to turn the crowd's attention away from Jura and Geralt.

"I knew you would come," Jura said, smiling at him. "You should have gone with the others but I knew you would not."

"Follow me," Rowan ordered, "and do not do anything foolish." He gave an angry look at the sword she had taken from the walls. "Do not hurt any of my people."

"These *people* tried to kill me," Geralt said. "I think—"

"Quiet!" Jura ordered. "And follow King Rowan."

Rowan blinked a couple of times at her words, then began to lead them through the shoving women. Every time a group of women stopped and stared at them, Rowan yelled, "Marek," and pointed toward the bowels of the castle.

They made it almost to the city gates before the women turned on them.

"There are two of them!" a woman yelled.

"They have kept us prisoners. They have denied us husbands and children. We will kill them and free ourselves."

The women stood in front of the open gateway

while other women tried to shove the heavy gates closed.

"Run!" Rowan ordered, "and kill no one."

Jura was not attacked but the men were. Out of instinct, she protected Rowan's body with her own as the women used what weapons they had. Rowan had his head down, trying to protect himself from the blows and so did not see Geralt knock one woman after another down. Jura knew that Rowan's love for his people extended to protecting them at the cost of his own skin.

They made it through the gate and the women chased them for a while but not for long as Jura, Geralt, and Rowan made their way toward the mountains.

After nearly an hour of running, they stopped for breath. "We must find the others," Jura said, and only then did she look at Rowan. His pale skin was white and beneath his cloak was a growing bloodstain. And his bare feet were also bleeding.

Jura put her arms around him in a motherly way and bade him to sit down.

"I must—"

"No," she said softly, "you have done enough for now. It is time that you allowed others to help you." She looked up at Geralt. "Go ahead and find the others. Tell them that our king is injured and tell them to send Daire to find Brita." She looked back at Rowan. "If that is what you think we should do. I mean—"

Rowan leaned forward and kissed her. "It is my idea also, and since we are one it does not matter who says the idea."

"Jura, I—" Geralt began.

"Go!" Jura snapped. "You have caused enough trouble. Tomorrow you may thank our king for your life."

Reluctantly, Geralt turned away, up the path to look for the others.

"Jura, I am not hurt so much," Rowan said softly. "You can bandage me and I can travel."

Tenderly, she used Rowan's knife to cut away his tunic and examine the shoulder wound he had received from an ax blade.

Rowan put his hand to her face. "You have called me king and Lanconian. Do you mean to say that you love me? Do you hope for my death so that you may marry Daire?"

She looked long and hard into his blue eyes. "I was raised by Thal to think of war first and I loved Daire because he caused me no conflict of interest. With Daire I would have chosen Lanconia over my marriage. But you have always confused me. You have shown me real love: a love for my country that goes beyond war and a love for a man that is . . ."

"Is what?"

"A love that permeates me." She put both hands on his face. "Rowan, my husband, if you were to die, I think my soul should die too. For every drop of blood that comes from your wound, my heart sheds an equal amount. This . . . this pain I feel when I am near you, I did not know it was love."

He kissed her softly. "I feel I have earned your love, Jura. I have suffered and bled and withstood great abuse to gain your love."

"That is not so," she protested, then a bit of a smile touched her lips. "It has been worth it?"

"Yes," he said softly. "I thought I wanted a woman

like . . . like these Ultens, who would soften my life, but you are more than a wife to me. You have helped me, Jura. You have helped me to understand the Irial way."

She pulled back from him. "Helped you? I have kept you from being killed. You would never have done what you have without me. If I hadn't been unconscious, I would not have let you enter this Ulten city alone. You trust too much. You believe everyone is full of goodness."

"Except you, Jura. You're full of fire and brimstone and you take credit for everything. *I* am the one who has united Lanconia. *I* am—"

"With *my* help," she said loudly.

Suddenly, Rowan smiled. "I guess we work well together. Perhaps we should continue to work together. Now are you going to let me bleed to death or are we going to stay here and let that stupid brother of yours go after Brita and start a war?"

"Geralt is not stupid. He is . . ."

"Yes?" Rowan asked, one eyebrow raised.

"Perhaps we should give him a tiny corner of Lanconia and tell him it is his own kingdom. He could cause much trouble to us as we unite the rest of the tribes, and we don't want him angering the Zerna men when we give them the Ulten women." She began tearing the bottom off her tunic to bandage Rowan's shoulder.

"What! Give those sweet little Ulten women to the Zerna men?"

"Those 'sweet' women as you call them nearly worked Cilean and me to death, and one of them took a whip to me."

"Yes, but—" he protested, but Jura kissed him,

and, as always, he thought of nothing else, not Lanconia or the Irials or where Brita was. He had loved Jura from the first moment he saw her and he would always love her. And now they had years ahead to unite the tribes and to love and argue. He smiled against her lips and hugged her to him. He was happy.

Over the top of the ridge came Cilean and Daire, and they paused when they heard the raised voices of Rowan and Jura.

Cilean smiled. "I think they are unhurt."

"Jura loves him," Daire said, and there was finality in his voice but no regret. "I think she would give her life for him."

Cilean looked at Daire. "It hurts you to have lost her so completely?"

"I feel like a protective older brother losing an adoring little sister. I know now that Jura and I never . . . lusted for one another." He smiled in memory. "Not like the Ulten women."

"So!" Cilean said coldly. "You like those soft women who do not know a sword from a hair comb?"

Daire looked at her in surprise, then his eyes warmed. "Cilean, I love the way your breasts move when you throw a lance. Shall we go down to our king and queen? The sooner we get out of here and find Brita, the sooner you and I can get married."

He started walking down the hill, but it took Cilean a moment to recover herself. Then, smiling hugely, she followed Daire.

# *Epilogue*

$B$ROCAIN DID NOT demand Rowan's life in payment for Keon's death. By the time Rowan saw Brocain again, nearly all the tribes were united, with Rowan as their king. Brocain wisely knew that if he harmed Rowan it would be the death of him and all the Zernas. So, in exchange for Rowan's life, he took a hundred of the most beautiful Ulten women.

Brita married Yaine and the two of them fought each other for power so fiercely that they were little trouble to Rowan. On Yaine's death, Daire and Cilean inherited what little wealth the Fearens had.

Rowan declared the rulers of each tribe to be dukes, and today in Lanconia, they are still the ruling families. Aria, in *The Princess,* is a descendant of Rowan, and J.T. is descended from Rowan's squire, Montgomery de Warbrooke.

 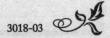